Encrypted Hearts

By E.V. Bancroft

2024

Butterworth Books is a different breed of publishing house. It's a home for Indies, for independent authors who take great pride in their work and produce top quality books for readers who deserve the best. Professional editing, professional cover design, professional proof reading, professional book production—you get the idea. As Individual as the Indie authors we're proud to work with, we're Butterworths and we're *different*.

Authors currently publishing with us:

E.V. Bancroft
Valden Bush
Addison M Conley
Jo Fletcher
Helena Harte
Lee Haven
Karen Klyne
Sydney Lear
AJ Mason
Ally McGuire
James Merrick
Robyn Nyx
JP Preston
Simon Smalley
Brey Willows

For more information visit www.butterworthbooks.co.uk

CATALOGING INFORMATION
ISBN: 978-1-915009-76-0
CREDITS
Editor: Nicci Robinson
Cover Design: Nicci Robinson
Production Design: Global Wordsmiths

Acknowledgements

I am so grateful to everyone who has given their time and expertise to bring Encrypted Hearts to life.

Firstly, thank you to Nicci Robinson from Global Wordsmiths/ Butterworth Books for putting up with my quibbles during editing and publication, particularly over the cover (again).

Special thanks go to the wonderful staff at Bletchley Park, who answered my queries and have a wealth of information available. That it took two days to explore and I still didn't seen everything says it all.

Every author needs a person to read and critique the roughest of drafts, and I'm very grateful to Annmarie for ploughing through my ponderous ramblings, challenging me and making suggestions. I'm lucky I have some awesome beta readers in the Swallows critique group: Joey Bass, Valden Bush, Jane Fletcher, Lee Haven, AJ Mason, Maggie McIntyre, and Sue Still. I know the book is so much stronger because of all your input. Thanks also to my puzzle testers, in particular, Alison, Em, Hazel, and *The Blue Stockings*: Caroline, Joy, Jeannie, and Roy.

Thanks to Em, who has been supportive in her unique way, and Jerry the cat, who has been a total distraction as I've tried to work.

Finally, I'd like to thank you, the reader, for taking a chance on me and giving me such wonderful feedback. It's such an honour. Thanks.

Dedication

To Em, for helping with the puzzles.

And to all the "bright buggers" who cracked the
codes that shortened the war and who
never revealed their secrets.

Author's Note

Inevitably with an historical fiction, you have to decide whether to be absolutely faithful to the timeline and sensitivities of the time or alter things slightly for a modern audience. Throughout, I have attempted to be as authentic as possible, while tweaking the timeline a little for the sake of the narrative. If anything offends, that's at my door.

Chapter One

1943, London

GLORIA EDWARDS BLEW OUT a breath. *This better be the right place.* With the windows being shuttered and the numbers removed because of the war, it was just another anonymous stone building with a crown on the brass letter plate. Inside was the ticket to freedom—if she passed the test. She pushed open the solid wooden doors and entered.

Her uncomfortable heels clattered as she crossed the tiled lobby to the wooden reception desk where a young woman scanned her from head to toe with a barely disguised look of disdain. No, she didn't have London clothes and hadn't had time to freshen up after her long train journey. Gloria slapped her letter of invitation on the high counter and flashed her warmest smile. She almost said "'Ow do?' but remembered her manners just in time. "Good morning. My name is Gloria Edwards. I'm to report to room 204."

The woman cocked her head. "You're late. The rest of the candidates went upstairs for their test a few minutes ago."

Gloria glanced at her watch. She hadn't caught the earliest milk train and lied to her parents just to be turned down now. "No. I'm three minutes early."

The woman shrugged and pointed to an appointment book. "Sign in there. Second floor. Turn left out of the lift and it's the second door on the right."

Gloria scribbled her name, then snatched up her letter and hastened to the lift as fast as politeness would allow. It was one of those ancient lifts with metal gates and outer doors that would take half a minute just to open up. "Sod that," she whispered under her breath and raced up the stairs two at a time onto the second floor, ignoring the pinching on her heels. Hardly pausing to catch her breath, she flung open the door to the dark green institutional corridor to the left. A man was closing one of two doors on the right.

"Ay up, is that room 204?" She hurried towards the man and stopped with a foot just within the inner sanctum.

He towered over her, barring her entrance and peering at her through thick round spectacles. "Secretarial interviews are on the third floor."

Remembering her manners and ignoring his sneer, she smiled and thrust her letter at him. "No. I was asked to report to room 204 for the crossword test because I can complete it in under twelve minutes."

He winced and wrinkled his nose, although she was unsure if that was because of her broad Yorkshire accent or because she was a woman. She shook the letter in his face. "Look; that's me. Gloria Edwards." She peered beyond him into the room lit only by two large hanging lights, where thirty or so small desks were lined up examination style, all occupied bar one. "And that's probably my desk."

The man's nostrils flared as if he was about to say something else, then he strode to his desk outside the room and consulted his list on a clipboard. "It says *Mister* Gloria Edwards."

She gave him an arch look. *Idiots.* "I entered the competition, and this letter is addressed to *me*. I'm here now."

"ID number DT14. Leave your bag and coat on the coat rack." He pointed at the overflowing coat stands beside his desk.

There was no extra hanger, so she slung her coat over the top of another and dropped her bag to the floor. She patted her hair to make sure her curls were more or less in place and entered the room with a sway of her hips. All heads turned and fixed their eyes on her. She smiled at the examiner, who pointed to the empty desk. *I'm in.* Gloria exhaled like it was the first proper breath she'd released since leaving home this morning at crack of sparrows.

The door behind her closed, and the examiner glared at them all. "You have twelve minutes. When you've finished, please raise your hand. Please turn over your papers and begin."

Gloria did so, but there was no writing implement. *Damn.* She raised her hand and waved at the examiner, but it seemed an age until he looked at her. He rose with some difficulty and shuffled towards her. He was so old and crotchety, she was surprised he could walk at all. When he arrived, he barely contained his amusement, judging by the way his lips receded over his bared yellow teeth.

"Yes? Finished already?"

"No. Do you have a pen or pencil?"

He nodded and retraced his steps. Could he go any slower? In the meantime, she checked the clues. One across: a stage company, six letters. *Easy. Troupe.* Four across: the direct route preferred by the Roundheads, five and three. She smiled at the bad pun. *Short cut.* Nine across: one of the evergreens, six letters. That could be either laurel or privet; she'd come back to that.

Finally, the examiner handed her a wooden pencil with a crown embossed on it and the letters S.O. for His Majesty's Stationery Office. "Thank you," she whispered and proceeded to complete the clues she had already solved, conscious that she'd already lost a few precious minutes. When she'd finished, she raised her hand and looked around. Everyone else still had their heads bowed, scribbling away. *Hah!* All these men beaten by a northern lass, not that they'd ever acknowledge that.

The examiner sauntered down to her desk. "What's the problem this time?"

Did she really want a job with these unfriendly people? No, but she wouldn't be working with them, and she wanted to do her duty. Besides, anything was better than where she was now. "No problem. I've finished," she said, lowering her voice when she caught sight of a man on the next desk over glaring at her. His grid was only half complete. It was worth the very early start if she changed her life and proved herself equal to the task. "Pride comes before a fall," her da would say, but just as he was proud he'd made something of himself, so she was proud of her achievement, beating these men from all over the country. She handed out her paper.

"Oh... Put your name and ID number on the back and leave it on the table. Report to the clerk outside."

She grimaced, hoping it passed as a smile. Why report to the clerk? Had they already decided they wouldn't let her through?

Two men raised their hands, and the examiner went to them. Gloria waited to check they were given the same instructions before she rose. As she followed them out, a man standing at the back, whom she hadn't seen before, nodded at her. What was that supposed to mean? It wasn't the usual leering stare of a man who admired her looks, but an acknowledgement of her intellectual prowess and that warmed her to her soul. Sometimes being attractive was a curse, because people looked no further and expected nothing more from her than a smile and good cheer. But she was more than a pretty face, and if she was lucky, she'd show them. She didn't think she was too big for her boots, whatever her da said.

The clerk pointed to a door down the corridor. "Room 207," he said to Gloria, then allocated 205 and 206 to the men. "Leave your bag here," he added as Gloria stooped to pick it up.

Fine. There wasn't much to nick from there anyway: what would the men want with a Dorothy L Sayers Penguin paperback, that was easy to tuck into a bag? They would judge it unsophisticated, but she was enjoying it. She walked along the corridor to her room and rapped on the door. She had a right to be here. This was her opportunity to impress.

She heard a muffled "Come," so she pulled herself to her full height and exhaled noisily before clasping the brass handle and entering. "Good morning," she said, but there was no one behind the desk.

A bulky man stood at the window looking down at the street below. "You finished third then?"

She frowned. "First, actually." *Put that in your pipe and smoke it.* She'd just about had it with the superior attitude of the people she'd met so far.

Now he turned. His greying, shaggy eyebrows met in the middle, and his side whiskers reminded her of a gorilla she'd seen in London zoo before the war.

He peered at her with small bright eyes. "Any languages?"

"Apart from Yorkshire you mean?"

Not a whisper of a smile crossed his lips. Fine. No sense of humour either, then.

"Can you keep a secret?"

She swallowed hard as he lumbered across to the desk. From a drawer, he retrieved a revolver, and she shrank back. *What the...?*

He placed it on the leather top. "I repeat. Can you keep a secret?"

"Yes, sir."

"Good. We'll get back to you." With that, he flicked his hand at her in dismissal.

"Is that it? I'm not even sure what job I'm applying for. I'm guessing it's super important war work." Perhaps she should learn to keep her mouth shut as his eyebrows lowered even further. "But I'm assuming you can't tell me that." No formal interview then. How bizarre. There was no way she'd allow anyone into *her* cash office on the basis of such scant information. Or maybe they'd already decided she wasn't for them. Not stuck up enough, probably. Squashing down the disappointment, she flashed a bright smile. "Thanks for the opportunity."

Was that a hint of an incline to his head? "We'll get back to you."

Well, he was the life and soul of the party. She scuttled out of the room and retrieved her bag. As she stood, she came face-to-chest with one of the other examinees.

"Hello," he said. "My name's Jamie Gordon. What did you think of that?"

He stuck out his hand and smiled. He was quite handsome in a rather rakish way, with auburn hair that had been slicked down but for one lick that defied the comb. It gave him a boyish air that was sure to charm the girls. It was nice to see a friendly smile unlike most of the toffee-nosed officials she had encountered so far. At least one person today was friendly.

She returned the smile and accepted his handshake. "Gloria Edwards. 'Twere all right. I was a little confused by six down, but think I got it. And I had a rather strange interview."

"Right. Me too. Anyway, my friend and I are going for refreshments. Would you care to join us? You can tell us about your strange interview."

His friend shook her hand and peered at her through wire-rimmed glasses. "Archie Timlock. Pleased to meet you, I'm sure."

That's not what your face says. "And you." Gloria checked her watch. "I'm meeting my cousin in two and a half hours in Coventry Street, so I don't have time." Her visit with Hatty was her alibi for this trip and in her hastily scribbled letter, she'd promised she would tell her all about it when they met.

Jamie bowed like an old-fashioned courtier, and Gloria eyed him suspiciously. He raised his head and grinned at her, all freckles and turned-up nose, like a cheeky boy.

"Oh, come on. We'll get you a cab to your meeting place. Where is it, the Lyons Corner House? I promise you we're gentlemen."

How did he know that's where they were meeting? Presumably it was a standard place for unaccompanied young women to meet without causing a scandal. "I'm sure you are."

A taxicab seemed very decadent, and she could almost imagine her father saying, "A fool and his money are soon parted." But this was her adventure. Who knew when she'd get another chance to come to London, even if this trip had been in vain. She sighed. "Sure. Why not?"

"Great! Here, let me help you on with that."

He wrestled her coat from her and held it up so she could slide her arms in. That she was quite capable of doing it herself didn't seem to matter as long as he could demonstrate proof of his gentleman status. Like the best swindlers didn't charm their way into people's wallets.

Out on the street, Jamie hailed a cab. "We're going to the Savoy. Have you ever been, Gloria Edwards?"

She couldn't decide if he was mocking her but decided to give him the benefit of the doubt. "I've only been to London once before, to the zoo," she said. Her confidence dimmed a little against the barrage of superiority.

A cab pulled up, and Jamie opened the back door for her. She plopped herself on the hard leather seat. Archie took the pull-down seat to face Jamie.

Jamie offered her a cigarette, but she shook her head.

"Do you mind if I do?" he asked.

With the cigarette already clamped between his lips, no wasn't an option. He lit up a strong tar-smelling cigarette, exhaled and leaned against the seat.

"And where in the world do you hail from with your thick northern accent and unpretentious clothes?"

Gloria's cheeks heated, unsure whether he was judging her or just teasing her. A bit of both, she suspected. "Bradford," she said and checked her watch again, wondering whether to cry off and just make her way to Hatty on her own. She'd been undermined enough today.

"Well, Bradford, let me treat you to a drink at the American

Bar. And don't worry, even if there's an air raid, the hotel has a secure basement and its own power supply."

They were going to the world-famous art deco bar she'd read about in the *Picture Post*? This was certainly part of an adventure. "Do you go there often?" She shifted sideways to look at Jamie when Archie glowered at her. *What's his problem?*

Jamie smiled. "Whenever I come to London. It's the best place to see life. I even saw Winston Churchill there one time."

She had to remind herself to listen to what he was saying rather than gawping at the sights that she'd seen in pictures but never in real life. It must have been marvellous before the war started, when there weren't piles of rubble from bomb damage, where railings hadn't been removed, and paintwork wasn't shabby and flaking. The cab circled Trafalgar Square, and she wondered if London would ever be the same.

When they finally arrived at the Savoy off the Strand, Jamie helped her out of the cab. He indicated towards the entrance, where two older footmen welcomed them. They could be stepping into a world of flappers and frivolity in the 1920s, before depression and the bleakness of war.

"This way," Jamie said.

He led the way through the opulent lobby with shiny marble floors, comfortable chairs, and rich wooden panelling over a marble surround fireplace. She could almost believe there was no war on given the well-stacked roaring fire, spreading warmth and glamour to the room. This was a space of old money and privilege, and no matter how wealthy her da became in his factory she would never belong here. She would have loved to sit and relax and soak it all in and pretend there was no fear or rations or carrying on regardless, but Jamie had bounded up the stairs to the left and was chatting to the elderly host dressed in white tie and tails.

A few minutes later, they sat in the glossy art deco bar sipping pink gin, which was rather sour. It was very different from her usual port and lemon. She felt conflicted, drinking at lunchtime as if she hadn't a care in the world, when people struggled to put food on the table, and worked long hours to help the war effort. Guilt had a tight stranglehold, crushing and distorting the beauty of the moment, but she pushed it aside.

"They say lots of spies and politicians come here, and the diaspora of European royalty stay here," Jamie said, draining his drink. He checked his watch. "Excuse me I need to go to the bathroom."

He sprang up and weaved his way through the tables. There was a pause and awkwardness as Archie sipped his drink and avoided her eye.

"Do you have a problem with me, Archie?"

He blinked, and his mouth curled upwards. "No. I just... No."

He had the air of someone observing his surroundings all the time, as if he was protecting Jamie. *Curious.* But it wasn't her place to judge their arrangement. At least he seemed less hostile.

"How did you meet each other?" she asked, glancing at Jamie, who paused to chat to people near the entrance. He clearly enjoyed being the centre of attention.

"Same college, and we travelled in Europe before the war."

Archie offered her some crisps and green olives in a bowl. If that was him offering a literal olive branch, she wasn't going to say no and grabbed a handful. He helped himself but didn't savour them one by one as she did.

"And what do you do now?" The subtext, which he probably understood, was, "why aren't you in uniform?"

"We've been working in London." That was a bit of spurious deflection if ever she heard it, but in the interest of keeping the peace she let it pass.

She smiled. "I wasn't trying to be rude, it's just unusual for men your age not to be in uniform." Maybe they were older than they seemed. She would have put them younger than twenty-five, but what did she know?

"Yes, it is, but we all serve the country how we can."

There was a slight awkwardness in the air, and Gloria was eager for Archie to continue to soften his stance towards her. "Exactly. Do you have any idea what this job entails, assuming we are offered a place?"

"No idea, but I'm sure it's secret."

Gloria took a sip of her gin. Was it spy work? But why crosswords? Was that an indicator of intelligence? Archie drummed his fingers on the table, as if he was playing a melody only he could hear. "Do you play the piano?"

His head shot up. "How did you know?"

Gloria indicated his phantom playing, which elicited the first smile she'd seen him make.

"Do you play?" Archie asked.

Bingo. Men were so simple; all she needed to do was discover what interested them and ask them questions. "Badly. I do sing though, which I enjoy. What music do you like? Classical...jazz?"

"Anything."

The tension eased as they discussed music, and Jamie returned a few minutes later, followed by a waiter carrying three more drinks. Jamie's presence was like a sun breaking through cloud, and they both basked in the warmth of his charm.

"I took the liberty of ordering some more while I was up."

Gloria stood. "That's very kind of you, Jamie, but I must go, otherwise my cousin will be worried. Thank you so much for whiling away the time with me and showing me the sights."

"No problem at all. Hold the table, Timlock. I'll just walk Bradford to a cab."

It must have been marvellous before the blackouts of the war, when the marbled tiles would reflect the light of the chandeliers, and the whole place would be lit up, welcoming patrons in from outside. She wished she'd had a quick peep in the powder room, but she needed to hurry or she'd be late.

Jamie shook her hand as the doorman hailed a taxi. "I do hope we meet again, Bradford. I've enjoyed our short time together. Here's my card. Look me up next time you're in London."

He turned to the cabbie and gave him a five-pound note. The cabbie grinned. That would cover her ride *and* a very generous tip. That was a week's wages to the male workers in her father's factory, and the women received about two thirds of that. No wonder they said London's streets were paved with gold.

Chapter Two

Just outside Bletchley, 1943

CAM LANGLEY FIDDLED WITH the icy lock on the henhouse. It held fast. She stamped her feet and huffed, emitting curls of vapour, like dragon's breath. She poured boiling water on the lock from the kettle she'd brought with her, then tried again. This time, the bolt slid out easily, releasing the hens for the day. There was still a five per cent chance that a fox would attack before she got back to pen them up in the evening, but Aunty Florrie couldn't manage the locks with her arthritic hands. Perhaps she could rig a simple wooden lever system that Aunty Florrie could use. She would manufacture it on her next day off.

The hens squawked and clucked as Cam scattered the food, distributed randomly so they would have to work for it and pick up grit in their diet that would help strengthen the eggshells. Cam stepped into the huts with the laying boxes, and the cacophony increased. Three, Four, and Seven had laid that day in their favourite nesting spots. She placed the warm eggs in the bottom of her metal bucket. She closed her eyes for a second to recalculate the averages to record in her notebook. Three, her favourite, was in the lead with an estimate of 247 eggs a year, a massive average of 4.75 eggs per week. The other hens had an average ranging from 2.3 eggs to 3.8 per week. She would need to change their bedding this weekend, even if she had to use shredded newspapers. The ink was probably not good for them but with the bedding shortages, she didn't have a choice. She stroked Three's beautiful feathers. "Goodbye, hens. Have a good day."

Cam headed towards the house, now shrouded in black silhouette against the violet sky. That usually threatened more bad weather. So much for March. She shivered. Today would be a full three-piece suit day. She strode back to the house, hurrying to get into the warmth.

Back in the kitchen, she refilled the kettle with exactly one and a half pints of water and placed it on the range's hob. She washed the eggs and mulled over the problem from work she'd struggled with the previous day. Her hope of having inspiration overnight had not thrown up anything worthwhile.

At the creaking of the floorboards upstairs—a sure sign that Aunty Florrie was up—she pushed two pieces of bread into the toaster, poured boiling water into the saucepan, and checked her watch as she placed the eggs inside, timing everything precisely to ensure the perfect boiled egg.

The latch to the kitchen opened, and Aunty Florrie shuffled in, her hair mussed from sleep. She raised her hand, then went through to the facilities behind the kitchen, the speed of her traverse indicating the need for the bathroom. While she waited for her aunt to return, Cam set the breakfasts and tea on the table and folded the newspaper by her plate.

Her aunt re-entered and dropped into the nearest chair, which creaked under the strain, and Cam hovered, waiting to pounce if it should topple. It was strange to think this frail old lady had once been a bigwig in a publishing company in London, one of the very few women who held a non-menial position before the war.

Aunty Florrie smiled and picked up her cup. "Good morning, Camilla. Did you sleep well?"

Cam winced. Her aunt was the only person she allowed to call her that. "I've left a stew to cook slowly for you to eat later," Cam said.

"Thank you. That's very kind of you, dear, but I need to keep doing things for myself. When you leave, I'll need to manage on my own."

"I've told you, Aunty, I'm not going anywhere." Cam sliced her egg and smiled at the perfect consistency of solid white and runny yolk. She poured a pinch of salt and pepper on the side of the plate and picked up her tiny egg spoon, then waited until her aunt took her first bite before she slipped the spoon into the yellow liquid.

"But what about after the war? You'll go back to your job in Cambridge. Or what if you find some nice young man to share with you?"

Not this conversation again. "Did you see in the newspaper that the Eighth Army is making headway in Tunisia." There was no way she would break the Official Secrets Act and reveal what she had decoded the other day, including the details of the German retreat.

"Yes, dear, I'm sure the war will still be there if I listen to it later. I'm worried about you. You need to spend more time with people your own age. I hate to think of you being so lonely."

"I'm not lonely. I've got you."

Her aunt's raised eyebrow indicated she knew Cam was lying, but how could she explain she was the oddball that people only spoke to when they needed something at work? And that people her age weren't interested in her company. But at least they treated her with respect. Work was the first time in her life that she'd put her mathematics skills to the test, trying to change the trajectory of war. "I have my work, and it's important to the war effort."

Her aunt shook her head and replaced her cup on its saucer.

Desperate to get her off that topic, Cam held up the teapot. "More tea?"

Even before her aunt spoke, Cam knew she would quote the same catchphrase from her favourite radio show, *It's That Man Again*: "I don't mind if I do."

Cam didn't understand the humour, but it made her aunt laugh, and it was worth enduring the comedy if it made Aunty Florrie happy. She flashed a smile. "Three, Four, and Seven laid again this morning. Three's laid an average of 4.75 eggs a week over the last year—"

"Perhaps you should have the extra .75 of an egg then. I'm sure one isn't enough to keep you going all day."

Cam scoffed her breakfast, not talking until she had finished, then laid her cutlery perpendicular to the table edge. "We have a canteen, Aunty, and I take my sandwiches, I told you. Now I must get ready for work."

Aunty Florrie set down her spoon. "I'm worried about you. The only things you have are work and looking after me. That's not enough for anyone."

"You said that already. I enjoy looking after you, and I love my work. Work gives me a sense of purpose. I don't need anything but that and you. And music."

Aunty Florrie shook her head and sighed as if Cam was being difficult or awkward. It was a look Cam was familiar with, having received it all her life, but usually not so kindly. It was all part of being different, she guessed. She stood and stacked the china into the bowl of water in the sink.

"Leave the crocks, I'll do them later."

"Are you sure?"

"Yes, dear. I've got all day, and you don't want to be late."

Cam nodded. "I'll see you later then, but don't wait up if it's very late."

"You work too hard."

"There's a war on, Aunt." She took the stairs two at a time and changed into the outfit that reflected her real self, one piece of men's clothing at a time. She fixed her tie expertly, straightened her waistcoat, and checked herself in the mirror. A little Brylcreem to slick down her hair, and she was ready. Transformation complete, she attached her bicycle clips around her trouser legs and let herself out of the front door, calling out goodbye to her aunt.

Chapter Three

GLORIA PUT HER CROSSWORD down and drained her cooling cup of tea. She glanced at her watch. Eleven minutes and twenty-one seconds: she was slipping, and the highlight of her day was now over. It had been three long weeks since she had bunked off to London, and she'd heard nothing. Reluctantly, she had to accept there'd be no secret role for her in the war, so she'd need to settle herself back into the mundanity of her life.

But she'd seen a glimpse of life beyond her cage and wanted more of it.

She glanced up to meet the glare of the office manager, Nancy Ramsbottom, from across the canteen. Doubtless, Nancy would make some sarcastic comment about Gloria not getting back from tea break five minutes early to set an example to her department. Gloria sighed and rose to approach the table where a gaggle of middle-aged women chattered. The moment they saw her, they fell silent and sullen expressions abounded.

"Tea break is over." Without waiting for a reply, Gloria whirled around and marched to the door.

"Who does she think she is, lording it over us?" Edith Lofthouse, ever the troublemaker said. "She only got the supervisor job because her da's the gaffer."

She pretended she didn't hear, even though Edith had raised her voice deliberately. If only they knew how she hated doing what she did. But she could never say anything as they'd say she was an ungrateful bairn who didn't know which side of her bread was buttered. She unlocked the heavy metal door and accessed the safe to retrieve the bags of cash that the women would sort and place into little tins with their number on for the workers to pick up this evening. When the last woman, Edith of course, dallied into the room surrounded by a miasma of smoke from a hastily extinguished cigarette, Gloria locked the door behind her and slid open the small window in the wall, where people could pick up their wages when the factory hooter went.

Her new system worked so well, with checks and counterchecks, that Gloria had little to do until the women completed the wages. When she had rearranged her desk for the third time that day, Anne Coggins gave her the second listing to be calculated and brought across the tray of tins and supporting documentation for her to check.

Gloria devised a game with herself of trying to beat Edith, the comptometer operator, to tally the columns. Not that she'd ever admit that, even though she usually won. She traced her index finger down the list of employees, then frowned. "Is this right? Richard Kirby is on a lower piece rate than the other workers."

Anne shrugged. "You'd better talk to Nancy Ramsbottom about that. She said summat about the union being narked how fast he worked, so your da agreed to a lower amount until he kept to the official work rate."

Gloria heard the slight sneer. It didn't take a genius to work out that the women resented her. That she didn't want the job apparently counted for nothing. "But that's ridiculous and unfair. There's a war on; we should be maximising output to help the war effort."

"Nowt to do with me. I just follow orders."

"Aye, thanks, Anne. Will you supervise the others while I go and talk to Nancy about this?"

As Gloria click-clacked her way down the corridors, the constant thumping from the presses vibrated through her entire body and the heat from the furnaces increased until she opened the door to the factory feeling like she was teetering on the entrance to hell. Steeling herself to face the incredible heat and noise, she threaded her way through the workstations till she came to the corner, then clanged her way up the metal stairs to the office that oversaw the entire building. She knocked on the door.

"Wait a moment."

The squeaking of the office chair, whispers, and the sound of the inner door closing followed. Gloria tried not to imagine what was going on behind there and wished she hadn't come, carried along by a wave of righteous anger. Her mam always said her temper would get her into trouble.

A minute seemed like eternity before Nancy called out, "Come in."

On seeing Gloria, Nancy's false, sweet smile dropped. "What do you want?"

Nancy was the epitome of mutton dressed as lamb, with her black silk stockings, her skirt twisted and way too short to be respectable, and make-up so thick, it'd take a trowel to scrape it off. Her bright red lipstick was smeared, and one button on her blouse was adrift, revealing pale skin and the hint of a white bra.

Gloria didn't need any more evidence of her da's infidelity with his secretary, whom he'd promoted to become office manager. She seemed to do the same as she had always done: take care of all his needs—including those non-work related, judging by Nancy's appearance. His hypocrisy of playing the doting husband and upright citizen sickened her. But she didn't even know if her mam would register the insult. She needed to focus on now. "There's a problem. Young Richard Kirby is being paid at a lower than standard rate for every tank track he produces even though he works through twice as much as anyone else. Is it correct that he's being punished because he's working too hard?"

Nancy's eyelids fluttered, and she opened her mouth but before she could utter a word, the inner door opened, and Da emerged.

"That's none of your business."

Gloria wasn't about to be intimidated; she wasn't her mam. She stood to her full height and stared him down. "Yes, it is. My job is to ensure that all payments are correct and legal—"

"We can't afford a strike over this. We're on a tight deadline to get the tank tracks to the Army, and I'm going to double the overnight shift. The rate stays."

His thick eyebrows formed one deep V-shape, and his eyes were hard without any trace of affection. Long gone was the indulgent smile he'd once reserved for her, when she could wrap him around her little finger.

"In that case, I would like your signature on the payroll documents by his name."

"Don't trust me?"

Gloria handed over the pages. She wasn't going to fall for his inconsistencies again; she'd been caught too many times over the years. With a huff of barely disguised exasperation, he snatched it from her, took the pen Nancy offered, and leaned against the desk to scribble his name. He thrust the papers back at her but carefully replaced the cap on the pen that he handed over to Nancy with a sweet smile. Gloria squashed down the nausea.

"I don't want my time wasted again. We're very busy up here."

Gloria coughed to disguise her laughter, which elicited another glare from him. Nancy lifted a letter from her pending tray and tipped her head to Gloria.

Her father snorted. "That's another waste of time. She's not going."

Gloria tried to glimpse at the letter. "What's that?"

"Nothing you need to worry about," he said.

Nancy looked up at him. "I think she should know."

"Know what?" Gloria hoped but didn't believe that the letter might be from the Foreign Office.

On her father's tiniest of nods, Nancy smiled and retrieved the letter from the envelope. "It's from the Foreign Office asking for a reference for you. Something about a crossword puzzle exam."

Gloria's heart sped up, and she couldn't conceal her grin. "They're interested?"

Nancy nodded, but her father snatched the letter from Nancy's hands. "It doesn't matter. You're not going to some stuck-up Foreign Office, where they'll look down at you because you don't talk with a plum in your mouth. You can be here where you're doing important war work—"

Rage pounded in her head. "Where you can set me up with your selected successor, you mean. If you're so desperate to retire, do it now and hand the business to Stanley Arkwright, assuming he's still the latest flavour of the month. Leave me out of it." Words spewed out before her brain could modify them.

"It's not the same. I want an Edwards to be involved in the business. Our name is over the door. If your brother was still alive, well, it would be different..."

A sudden sadness misted his eyes, but she wouldn't feel guilty. It was over two years since Ben had been killed in the Battle of Britain, and there was a hole in their family that couldn't be filled by any of the jingoistic rhetoric. She couldn't believe they'd never sing together again, or play cricket or chess, or bicker about who would get the first piece of cake. She inhaled and pulled herself away from that abyss. "If you want an Edwards to run the company, choose me. I could make it so much more efficient."

He shook his head. "You'd have the unions out on strike before you could utter the word efficiency. This is Yorkshire, lassie. No men are going to take their orders from a woman. They respect Stanley Arkwright, and he's a fine young man—"

"Who's ten years older than I am and has bad breath, and whose sole topic of conversation is the respective attributes of different furnaces. Oh, and the Yorkshire cricket club. Don't force that on me, Da. This way, I'll have a genuine opportunity to do important war work, and it'll make me happy."

His mouth puckered like a duck's arse, and he inhaled as if he was on the brink of declining.

Nancy took the letter back. "Perhaps you should let her go, William. She's never going to be happy here. None of her colleagues trust her, and that can't be easy."

Gloria clamped her mouth shut. Nancy supporting her was an enormous surprise, but it *would* be in her interest to get Gloria out of the way. Whatever the reason, she didn't care. "Nancy's right. Besides, I'd hate to accidentally stumble into something at work I shouldn't see."

Her father's neck turned as red as the factory furnaces. "I don't know what you mean."

Nancy's mouth tightened into a thin line.

Perhaps she'd overplayed her hand. "I understand. Mam isn't herself and hasn't been since Ben died. But why should you be the only one who gets to do what they want? I hate it here, and you'll never make me the boss. The workers resent me because I'm the gaffer's daughter. But I could contribute to the war effort here," she gestured to the letter, "on my terms and through my own skill. Anne Coggins could easily do my job now I've set up a new system, and you could save my salary. And I've organised for Mrs Henderson to help Mam at home. If Ben were alive, you wouldn't hold me back." She paused, hoping her words would penetrate her father's armour like a bullet.

He crumpled for a second before forcing himself upright. "But he's not alive. The answer's no. You're needed here. Now get back to work, the hooter for shift end will go off in ten minutes."

"This isn't the end of this." Gloria snatched up the signed wages documents and hurried out of the office. As the door clicked shut, she heard her father's whisper, "Now, where were we?" She really didn't want to picture where they were or where they were going. She had to escape here before she went mad, or worse, was forced to submit to her da's wishes and live with a crushed soul.

Chapter Four

A FEW DAYS LATER, Cam ran her hand through her hair for the umpteenth time, no doubt ruffling her pristine look. Could this day get any worse? The Germans had recently changed their Enigma coding machines and had left the allies no longer able to decipher the codes. Consequently, the messages they received from the Y radio intercept stations were just lines of garbled text. Their job in the Duddery was to take the information and decipher the failed messages manually. They were back at stage one, and the hollowed eyes and grim determination reflected the knowledge that every message unsolved could be the vital one in the action. That didn't stop them trying though; hours and days of scrabbling and scratching, but all to no avail.

Her stomach rumbled, reminding her she hadn't eaten since early this morning. Aunty Florrie hadn't come down for breakfast. She said she'd been tired and her arthritis had kept her awake most of the night. The cold certainly didn't help. It had taken Cam nineteen minutes to help her aunt downstairs. Nineteen minutes that meant she wouldn't have time to make sandwiches. She would need to go to the canteen to grab some food, even though she detested the place. Sighing, she rose, collected her jacket, and made her way outside towards the dining hall.

When she heard her name being called, her spine stiffened. A woman approached her smiling in recognition. Beatrice Williams looked very dapper in her Wren's uniform, but her gaunt face and shadows around her eyes probably reflected Cam's. It shouldn't have surprised her when Bea ended up at Bletchley Park. Not that their paths crossed very much; they were on different shifts, and people had to be discreet about what they were doing. And Cam never joined the men in the hut for drinks after their shift finished.

Beatrice bounced up to her, her blond curls threatening to spill out of her bun. "Hello, Cam. Just the person I wanted to see."

Cam didn't believe that as no one ever wanted to see her except if they wanted something, but she smiled anyway. "Hello, Beatrice."

Bea laughed. "How many times do I have to tell you to call me Bea? If you persist, I will call you Camilla." Cam scowled, but Bea just laughed again. "I'm only teasing you. I'm arranging a concert. Do you still play cello and sing?"

That was the problem with having been known in a previous life. She couldn't deny that she had played cello and sung in a concert once at Cambridge. That she'd done it to please Mary Orme, whom she admired from afar, was irrelevant. Playing with associates was fine, but performing in public made her skin crawl, being on display for jeering and mockery. "Yes, but I haven't practiced for a long time."

"Perfect. We're getting together a small orchestra. Not me, of course. My violin playing was worse than cats scrapping at night. You're on the C shift rotation, aren't you? You could come along after work on Tuesday evenings."

"I don't want to join the orchestra. I can't commit to it, you know how little time we get, and I'm not interested in performing in public."

"Remind me. What do you sing? Alto?"

Bea was worse than a dog with a bone. "Tenor."

Bea clapped her hands together. "Ooh, a tenor. We're always short of tenors. Probably because most of the men here are rather long in the tooth, and their range is in their boots. You must come along. Tenors are so welcome. We need you; please say yes. We sing a range of–"

"I hate Gilbert and Sullivan."

"That's fine. Almost all the repertoire is classical choral music. For the last concert, we did Verdi's *Requiem*. If you come along to choir on Wednesday night, you can make a request for our next concert. There are some wonderful tenor parts you could take on."

Bea touched Cam's forearm, and for once, she didn't flinch.

"Come along on Wednesday for the choir auditions. You can choose a song to sing, and if you really hate it after that, you don't have to come again. Or you could do a solo, where you could practice on your own. Or a duet from one of the operas maybe?"

Arguing with Bea was like swimming against a rip tide. "I'll think about it. Now I need to eat."

"Perfect."

Bea's full bloom smile made her look much younger, like when they were back at Cambridge together. Even now she was still radiant, despite the long hours and the nature of the work they did, and the privations and uncertainty of the war.

When they parted, Cam straightened her tie, pulled down her waistcoat, and headed towards the dining hall. The noise of chattering people, scraping chairs, and clattering of cutlery on crockery exploded in her head and confirmed why she hated the canteen so much. Her heart began to race, and the crowd of people seemed to press in on her. She pulled at her collar and was about to flee, when her colleagues entered and fell into the queue behind her. Their discussion about cricket and the pub was too loud and braying. As if any of those things mattered anyway. She was caught between her growling stomach and her need to escape.

"What are you having, duck?" the canteen assistant asked, looking bored.

Cam tried for a smile and scanned the meagre fare. "Spam fritters, mashed potato, carrots, and a cup of tea, please."

The assistant slapped a small portion onto the plate, and Cam helped herself to a cube of sugar. With rations, it was hard to satisfy her sweet tooth, so the sugar in her tea was a little treat. At home they saved the sugar so Auntie Florrie could bake cakes. Cam picked up her tray and scanned the crowded hall. There were a few empty tables in the far corner by the open door. It probably meant they were in a draught, but it still offered a refuge. Anything that minimised this jostling, seething mass of humanity was welcome to stave off the headache that had her in a vice grip. The effort required to block out the noise and commotion of the crowd left her drained, and she almost turned around.

Instead, she threaded her way through the noisy hall and positioned herself so she faced the outside where she could enjoy the view of the late daffodils fringing the lake and imagine she was alone in the countryside. The wind whipped in through the gaping hole, and she pulled her jacket tighter. Cam exhaled her anxiety and picked up her cutlery, but she had hardly taken her first mouthful when her colleagues arrived in a torrent of noise and laughter.

"Thanks for saving the table. We couldn't see you for a minute."

That was the plan. Her aunt's warning flitted in her brain: "Play nicely." They meant well, so she forced a smile. "It was the only spare table away from the noise." It was an almost truth and they didn't question it.

The men sat down and conversed around her, which gave her the opportunity to reflect on the morning's work. It had been so frustrating trying to guess the key to the cypher they were working on. Maybe they would have to go back to when they'd first solved the Italian maritime codes. She would never forget the thrill when she had worked out that the first few letters of the Italian message weren't "per", the Italian for "for", followed by X to indicate a space, but "personale" followed by an X. From there, the code had flowed as easily for her as solving a crossword puzzle, and they had read the messages from the Italian navy detailing the plans to attack the British fleet in the Mediterranean. That major sea battle had taken the Italian navy out of the war.

Their section of "Dilly's girls" had been commended, and they'd received a visit from the admiral some weeks later. She hated being thought of as a girl. Dilly didn't care that Cam dressed in men's clothing; he was only interested in what their brains could uncover. Dilly had died from cancer a month ago, but his work continued. And though the awful war dragged on, she'd found it was where she came alive. Now they'd transferred her to the Duddery with a new set of men to work with, and they circled each other, not trusting or helping anyone but themselves. If only she was back in the cottage with the rest of Dilly's girls. The Germans must have changed the machines or the cyphers again as they were getting more messages that couldn't be resolved by Alan Turing and Welchman's Bombe machines. And each night, the machines slipped over to another setting of the Enigma machine rotors for the day. The cribs they used to prompt the machines, using the weather station codes and looking for standard phrases, didn't seem to work. Maybe if they went back to looking at the end of the codes, they would include the words "Heil Hitler," which they could then use to work backwards. She hadn't double-checked that this morning.

Cam stood abruptly and took her tray to the collection point.

"Rude invert," someone muttered.

She realised she hadn't excused herself. Rude, she understood, but the latter word threw her back into her childhood of being mocked and bullied because she was a tomboy. Cam picked up her pace to go back to their hut and pulled her jacket closer to keep out the wind. Even the ducks huddled near the edges of the lake. So much for spring. The hut smelled damp, and the single pane windows misted with condensation. She dropped into her creaky chair and stared at the codes. Nausea bubbled up unbidden. She'd felt respected here, but they were just as judgemental here as everyone else had been all her life. No wonder she was alone.

When her colleagues returned to work, she nodded at them

but said nothing. She worked on a different crib for the cypher. An hour later, the message revealed itself. *Bingo.* She passed it on to be translated, encrypted, and sent to the powers that be who would decide what to do with the information.

"Well done," Jamie Gordon said.

Her deputy section and head of shift had been the ringleader at the lunch table. Did he think she was an invert too? Did he consider her an oddity who dressed like a man? She acknowledged his praise with a blink, unsure if he was being sarcastic or not.

"It's way past shift end. Go home now, but don't forget to clear out your locker."

He didn't need to tell her the daily security protocol. Cam glared at him. "I know."

Jamie held up his hands. "Prickly. I was only saying. You've worked hard, and you seem tired."

"We're all tired. I would not forget to clear my desk and locker. I've done it for one year, eleven months, and two days now." She picked up her bag, straightened the pleats on her trousers, and affixed her bicycle clips. "Goodnight," she said as an afterthought, not wishing to be called rude again.

She strode to the bike racks, then exited through the security gates. As she cycled away, pumping hard on the pedals and peering into the gloom with the partially covered lights, she tried to expunge her anger before she arrived home to Aunty Florrie. Just once, she would like to be accepted for who she was.

Chapter Five

GLORIA UNLOCKED THE FRONT door and had to push against the pile of newspapers and letters behind the door. That was not a good sign. "Ay up, Mam, I'm home," she said as brightly as she could manage. Silence. She stooped to pick up the *Telegraph and Argus* paper, covered in tiny print to save paper, three letters for Da, and a thick brown envelope with a black crown on it addressed to her. She threw down the other mail on the sideboard and clutched the letter to her chest. Surely it wouldn't be thick unless it was good news. She ripped it open, and her heart raced at the sight of a rail warrant and a letter.

"Congratulations. Subject to a suitable reference, you are invited to arrive at Euston Station," she read out loud then let out a whoop.

"Gloria, is that you?"

In her excitement, she'd forgotten anyone else would be in the house. "Yes, Mam." The letter would have to wait until it could be read in private, but she didn't trust her da not to burn it if he saw it. She slipped the envelope into her handbag and placed it at the bottom of the stairs.

"Gloria?"

"Coming, Mam." She set a smile on her face and swallowed hard before entering the dining room. Her mam was exactly where she'd been when Gloria had set out her breakfast this morning, and the cereal was congealed in the bowl. Gloria glanced at the clock on the mantelpiece: five thirty already. When her da came home, he'd expect his food on the table.

"Come on, Mam. Da will be home soon. Go and freshen

yourself up, then lay the table while I make the tea." She snatched up the bowl and cereal packet and hurried into the kitchen. He would have eaten in the works canteen, but he always liked meat when they could get it. She checked on the settle in the pantry where three slices of bacon were wrapped in wax paper. Bacon butties would have to do.

She washed her hands under the tap, but the water was cold. Clearly, her mam had forgotten to switch on the copper. Her dad would want a bath before he went out this evening. Aware of only having a few minutes before he arrived, she ran to fix the water, then hurried back to cook the bacon. Anything to cover that her mam'd had a bad day. The sooner Mrs Henderson arrived to help, the better. Their old housekeeper had been willing to return and help cook and clean for her mam as it gave her "summat to do to keep my mind off the war." Gloria suspected Mrs Henderson's enthusiasm came more from not having to heat her house during the day and being able to stash extra cash into her war bonds. Gloria shook her head at herself. That was churlish. She was overwhelmed with gratitude for the support even if the woman had terrified her when she was a child.

The bacon spat and sizzled as it fried, the smell causing her to salivate. She smeared the butter over the loaf, then scraped it off so only a sheen remained. Finally, she cut the thinnest slices of bread to eke the loaf out for another day.

Her thoughts were a jumble: excitement that she could escape mixed with guilt and concern for her mam. Her mam made her way upstairs slowly, heaving up each leg as though it weighed a ton. Gloria was thankful that Mrs Henderson was coming from Monday. It eased Gloria's guilt at abandoning her mam, but there was little more she could do.

A thrill ran through her as she took another peep in the official envelope, just to confirm it didn't say something different when she looked again. But there it was: a rail warrant and an invitation to London at ten a.m. on Monday morning with enough clothes for a two-week stay. So soon. How would she get to Euston that early? She would need to stay with Hatty in Watford the night before. A hotel would be an unnecessary expense, and she really wanted to buy a pair of stockings to take with her for best. She bit her bottom lip, weighing whether she should go or not. No one would miss her at work, her old school friends had moved on, and her mam would be okay if Mrs Henderson worked out all right. Her da was mainly absent, so he didn't count. And she wasn't going to wait here until he insisted she get married just to continue the Edwards' bloodline in the factory. No, she needed to escape. Gloria went to the hall, picked up the phone and asked the operator for Hatty's number, hoping she would answer rather than her mother, Aunty Barbara.

"'Ow do, Hatty. I have to be quick as Da will be home any minute. Can you ask your mam if I can stay on Sunday night. I have to be at Euston at ten o'clock on Monday. They offered me a job. I'm not sure what I'll be doing, but anything's better than here."

"I'm sure that'll be grand. Let me check."

While she waited for an answer, Gloria rushed to put the bacon in the oven to keep warm and hurriedly laid the table as her mam had yet to emerge.

"That's fine," Hatty said when they reconnected.

Gloria jumped when a key in the front door lock rattled. "I must go. Da's just arrived, and I need to sort out the tea. I'll call when I can with the details. Thank you." Bless her, she owed Hatty a huge favour. Maybe she could take her down some sticky parkin cake, which was very difficult to get in the south.

She hurried back to the kitchen and switched on the kettle. She removed the bacon from the oven and used two pieces to make her dad's butty and half each in hers and her mam's.

Gloria knew she was in trouble when her father put down his food halfway through tea. He was clearly still seething about their conversation earlier. He must realise she had a hold over him because of Nancy. She didn't want to use it, but she would if he forced her hand.

"I've had a letter today from the Foreign Office commanding me to report for duty on Monday morning at Euston station." Better get her defence in first before he worked himself into a rage.

"What's that?" Her mother looked up with milky eyes. "Is our Ben coming back?"

Gloria exchanged a look with her da. Her mam's grasp of reality was tenuous, and she would recall little of it later.

"No, Mam. I've had a letter calling me up to work for the Foreign Office," she said softly.

"As though the only bloody work that's important in this war is pushing papers around." Spittle flew from his mouth. "The real work is done by those producing the goods, the people keeping the factories going to build the tanks that mean we can win this war."

Gloria patted her mother's hand gently then glared at her da. "You're like a broken record. We know it's important, but so is the work other people do—"

"What's so important that you have to abandon us in our hour of need? How will your mam cope?"

He must know he was losing the argument if he was resorting to emotional blackmail. She smoothed down her skirt, wondering how best to approach this to elicit a yes. She didn't really want to leave with bad blood between them. "I'm not sure. It's secret."

His face coloured red. "You're not sure? How do you know it's not some cock and bull story to get you to be some prostitute to the high-ups?"

"Don't be ridiculous, Da. There are hundreds of secret jobs that need doing for the war effort."

"You fancy yourself as a spy? You'd be bloody useless the moment you opened your mouth; the only language you speak is Yorkshire."

"No, I don't think it's spy work, Da, but it does involve secrets. I want to do my duty, and I can make a bigger contribution to the war than I am here."

"Is this to do with the crossword nonsense? Where did you go for the test?"

Gloria exhaled noisily. "In London when I went to visit Hatty. I did the test first then met her for afternoon tea." She avoided mentioning going with strangers in a cab to the Savoy; it had been risky but it seemed exciting at the time, and she'd thought of Jamie a lot since. He reminded her of Ben.

Her da slammed his fist on the table, making the cups rattle in their saucers. "You lied to us."

Gloria hardly contained her contempt. "Like you've never lied? I kept it secret because you would never have agreed to me going."

He looked as if he was about to argue on both counts, but she could reveal his illicit affair, and that realisation seemed to cross his face. She glanced at her mam, who looked puzzled. It was hard to believe this woman had been a community-respected maths teacher once. "Perhaps mam can take my place doing the calculations?"

Mam looked up and for once, her eyes seemed clear. "What's that, dear?"

Da glared at her. "She can't go to the office, you know that." The real reason hung between them, charging the air with anticipation. One sentence could change their whole lives. "She would hate the noise and the bustle," he said. "And she's in no fit state."

"Maybe she needs to do something rather than sitting around moping and feeling sorry for herself. Sorry, Mam. We shouldn't talk about you as if you're not there." Gloria sat up straighter. "I need to do my duty."

"Duty? What do you know about duty? Duty isn't just a word to toss around. It's a code of honour, a value to aspire to. It's something that keeps you going when it gets tough. Your duty is here looking after your mam and making sure there's a meal on the table when I get home."

"All of which will be done much better by Mrs Henderson when she gets here next Monday." Her heart thundered in her chest as fast as any of the mechanical factory hammers. "What about your duty as a husband, making sure Mam gets the help and support she needs?"

The sudden pain across her cheek was such a shock that she didn't understand what had happened at first. *You hit me.* His Masonic ring had caught her cheekbone. Her face throbbed and her eye began to close. Something wet trickled down her face. She wasn't sure if it was blood or tears. She tenderly touched around the wound. When she pulled away her hand, the telltale red stained her fingers. Her eyes watered, but she didn't cry. The sting and swelling of her cheek were nothing to the realisation of what had happened. The ache jolted her into a pulsing rage. "How dare you?" It took everything she had not to retaliate by raining blows on him.

He seemed as shocked as she was. She'd always been the apple of his eye—until she wasn't. The disintegration of her family, Mam's disengagement from the world as she suffered from her nerves, her da's cheating and staying away from home, and her own grief that still came in waves all stemmed from Ben's death.

Her da had never been violent before, and he stared down onto the tablecloth as though he couldn't believe it either and was having to reassess who he was.

"Sorry, lassie, you drove me to distraction."

Blood throbbed in her ears with a rush. She picked up her plate and pushed away from the table. "Don't blame your weakness and lack of control on me."

"Where are you going?"

"To the kitchen to clean up my face and wash my plate. And then I'm going to pack."

"You can't go."

She ignored his desperate-sounding plea. "I have a letter, a travel warrant, and instructions. I'm not staying here to be assaulted." Her voice was remarkably calm, at odds with how her nerve ends fizzed beneath her skin.

"As your father, I forbid you to go."

"As my father? The father who supposedly loves his daughter yet hits her across the face. You've just lost your daughter." Gloria caught sight of her mam clutching her chest, her eyes as wide and round as her mouth. Gloria wiped at her cheek with a handkerchief. "I'm going to put a cold compress on to stop the swelling."

Her mam cleared her throat. "Let her go, William."

"She's not twenty-one yet. I say she stays. And what about her part as Mimi?"

Interesting that he hadn't wanted her to sing in the local amateur operatic society before but was quick to use it as an excuse for her not to leave. All the filial duty and respect she'd had for him gushed out along with the blood that seeped from her skin. Her handkerchief was soaked a deep red, and it still wasn't stopping. Maybe this moment had been coming; the thin layer that had held the family together split and melted, leaving three lonely individuals with nothing bonding them together. She was done. She needed to start a new phase of her life.

"She wants to go. What life is it here for her to follow in your footsteps? She's a good girl; she's been cooking and running the house single-handed, but Mrs Henderson is coming on Monday. If she can use her brain and be part of the war effort, she should."

Gloria stared at Mam. She hadn't been this animated in years, as though the slap had jolted her awake. And she had sided with Gloria. She stepped across and gave her mam a hug, being careful not to drip blood on her.

Her mam clung to her. "Sorry I haven't been here for you... to protect you." She turned to Da with just a hint of mischief in her eyes. "Gloria's right. She can make a bigger contribution elsewhere. And I might come along to the cash office."

Now Da looked slightly panicked and sweat formed on his forehead. "No. The factory wouldn't do for you, love. Maybe we can get you something else. You're too frail for factory work."

"I know why you don't want me in the office. I'm not blind or stupid, William. Do you hate us so much that you're prepared to ruin our family?"

Da wiped his brow with his monogrammed handkerchief. In the past, he would have thought such an article to be ostentatious. Now his war contracts had made him a wealthy man, he was adopting the signs of capitalism. Yet another example of how they had all changed.

"Our family was ruined when our Ben died," he said, his voice choking a little.

That's what it always boiled down to: Ben being killed and not stepping into their father's footsteps. Da slumped in his chair and rested his head in his hands as if he could no longer support himself or his family.

"I'll leave tomorrow morning and stay with Hatty until Monday. Goodnight." Gloria managed to retain her composure until she reached the kitchen sink, where tears stung the graze on her face, and dropped salt on her lips. Her cheek felt huge and sore to the touch. She could see the swelling in her peripheral vision, so she extracted a flannel from the cabinet, soaked it, and placed the cloth over her handkerchief. She sagged onto the kitchen chair and tenderly dabbed around the wound.

A gentle grip on her shoulder made her look up.

Mam stood beside her, her expression clear but sorrowful. "Let me help."

Her mam took the flannel and caressed her cheek, like she had when Gloria was a child. Her old mam seemed to peer from behind the usual mask. It probably wouldn't last, but Gloria was grateful for the glimpse of what once was.

"I'm proud of you wanting to do your duty, and I'm envious you get to escape. It's exciting, and you need that. You always were headstrong and determined. You need to fly. It's what our Ben would have wanted."

Gloria placed a hand on her mam's arm. "I'm sorry I'm leaving you with him."

"We'll be fine. Mrs Henderson is coming on Monday. And you're right; I should do my duty too. I'm sure the school needs teachers now that so many of them have been called up. Perhaps I'll go back there. Now, look up. Let me put this on you. This will sting a little." She dabbed the cut with TCP.

"You always used this as a cure-all when we were kids, from cuts to sore throats. Thanks for standing up for me."

Gloria doubted her mam would cope with the demands of a school, but she wasn't going to be the one to say that. Maybe things could change for both of them. She stared into her mam's eyes, grateful for the flicker of intelligence and kindness that had been numbed these past years.

The antiseptic made Gloria wince. "I think I'll have a big bruise there tomorrow."

"You will, my love. Put on a bit of foundation and hopefully, no one will notice. I can let you have some."

The thought of two-year-old foundation made Gloria shudder. "Thanks, but I've got some. Will you be all right with Da on your own?" She searched her mam's face.

"Yes, love. And if I'm not, I'll see if Ailish needs help with little Benji. Or I'll go and stay with Aunty Barbara. She'll probably need some help in their store, especially when Hatty gets married and has her baby."

So, her mam did know about that. Had Gloria been doing her mam a disservice over the last couple of years by doing everything for her?

Mam put the bottle down. "How exciting. Almost exciting as you doing secret work. Go and fly Gloria."

"Thank you, Mam. I love you." Gloria held her mam close and let the excitement wash over her. She was going to escape this life and contribute to winning the war. She would do her duty and live a different life, a stimulating life. A real life. "I hope you fly yourself, Mam."

Her mam shook her head but smiled. "I need to walk first, but maybe there'll be a path I can tread."

"I think it's what Ben would have wanted." Gloria returned the smile and recalled one of the last conversations she'd had with Ben before he left to join his squadron.

"I want to serve my country, to save it and keep it safe, so we can all have tea and cake and sing around the piano. If anything happens to me, GeeGee, please keep singing."

I'll keep singing, Ben. I'll keep singing.

Chapter Six

CAM PUNCHED AND PUMMELLED the heavy bag swinging from the beam in the old stables till the sweat from her brow mingled with the tears. "Invert" screamed round her head. She hadn't heard that used as a taunt against her since the publication of Radclyffe Hall's *The Well of Loneliness*, and in the place where she thought her colleagues respected her. *Thump.* She needed the physical exertion to sweat out the toxicity of their words and judgement, but it was taking longer and was harder than she anticipated.

She wiped her eyes and nose with the back of her wrapped hand then gave a particularly vicious hook that swung the bag with an ominous creak. Not that she would stop. Just as she had channelled her fury as a child by running until she was exhausted, now she boxed.

It was curious how the insult only landed because she believed it at some level. She knew she was an invert, and she was proud of it. She loved how men's clothes looked on her, how she stood differently, how she felt within herself. So why was she so upset? Because she knew she would be like Stephen in *The Well of Loneliness* and never find reciprocated love or happiness. The constant jarring against the bag was making her shoulders ache and her hands tremble. But she couldn't stop until she had beaten out the frustration and fury in full. She wouldn't stop until she was spent and dripping sweat on the floor.

A few minutes later, just before she got to that state of exhaustion, the door creaked, and her aunt shuffled in.

"Cam, stop. You'll pull the rafters down. I can hear you from inside the house. What's the problem?"

Her aunt caught the bag, and Cam dropped her gloves to her side. She faced Aunty Florrie and saw her worried frown. Auntie Florrie opened her arms and without thinking, Cam stepped into them and laid her head on Florrie's shoulder and she let the tears flow.

"Come, my precious soul, what is it?"

The rough wool of Aunty Florrie's cardigan did almost the same trick as the boxing. "My colleagues called me rude in the dining hall."

"Why would they do that?"

Cam looked up into her kind eyes. "I was thinking about a problem at lunch then suddenly thought of something I hadn't tried."

"So you got up and walked away without excusing yourself?"

The sweat cooled on her body, and Cam shivered. "Yes. I wasn't trying to be rude. But they talk such facile nonsense, I hate it and get bored. I lose myself in thinking about what's important."

Aunty Florrie nodded. "You always did that as a child too, working out whatever was on your mind. There's nothing wrong with that. Look where it got you with your good job at Cambridge, one of only a few women to be given that honour. And in mathematics too. You're so clever."

Cam gave an exasperated huff, pulled away from her aunt, and wiped at the damp patch on the cardigan. "Sorry. I've made a mess on your shoulder."

"It doesn't matter, Cam, dear."

She could hardly look at her aunt. "And they called me an invert." If she'd expected judgement in her aunt's expression, she found none.

She shook her head and grabbed Cam's wrapped hands in her frail ones. "You are you. You were always a tomboy as a child. I remember you standing in the stream, so proud you'd built a dam so you could watch how the water flooded. It would have been okay except you drowned your mother's garden and ruined all her flowers."

"I remember." Cam shared a rueful smile with Auntie Florrie. "Why can't you just be normal, like other girls?" her mother had said with an exasperated huff. She still didn't have an answer. Cam stared down at their joined hands and then pulled away. She jerked the string of her wraps between her teeth to untie the knot.

"You've always been uniquely you, and I love you for it." Her aunt reached out but stopped before touching her.

Cam unwound the wrapping, exposing her emotions as well as her reddened hands. "Thank you, Aunty. But am I always destined to be alone? To be unhappy?"

Aunty Florrie cocked her head. "Are you unhappy? I thought you loved your job."

"No. I use my skills, and it's challenging, and I'm making a difference. You know I can't tell you how, but I love it."

"I don't see what the problem is."

"I thought my colleagues respected me, but then they insulted and mocked me."

"I'm sure they respect your work. But it seems as though the loneliness is getting to you. Perhaps you could join in with the activities I've heard go on there, concerts and the like. You've got a beautiful voice. It seems a shame not to share it with the world."

Cam gave a watery laugh. "It's funny you say that. Bea Williams, who was one of my students at Cambridge before the war, saw me today and asked me to join the choir."

"Perfect. I hope you're going to."

"I don't know. I'm not very good at social things. I get tongue-tied and panicky."

"Oh, Cam, you're like a volcano. There's so much going on underneath, and it all builds up until it explodes."

"I find it difficult to express my emotions."

"I know. I think sometimes people forget how much you feel because you seem so calm and logical."

Cam snatched up her towel and started to rub down some of the sweat. "Like my parents, you mean?"

Aunty Florrie sighed. "I'll never understand how they turned their back on you because you don't fit in with their expectation of a daughter. They've missed out on a kind, intelligent, wonderful person, and I've gained so much. But I shouldn't be the only person you see outside work."

Cam had never been sure if her parents had explained to Aunty Florrie why they had cut Cam from their lives, but she clearly wasn't fazed. "I'm too busy for friendships."

"Maybe just pop along to the choir and see how it goes. Bea sounds like a nice woman. Why not just do a solo or duet?"

Cam looked up sharply. "Has Bea been speaking to you?"

Aunty Florrie laughed. "Of course not, dear. I've never met her, but she sounds like a good soul. Why don't you invite her around for tea?"

"Oh, no, I can't." Something pulled at the corners of her consciousness. "Wait. How do you know about the expression invert?"

"Wasn't it all the topic of scandal in *The Well of Loneliness*?"

There was something about the mischievous gleam in her aunt's eye that prompted Cam's suspicion. "Have you read it?"

Her aunt gave a cheeky smile. "I was curious to see what all the fuss is about."

"But how did you get a copy when it's banned? I only read it because Mary Orme brought over a copy from America covered in brown paper and slipped it in between her other books. It did the rounds in Cambridge."

"Well, I do still have contacts in the publishing business. And no, you're not Stephen, you are not going to be a martyr, and why shouldn't you have a happy, fulfilled life? You've no need to be lonely. You shouldn't spend all your time looking after an old biddy like me." Her aunt grunted and shuffled to get herself moving again.

There was so much more to be said, but Aunty Florrie was too uncomfortable to continue with the conversation. Cam hated it when people pushed her to reveal more than she wanted, so she'd never do the same. "Of course. Are you getting cold? Let's go in and have a nice warm cup of tea."

"Sod the tea. Let's have a whisky. It cures all ills from matters of the heart to stiff joints."

Cam laughed. "If you say so!"

"Just think about the choir. Sometimes doing the little things for other people and saying yes when you want to say no can set you on a different path. Now if you've finished destroying the beams in my stables, how about coming in and having that drink? And I'll put the copper on so you can have a bath. You need it." She wrinkled her nose.

Cam laughed. "Yes Aunty." She opened the door for her aunt and offered her arm to lean on as they returned to the house. Maybe she could try out for a solo. At least she could reacquaint herself with Bea, who would be an ally if not a friend.

Chapter Seven

GLORIA STARED UP AT the ancient manor house surrounded by various huts and concrete blocks, all of it behind barbed wire and with armed guards at the entrance. It reminded her of a prison. Andrew Tadcaster had been her official guide, pointing out the dining hall and referring to some of the buildings by the names of fish. Then he darted off as though he had something much more important to do. He probably did. When she called out to ask where she should go, he just waved his hand and hurried off.

A smiling woman in uniform approached her. "Hello. You look lost."

"I am. It's my first day, and my guide showed me around but had to rush off, and I don't know where the accommodation office is."

"Perfect. I'm just going there myself. I'll show you the way."

She smiled and shook Gloria's hand. At last, someone with courtesy. She sounded posh, but she was also friendly. In her experience so far, people seemed less affable the further south she'd travelled.

"My name is Beatrice Williams, but everyone calls me Bea."

"Gloria Edwards. Lovely to meet you. Is there a map of this place? I'll never find my way around otherwise."

Bea started walking the opposite way to where Gloria had been heading. "Unfortunately not. It's classified under the Official Secrets Act. You must be bright to be here, so you'll find your way. You could orientate yourself from the lake, the dining hall, and the entrance. That should give you a clue. I'm guessing you enjoy puzzles."

Gloria grinned. "I do. I was invited here on the back of a crossword test."

Bea returned the smile. She seemed relaxed, but the shadows under her eyes betrayed her tiredness and presumably years of strain.

"I'd heard rumours about that. It's certainly a way of getting the right people. We've got so much work to do now that we're desperate for more willing hands and eager brains. Welcome."

"What's everyone doing here?"

"That's classified too, I'm afraid, but you'll understand soon, depending on the section you'll be based in."

"It's so frustrating."

Bea laughed again, a warm rich sound. "Which part of Yorkshire are you from? That's a wonderful accent you have there."

"Bradford. Are you sure you're not teasing me?" She'd caught herself from saying something stronger just in time.

"Not at all. Through here, Gloria."

"Thank you."

Bea paused. "Do you know where you're staying?"

"I was told in one of the new dorms, but I don't know where it is."

Bea tilted her head. "I wouldn't normally do this, but my housemate, Edith, has just left to have a baby, and I told my landlady I'd look for a replacement to share the costs of the lodgings. It's a bit more expensive than the dorms, but it's warmer and within cycling distance. Edith left her bike because she didn't need it anymore. And if that doesn't sway you, we have proper toilet roll, not the thin, hard government paper you'll get in the dorm."

Gloria laughed.

"Oh, you're not allergic to cats, are you? A stray found me and has moved in."

"No." Was she mad to even contemplate living with a stranger?

But everyone was a stranger here, and Bea was so friendly. This was part of her new approach to life, to have her adventure and always say yes. "Okay, that sounds like fun. Thanks, Bea."

Bea pushed down the handle and opened the door. "Great, let's get this sorted."

Making arrangements happened quickly and efficiently.

After she'd made a few phone calls, the admin clerk, Josie, turned to face them. "Officer Williams, thank you for letting me know about the change. You're all sorted, Gloria." She checked her notes. "You've been asked to report to Block C at 0800 hours tomorrow morning. In the meantime, I'll leave you in Officer Williams' capable hands."

"Thank you, Josie." Another friendly person to add to her tally. Gloria happily trailed Bea outside again, but Bea frowned. "What's wrong?"

"I'm just curious. You said you were invited on the strength of completing a crossword puzzle, but you're working in Block C. No one will say what they're doing there, but that's unexpected. Let me show you where you need to turn up tomorrow. I'm on nights again tonight, so do you fancy something to eat before we go back to the lodging?"

"Yes, please, but aren't you tired if you're working nights?"

"We're always tired. But I was working on something, so I'll go back for a quick kip first. Grabbing some food will save me cooking later. We give our ration books to our landlady so help yourself to tea and milk. Who are you working with?"

"Agnes Black."

"Shall we see if she's here today and I can introduce you?" Without waiting for a reply, Bea hurried into the bare brick block.

The dull thumping became a heavy roar, clanking like some wild factory animals. The room was crammed full of women typing holes in four-inch by six-inch cards before they fed them into banks of machines. The women's faces were wan and weary, and only a couple of women glanced up at the visitors with dull eyes. Mercifully, Bea turned to another door and knocked.

"Enter."

It was difficult to hear above the noise of the machines.

"Agnes Black?" Bea asked.

The woman behind the desk rose and saluted Bea. So Bea was a higher-ranking officer then. She was very smart in a double-breasted jacket, skirt, and tie. Gloria felt a twinge of envy that she wasn't in a uniform, but she'd never cope with the rigid structure and discipline in the armed forces. She would kick back at control, probably a result of all the practice against her father's domineering in recent years. At the thought of him, she gulped back her discomfort and consciously avoided touching her face where the bruise had now yellowed. She'd hoped to leave on better terms, but it was too late. With every day, the chasm grew wider, and she no longer expected an apology or a reconciliation.

The woman held her hand out to shake. "Welcome, Gloria. We're grateful for the help. We'll show you what's needed tomorrow, but I hope your typing skills are up to date."

"I don't type." Gloria had an uneasy feeling in her stomach she wasn't going to be doing what she was hoping for.

"Oh? But that's what they've recommended for you. I'm sure you'll be fine. Accuracy is critical, as well as secrecy, of course."

"Yes. Thank you." Like *Alice in Wonderland*, she almost expected the rabbit to go hurrying past, consulting his pocket watch.

"See you at 0800. Make sure you're settled in your lodgings and get some rest. It will be very busy once you get started."

"Yes, thank you."

Gloria followed Bea's brisk march to the dining hall. For someone quite short, she covered a lot of ground fast. Gloria selected cottage pie that seemed to be more mash than meat, then covered it in watery gravy and sloppy carrots. But it was food, and it was a long time since she had a piece of toast for breakfast at Hatty's this morning. She'd promised her mam she'd write to say she'd arrived safely.

As she took her place opposite Bea, she couldn't help but feel disappointed she'd just be typing. She wasn't exactly out of the frying pan into the furnace, but the noise from the machines was akin to the level in the factory. She could type a little bit but found it even more tedious than calculating wages and managing a cash office. Not that she would ever say that to her da, who would be smug and say "I told you so" if they ever spoke again.

Bea seemed to study her curiously, and Gloria resisted the urge to check the thick foundation was still hiding her facial injury. It would take time to heal, but the emotional impact would take even longer. Although Mam had been aware at the end, and their parting was more tearful and genuine than she'd imagined it would be. She sniffed back the tears that threatened to break free again.

"Are you okay, Gloria?"

Gloria flashed a smile. "Yes, thanks. I was thinking of my parents. My da really didn't want me to come here, and I'd arrogantly assumed I'd be able to do more to help to win the war than overseeing the cash office in his factory."

Bea tilted her head. "I don't think it's arrogance. We do vital work here, as I'm sure you'll discover when we start. Some of the work is boring or frustrating, and you may wonder how it fits in. Everything is covered by the Official Secrets Act, and nobody can say what they're doing, even with other colleagues, but everybody here is working as hard as they can to win the war. Can someone else not look after the cash office?"

"Oh, aye. Anne Coggins is chuffed to take over as the promotion means she gets more money to take home to her family." She imagined that would have been her reaction anyway. And she was probably just as delighted to see the back of Gloria.

"It sounds like a good solution. Now, on to more cheerful things. Do you play an instrument or sing? We've got an orchestra and choir. We're putting together a concert, and we're looking for new members."

"I can't play an instrument, but I sing in church, and I was due to play Mimi in *La Bohème* at my local amateur operatic society."

Bea clapped her hands together. "Wonderful. So, a soprano then?"

"Yes, but I'm not sure about singing in a choir."

"Just come along and see. Maybe you could just sing one song, or maybe do a duet? Cam, an old Cambridge friend, sings tenor, and she's a bit reluctant. You should sing together. I'll introduce you, and you can encourage each other and practice separately if that's easier. Our first audition for the soloists is on Wednesday evening after the day shift. Do say you'll come."

Gloria grinned. "Or you'll throw me out of my lodgings?"

Bea laughed. "You haven't met our landlady yet. You might run away screaming to get a dorm room."

"Now you tell me."

"We'll be fine. It'll be fun. Now if you're finished, I need to get home, to get a few hours' sleep before I have to be here again."

Gloria followed Bea, clutching at her kindness like a drowning woman clinging to flotsam. She just hoped she'd learn to swim soon. Had she just made the biggest mistake of her life? Well, she'd made her bed. The warmth of Bea's welcome seeped into her bones and for the first time since she'd left her da's house, she could see herself fitting in. If the rest of her workmates were as friendly as Bea, she'd cope with the work being tedious, and she'd learn typing or administration or whatever task they had for her. Maybe they could make that fun too. Between homelife and work, she would make the best of it.

Chapter Eight

CAM LOOKED UP FROM the message and grinned. It was definitely Japanese. She held out the page to Jamie, who strode across the hut to her desk by the door.

"Well done, Cam. I'll pass it on up the food chain."

Jamie snatched the paper from her hand, and she could almost feel his irritation that it was she who had broken the cypher, not him. He placed the paper in the cylindrical container to be sent through to another part of the complex by a pneumatic tube system. Cam was glad they didn't have to deliver their solved messages by hand because the noise and the smell of the machines in some of the huts made her want to shut down and crawl into a ball. Not that she would ever show that weakness, certainly not in front of Jamie or Archie, his shadow.

Richard, the older ex-don she'd studied with, clapped his hands together. "Another one for Cambridge."

Drew, who had taught at Oxford, scowled at him but gave her a thumbs up. Even Archie gave her the ghost of a smile. None of them hugged her or clapped her on her back as they would have if one of the men had achieved the breakthrough, but since she hated being touched without permission, that was just as she liked it. She tapped her pencil on the desk, trying to hide her disappointment at their reaction. Just once, it would be nice to be treated the same as the others, even though it made her a hypocrite, desiring what she hated. With every interaction, she was aware of her difference.

With the drop in adrenaline that had been driving her forward, exhaustion swept over her. She rubbed her face to shift the gathering headache and raised her head to see Richard observing her with a look of compassion.

"Well done. I thought after they changed the key, we'd be at it for weeks." He stretched back and tamped down on his pipe. "But I suppose we've done a few weeks' work at it during the last few days. Who knew the Japanese ambassador to Paris would be so forthcoming?" He grinned. "I'm sure the higher-ups will be delighted." He flicked a lighter and puffed hard to get the tobacco to light. "What helped get the breakthrough?"

"Honestly? Exhaustion, I think. I lay in bed the last two nights, trying to make sense of the patterns, but I just thought I'd try something based on the Japanese military manual to see if any words fit. They did."

"What they'll do with the information depends on how much they want to keep it secret that we've broken Enigma," Jamie said as he picked up another unsolved message from the pile in the table at the centre.

It was typical of Jamie to act as a dampener, and Cam gritted her teeth. Doubtless if he'd deciphered it, he'd be shouting it to their superiors, telling them how brilliant he was.

"They didn't reckon on a bunch of bright buggers breaking the codes," Richard said and grinned at Cam, picking up his pencil again.

She was proud to be one of those bright buggers. That look of wonder in the eyes of her peers was worth any of their insults.

Though she still needed to remember not to be rude. "I'm going to get a cup of tea to celebrate. Anyone want one?"

Richard jumped up, still puffing at his pipe. "We should make you one in celebration. I might have some biscuits too."

He caught her gaze, and his look of acceptance warmed her. Admiration was written in his expression, and for an oddball like her to be valued was pure joy. "Thank you, Richard."

Richard stepped away, and she picked up an unsolved dud message from the pile on the table in the centre of the room. She tweaked her trousers at the knees to not ruin the crease and sat down at her desk again.

"I hear you're going to choir meeting this evening," Jamie said after a few minutes of working in silence.

Cam groaned. She'd forgotten she'd promised Aunty Florrie and Bea that she'd go. All she wanted to do was curl up in a ball and sleep, or failing that, to sit and read while Aunty Florrie listened to her radio programme. But she couldn't let them all down. "How did you know?"

He grinned and tapped the side of his nose as though he was privy to a secret she wasn't. If he hoped she would give him some attention and react, he was mistaken. She would not stoop to his stupid mind games. She shrugged and went back to her paperwork.

"Don't you want to know how I know?"

"Not particularly, no."

"Well, it was Beatrice Williams, the deputy head of the B shift. She said someone from my section had also agreed to come along. I asked the others, but they denied it, so it has to be you. She said she knew you in Cambridge."

"That isn't a secret." She hated that Jamie had gossiped about her. Bea knew more about Cam than she was comfortable being widely known, so she'd have to speak to her and ask her to desist. Now this damned idiot was trying to goad her into revealing more.

Fortunately, Richard returned with a tray of tea, which he set down on the table in the centre of the room. "For our resident savant, Cam Langley." He handed her a cup and saucer as though he was presenting her with a prize. She smiled as she took it from him. She had learned he was only teasing. He was always polite and was the closest thing she had to a friend in the hut.

"Thank you," she said. A biscuit lay in the saucer, and she scanned the rest of the crockery. "Is this the last biscuit?"

He bowed. "I'm honoured to give it to you."

"Cut it out, Richard. Some of us are trying to get some work done here," Jamie said.

Richard rolled his eyes and handed out the rest of the mugs, leaving the last for Jamie on the tray. When Richard sat down, Jamie rose muttering something like arsehole, but Cam wasn't sure. She grinned that Richard had wound him up and studiously stared at the papers in front of her until the letters morphed into patterns, and she settled again.

The rest of the afternoon passed in silence as they worked on their next set of messages from a pile that grew higher by the hour. There was always more to do, always the thought that if they could solve the next set of messages, they could shift the tides of war.

Cam checked the clock on the wall as the men packed up.

"Don't forget to empty your desks and lockers," Jamie said as he handed over their pending tray to the next shift coming in, and they signed the changeover.

"Are you coming then?" Jamie hovered over her desk.

Cam had hoped he would just leave. She might look in later, once she'd freshened up and built up her courage. "I'll see you there."

She dawdled packing up her belongings and then sauntered over to the education hut. When she entered the building, she slipped into the ladies' bathroom rather than make her way to the hall where the auditions were being held. She could hear someone warming up and a pianist practising a few scales. Did she really want to do this? But she had promised, and she always tried to keep her promises. She just hoped she wouldn't regret it.

Chapter Nine

GLORIA FOLLOWED BEA PAST the main manor house and lake. How different it must have been before the war without the wooden huts and the squat, blocky buildings. She imagined a quiet country estate, but now it teemed with the constant arrival of despatch riders and people streaming in and out of the main gate at the change of shifts.

"Sorry, I've hardly seen you since you arrived," Bea said. "As you may have gathered, it's been incredibly busy. How have your first few days been? Obviously you can't say what you are doing, but are you settling in, okay?"

"The women I work with are friendly enough, but everyone's so busy, there's no time to talk." The noise from the various machines was unbearable as they clacked and clattered with hundreds of punch cards rattling through the mechanisms and each night, she arrived back at the digs fighting off a headache. "I'm not even operating the machines and haven't been told what they do."

Her job was to type up snippets of notes in German, then attach the notes with the original deciphered sentence to the back of the message with glue. Those messages were then passed on through the pneumatic tube system to be translated and passed onto the great and the good, who would use the information. Gloria tried to amuse herself by guessing what the German words meant, but there seemed to be a host of military jargon and abbreviations that eluded her. With every hour she'd been there, her enthusiasm had waned.

She wrinkled her nose. "I'm not using my skills at all. I'm

a glorified clerk, and I'm rubbish at it, and I'm bored out of my brain."

Bea frowned. "I thought you came from the crossword test?"

"I did."

Bea opened the door and let Gloria enter first. "That's strange. I'll follow that up. Here we are. This is Hut 12, officially for education, but we use it for concerts and other entertainments."

Inside was not unlike a village hall, with a hatch leading to a kitchenette. In the main hall, chairs were laid out in a semicircle, and a piano was off to the side. She recognised Archie from London sitting on the piano stool, and she waved enthusiastically. He nodded in recognition. For the first time since she arrived, she felt as if she had some connection to someone familiar, even if it was Jamie's rather grumpy friend. The hope of being part of something greater and more exciting than the cash office had faded. Hubris was alive and well and festering in Bletchley Park.

The conductor tapped his baton on the music stand to bring them all to order.

"Good evening. My name is Romuald Skarbek, but you may call me Reggie. Before the war, I played violin in the Warsaw Philharmonic Orchestra."

Gloria shuffled her feet. "You didn't tell me they were professional," she whispered to Bea, hoping no one could see the sweat on her forehead. She shrank back.

Bea nudged her. "Don't look so worried. We have a range of skills, and Reggie will alter the arrangements for the troupe. There are quite a few talented musicians among the code breakers though. Something to do with correlating patterns, I think."

Gloria curled her lips upwards but doubted that it would pass as a smile. "Maybe I should sing in the chorus."

"Nonsense. I thought you said you were playing Mimi in La Bohème?"

"Only for an amateur group."

"Give it a shot for tonight, and if you're not comfortable, you can always sing in the chorus. We're playing a variety of classical pieces to satisfy a mixture of tastes." Bea smiled and handed over the worn and tatty sheet music. "Do you know this piece by Handel?"

Gloria glanced down at the music for Handel's duet *As Steals the Morn*. She had sung it in church a few years ago with a man who had more enthusiasm than talent. "I think so."

The door burst open, and Gloria's heart skipped a beat as Jamie strode in, sucking all the attention in the room.

"Sorry I'm late, Reggie, we were busy working on something important." He waved at Archie. "Archie, old thing. Long time no see. All of an hour, isn't it? Hello, Bea. Beautiful as ever." His eyes alighted on Gloria, and he lit up. "Well, well, well if it isn't Bradford."

He paced across to her and shook her hand. She reflected his warm smile, delighted to be recognised and acknowledged.

"I wondered what happened to you. I hoped your father hadn't stopped you from coming."

Gloria almost put her fingers to her cheek but resisted the urge. No one had said anything about the now-yellowing bruise, but she had concealed it. At this point, she was unsure whether she was doing anything more for the war effort than she had been working in the cash office, so had the bruise and the split from her family been worth it?

"Are you on a different shift from me? I'll have to get that changed," Jamie said, ignoring Reggie who frowned at the interruption.

"I don't know. I'm in Block C."

"Block C? But you're a codebreaker, surely?"

Gloria's cheeks were probably showing pink despite the heavy foundation she had slapped on. She shook her head.

"Well, that's a mistake. We need all the help we can get. Let me have a word."

Had there been a mistake? Her heart soared, not just from the possibility that he would help her but also from the friendliness of Jamie. "Thank you."

"Leave it with me. You sing? Why didn't I know that?"

Possibly because he had spent all the time talking about himself and telling jokes. But she just smiled. His exuberance reminded her of Ben. The ongoing pang of grief gripped her heart, so she turned away.

Reggie coughed to get Jamie's attention.

"So, Reggie, what have you got for me?"

Jamie didn't seem perturbed at all that he had crashed in late and disrupted the audition.

"I asked the potential soloists along tonight to see what we have to work with. We're starting with the tenors and the sopranos as the programme will probably focus on those arias. Can you take your seats, please. We've wasted too much time already."

Jamie looked annoyed. He must be a baritone or a bass then. It made sense as his speaking voice was deep.

Reggie turned his focus on Gloria. "Officer Williams tells me that you sing the soloist parts—"

"Only in amateur operatics and in church."

Reggie smiled. "We all start somewhere. I've been surprised by the talent. Do you know the aria in front of you? Archie will play the tenor part as well as the accompaniment."

Archie nodded. Bea poured out a glass of water from a jug on a side table and handed it over. Gloria took it gratefully. "Thank you." Gloria took a sip then cleared her throat, which had become uncomfortably dry.

"Break a leg," Bea whispered and sat down at the edge of the semicircle of chairs.

Gloria counted the bars and followed the music but still almost missed her cue and had to rush in to catch the note. Did Reggie wince? Well, if she wasn't good enough, she'd just join the chorus. As the piece progressed, she felt her way into the music and shrugged it on like a snug-fitting coat.

The door opened and shut with a click, but she was too engrossed in the music to look around. It felt slightly odd to sing a duet on her own, but Reggie was clearly working out if she could actually sing. She so hoped to do well. The piece ended with a flourish on the piano from Archie.

Jamie clapped and rushed over to her. "I'd no idea you could sing like that. You have a fantastic voice. We must sing together. I'll get Reggie to do a different number. What do you think, Archie?"

Archie stretched out his fingers. "Yes, she can sing."

His agreement seemed more reluctant though. *There's no pleasing some folk.*

She grinned. "Pains you to say that, does it?"

Archie shook his head and looked down at his sheet music as if he had something much more important to be fussing with.

"I'll see about getting you on our shift then we can practice after work," Jamie said. "Also, has Bea told you about the party she's having after the first rehearsal on Saturday night?"

"No, we've been like ships passing in the night. And I'm not sure I'll be invited to rehearsal."

"Are you kidding? Of course Reggie will include you. He'll have a riot on his hands if he doesn't—he can't lose his bass soloist and his accompanist."

"Don't speak for me," Archie said.

Gloria got the distinct impression he would prefer that she wasn't here at all. He was obviously besotted with Jamie and wanted him all to himself. She would wait for Bea to ask her and not foist herself on the party.

Reggie tapped his baton on the music stand. "Let's go again. From the top, please."

Gloria stood and inhaled deeply to fill her lungs. Why was she doing the duet on her own again? Had she fluffed it last time and he was giving her another chance?

This time she hit her cue spot on and was surprised when a warm tenor voice joined her, curling around her in a spiral of sound, echoing the phrases she sang. She took a quick glance at the man who stood near the back. He looked dapper in a three-piece suit and dark tie. His almost-black hair was short and slicked back, revealing sharp cheekbones and a rather delicate narrow face. She coughed and faltered a second. Reggie frowned at her, so she tried to catch up as her mind whirred. The tenor was a *woman*.

As she sang, her whole body thrummed in excitement. What a wonderful sight and a stunning voice. She'd heard of women who dressed in men's clothing before but had never come across it back home. She was stirred as never before and suddenly, the hall felt unfathomably warm, and she wrestled to control her breathing.

She must be Bea's friend, Cam. The confidence that rolled off her when she sang was intoxicating and sensual, and Gloria's pulse throbbed in more places than her heart. She had never had such a visceral reaction to someone before, and not just because of the singing, that mellifluous timbre of the tenor, but also because her whole nervous system tingled with delight at the contradiction of a female form in male clothing.

She stumbled again, and Reggie rapped the music stand.

"From the top, please," he said.

A hush settled around the hall as if the small crowd was holding its breath, expecting something to happen. The scraping of a chair and a brief cough broke the silence. Cam stood straighter and inhaled sharply. She resisted the urge to wipe her clammy hands on her trousers. This was her moment to shine. Playing music was the only time she had ever felt a sense of camaraderie with others and she'd missed it. The thrill of singing again and being part of something bigger took her by surprise.

Archie played the introduction and Cam stared at the woman in the green dress who sang the soprano part. She started with her first bars of "As Steals the Night," drawing Cam under her spell. The soprano sang with little vibrato, but it was very pure and clear. Cam joined in with the tenor part, and their voices blended in tense counterpoint and repeated phrases. The woman glanced across at Cam, her eyes widening as she stared at Cam, then she smiled and dipped her head, and Cam's heart fluttered.

Their voices melded into one euphoric sound resonating throughout the hall, causing the shuffling and murmuring around them to stop. Cam focused in on the singing, following the phrasing of the woman and anticipating her breath control. They held the long note and shared a glance. They sang with an understanding and sensitivity as if they had sung together for years.

At the end, Reggie clapped his hands. "Brava. That's just what we need. I'd like to take the middle section a little slower, but we can work on that. There's another aria I'd like you both to perform, along with Bea and Jamie. The quartet from *Rigoletto*. At the concert, it will be with the orchestra, but you'll have to make do with the piano for the moment. Cam, take the tenor part, and Gloria, the soprano."

Gloria, Gloria. What a wonderful, intoxicating, and joyous name. How she'd love to hear that again and again. Gloria: three light sounds. A triumvirate of exultation. Not that she could say anything, or do anything, or be anything but an admirer from afar, but what a voice, all wrapped up in a stunning package. Gloria had a lean body, her brown hair curled in the modern way spilling over her shoulders, and those dark eyes pulled her in as they sang, inviting her to abandon all her inhibition.

Jamie scowled at the conductor. "Why can't I sing that duet?"

"It will strain your voice. You have a natural bass, and I don't want you to sing falsetto. I want you to sing a solo of "O Isis und Osiris," from *The Magic Flute*. We can practice that after the *Rigoletto* quartet."

"But I'd like to rehearse with Gloria."

Cam snorted. He wasn't subtle about his intentions. Her protective ire rose, but it was misplaced, given that Gloria wasn't hers. Goodness, they hadn't even spoken to each other. She caught Gloria's gaze and smiled. Her responding smile warmed Cam to her toes.

Cam closed her eyes to concentrate on the emotions swirling in the depths of her consciousness. There was attraction, for sure, and fascination at the vibrancy of Gloria's presence. And that singing was little short of divine as she'd covered the difficult phrasing with aplomb. A thrill of delight passed through Cam, and her raised heart rate made her feel alive.

"Let's have a ten-minute break and restart with the *Rigoletto* quartet," Reggie said. "Cigarette, Jamie, Archie?"

"In a minute, Reggie." Jamie squeezed himself on a chair beside Gloria.

The other two men left, the doors swinging as they exited. Cam sat forward to hear what Gloria was saying, but she was deep in conversation with Jamie the gasbag. She had no intention of listening to him pontificating, so rose to join Bea pouring tea from an urn.

As she accepted the cup, Bea looked uncomfortable. "Are you cross with me?"

"What, that you tricked me?" The duet was one Cam had performed with Mary in Cambridge before Mary and Bea had had a short fling. Was Bea trying to embarrass her? Cam spun around to leave, but Bea caught her hand.

"Cam, don't go. I wasn't trying to make you uncomfortable. I knew you could sing this, and you said how much you loved it, so I suggested it to Reggie."

"But I sang that for Mary," Cam whispered.

"I'm sorry. I didn't know you liked Mary. She didn't either. I'm sorry if you resented us being together, but it was only a short affair. Cam, please. I want us to be friends. We have to look out for each other and stick together. And I like you as a friend."

Cam stared at Bea, but her open expression didn't look like she was dissembling. "Mary didn't know?"

"No."

"And you like me?"

Bea bit her lip. "Yes. As a friend. You must know that."

Cam searched her face again. How could she be cross with Bea, especially when she'd just introduced her to another soprano to sing with? And what a soprano. She cast a glance across at Gloria before turning to Bea with a broad smile. "Yes. Friends. I like that."

They raised their cups in toast and smiled. She was so lucky to know someone else like her, and she would love to get to know Gloria better. Singing a duet would be the perfect excuse.

Reggie and Archie returned and took their places. "Let's get started."

Cam could hardly keep her eyes off Gloria, even though she was singing primarily with Bea. Gloria had styled her dark hair with glamourous Victory Rolls, and her green dress seemed too classy for everyday wear. She looked like she'd just stepped from a Hollywood set. She didn't need the thick make-up she wore as she was beautiful. That she had more than a passing resemblance to Mary, the intriguing American heiress in Cambridge, added to the plus column.

The four voices blended well, and even Jamie nodded at her when they finished.

"Yes, that definitely works too. Cam, Gloria, I do hope you'll perform in the concert."

Gloria cast a soft gaze across. "I'll sing if Cam will."

Cam's heart beat double time as she nodded. Gloria wanted to sing with her. Maybe they could get to know each other in rehearsals and become friends. Or even more than friends.

Then she deflated and dropped from excitement to disappointment in a heartbeat. She closed her eyes to block out the world and help parse her emotions. No one wanted someone like her, an oddball who lived with an elderly and infirm aunt. Someone who had an unusual obsession with the laying habits of the chickens under her care, and who worked too long and hard at a job she loved, a job that fulfilled and challenged her. Cam reopened her eyes to notice Gloria still looking at her, not in disgust or horror, but in fond curiosity. Cam offered a small smile, and for the first time, she felt understood, as if Gloria had exposed her soul and was cradling it in her fingers. No one had ever looked at her that way. She wanted to capture it and never let that feeling go. She wanted to sing the "Hallelujah Chorus," another piece by Handel, and express the exultation of being truly seen.

Chapter Ten

IN THE FOLLOWING DAYS, Gloria's image, singing, and warm smile occupied Cam's thoughts and fantasies. To make matters even worse, during their shifts Jamie had droned on about how he liked Gloria and was looking forward to seeing her again.

Cam needed to get a grip. Gloria had just been friendly, nothing more. So after rehearsal on Saturday night, she resolved to make a quick getaway so she didn't make a fool of herself and say or do something silly.

On Saturday evening after the rehearsal, Cam thought she'd escaped when Bea held up Cam's bicycle clips. The grin on her face was mischievous. Bea teased but in a kindly way, so Cam trusted her.

"You promised me you'd stay for one drink afterwards." Bea leaned forward and whispered, "And a certain dark-haired soprano will be there."

Cam's cheeks burned. Had Bea seen what Cam felt? That crushing insanity of lust and attraction? Was it written on her face for all to see? How humiliating.

Maybe seeing her discomfort, Bea gently squeezed her arm. "It's just Gloria said how much she enjoyed singing with you and was looking to make a new friend, her being new here and not knowing anyone."

Friend. Cam exhaled noisily. Perhaps she hadn't given away her burning desire or her struggle to contain it. Yet there had been a moment when they sang, when their eyes met as they matched their phrasing, when Cam thought her admiration was reflected back at her. She should know better than to trust her emotions. All they'd ever done was land her in trouble and anguish. Her roles in life were to perform her job to the best of her ability and to care for her aunt. She didn't have any right to daydream about something that could never be. Everything else was a distraction. And she *had* been distracted this week. For the first time ever, she hadn't been one hundred per cent absorbed in the task at hand. And she needed to be focused. They all did. The war was taking much longer than they had hoped when the Americans joined, and more people died every day.

"I don't have any clothes to wear, and my aunt..." It didn't sound as forceful and determined as she hoped, and Bea had already linked arms with her to steer her away from the back exit.

"Cam, you always look so dapper and handsome. You should come as you are. I'm sure your aunt will be happy listening to the radio until you return. You could call her if you're worried." Bea held out Cam's bicycle clips, giving her a choice. "We're meeting in a private room at the Eight Bells pub. You can cycle there, and I promise you can go after one drink. Please come."

A flutter of disquiet settled on Cam, and she struggled to name what she was feeling. She'd only seen Gloria once before, but there was a definite pull at rehearsal tonight, and she wanted to see her again. "Okay," she said.

"Great. It is concluded. I'm just going to round up some of the others."

Bea smiled and left, humming to herself. Her turn of phrase always caught Cam off guard, and it had taken her some time to realise Bea often quoted Shakespeare, which gave her the air of someone who lived in a drama.

"Pull yourself together, Cam," she said and blindly followed the closing down task of emptying her locker. She wheeled her bike out through security and headed towards the village, pushing hard on the pedals. What was really required was a hard session at the punch bag to dissipate the stress of the day and to release the unspoken emotions that swirled in her heart. It was so tempting to turn left at the fork, but she willed the bike to turn right and cycled into the village before dismounting at the pub. She pushed her bike into the rack and chained it to the metal bars.

After she twisted the knob of the mediaeval door and peered inside, she almost turned around and left. Jamie was holding forth to the small gathering, and Gloria appeared to be listening with rapt attention. Cam straightened her tie, strode to the bar, and placed an order for a half of bitter. She glared at the barmaid, who did a double-take on seeing her. She didn't want to have to deal with judgements tonight, so she scowled until the barmaid hurried to get her drink. Cam hadn't minded at all when Gloria had almost choked when she realised Cam wasn't a man. That was probably because Gloria's reaction was a deep blush and a gleam in her eye as though she was excited at the sight. Maybe she was. Or perhaps that was Cam's imagination. She paid for her drink and joined the others after pulling a stool from the adjoining table to sit beside Gloria.

Jamie continued to pontificate and Gloria flashed her a small smile as if to say, "Don't mind him."

"So, I solved the mystery, and now we're back to business as usual, doing all the things we can't talk about," Jamie said to his crowd of onlookers.

It took Cam a couple of seconds to realise he was talking about *her* breakthrough as if *he'd* made it. She gripped her beer tighter. Aunty Florrie would advise her to just let it go, but she'd never been able to consciously censor herself. "How did you come up with the idea?"

Jamie coughed a little on being caught at the sharp end of her stare. "Of course, I came up with the plan with the aid of my colleagues, such as Cam. We're all about teamwork. Should we stop talking about work now? We don't want to get into trouble; walls have ears and all that. This should be a fantastic concert, now we have such a natural soprano joining us."

Gloria flushed, but Cam didn't know if that was embarrassment or delight. She didn't seem comfortable, but Cam struggled to tell such things.

The bar door opened, letting in a draught of cool air along with Bea, Reggie, and Archie.

"Hello, everyone," Bea said. "Didn't they say we booked a private room? Bring your drinks and come through to the back."

As Cam was at the outer edge of the group, it was easy for her to slip out of the main bar and take a seat by the fire in the private room. She stretched out her legs, aiming to get comfortable. A few seconds later, the rest of the group entered as Jamie bloviated—again. She looked around to see there were no further seats, so she rose, and indicated for Gloria to take her seat.

"I'll get some more chairs," Jamie said and left the room.

"Hello, Cam. It's lovely to talk to you. I really enjoy singing with you. I think our voices blend well."

All the witty conversation Cam had rehearsed all week disappeared. "Yes, they do." How banal. "You've got a lovely singing voice." Cam cringed. How had she turned from an intelligent being into a drivelling mess so quickly?

Gloria flashed her a shy smile. "Thank you. It's certainly nicer than my flat Yorkshire accent. I can't believe how posh everyone sounds around here. Like the king."

"Your voice may be flat, but your intelligence is sharp, and you seem very natural." Cam squirmed and wished she could take the comment back. That was too much.

Gloria laughed. "If that was from a man, I'd have thought it was a chat-up line." Perhaps realising what she'd just said, Gloria's eyes widened. "Musical puns. How quaint."

Quaint? Cam wasn't sure if that was a compliment or an insult, so she stared into her beer, hoping the world would right itself. Why was she always so gauche?

Gloria gently tapped her forearm. "Do you live very far away?

I'm in lodgings with Bea. She's lovely, but the landlady's a bit grumpy. Fortunately, Bea seems to charm her."

"I live with my aunt, an easy bike ride away. I'm glad you're with Bea, she's a kind person."

"She's been a godsend: taking me under her wing, finding me the lodgings, orientating me to the place, and being a friendly face. Not that I've seen much of her. She spends all her free time writing letters if she's not at work or rehearsals. Have you known her long?"

Cam couldn't really say how she'd met Bea at Cambridge, where they'd both lusted after the same woman, but Bea won Mary, of course. "We met at Cambridge. Did you say you're working in Block C?"

Gloria's shoulders sagged a couple of inches. "I do. I know it's important, but typing up snippets of messages isn't stimulating. And the hours are much longer than I thought. I'm not complaining though." She frowned. "Or maybe I am. But I shouldn't. It was a right wrench to leave home, but I knew I'd do more for the war effort by using my brain than being in my dad's factory."

Cam blinked at the information and latched on to the last comment. "Are you using your brain?"

Gloria blushed. "Oh, dear, does that sound conceited? It's not very ladylike is it? To be honest, I'm overwhelmed by how intelligent everyone is. I've never been in such exalted company before; it's like being in an elite university—and I've never been to university. Don't know anyone who has."

Cam smiled, glad she had something she could comment on. "We work harder here than at university. Did you never think of applying?"

"Oh, people like me don't go to university. My da would never allow it. He doesn't believe in women getting above their station. He thinks we should either be worshipped or be housemaids. Or he used to. He's found it difficult in the war as he's had to take on more women in the factory, but he's proud he's held onto a lot of men, as it's a reserved occupation."

Cam leaned back against the wall, warmed from the heat of the fire and the attention from Gloria, and let Gloria's conversation wash over her. She was happy to listen, to catch every word, and savour every nuance to be analysed later. "You managed to get away though?"

Gloria touched her cheek and seemed fascinated by her feet.

"I did, although I'm not sure my da will ever forgive me. At least my mam's got the help she needs." She took a long sip of her drink, emptying the glass. "I'm not sure why I'm telling you this. Probably because you listen, and that's such a novelty. No one else listens, or they're too quick to tell me what I ought to be doing. Or they did. Here, no one has much time, and if I'm honest, I wonder if I made the right decision coming here. I don't really know anyone, and you're all so posh and sophisticated. People like Bea and Jamie have been friendly, but Bea is always so busy and Jamie, well, Jamie doesn't listen. Oh, here he is."

Jamie crossed the room and held a drink out for Gloria. Archie shadowed him, gripping two extra chairs.

"Just set them down there, old chap," Jamie said and put their drinks on the table. "Thanks. Are you talking about me? Sorry it took so long for the drinks. The bar is filled with flyboys, with their pilot egos, flashing their cash. We're much better off here. They think they're the only ones doing anything important in the war."

Gloria sniffed, and a sadness washed over her features. There must be a story there.

"Everyone's trying to do their bit," Gloria said.

Jamie sat on the other side of Gloria, then took a gulp of his beer. "I'm sure they are, but are you telling me what we're doing is less important than what they're doing at the sharp end? And they get all the glory."

"I don't know what we're doing," Gloria said. "All I've done is type out snippets of messages and stick them to pieces of paper—"

"They think themselves so superior. Would you believe one of them had the audacity to ask why I wasn't in uniform? As if that's the only way you can serve. Tosspots."

"My brother, Ben, was in the RAF."

Cam almost choked on her beer and tried to hide her smirk as Jamie tried to backpedal like the cartoon character he was.

"Of course, I didn't mean all flyboys are arrogant. Just the ones in the bar. Which squadron is your brother in?"

"He isn't. He was killed in the Battle of Britain two weeks after he'd join his squadron. We were informed by his squadron leader he hadn't even unpacked all his belongings."

There was a world of grief in Gloria's words. Cam reached out to touch Gloria's arm but stopped before she did. It wasn't her place. But the rawness of Gloria's expression made Cam want to take her in her arms and hold her tight. Her need to comfort overrode her dislike of physical touch. "I'm sorry about that," she whispered and received a small smile that made Cam's heart ache.

Gloria disturbed Cam's equilibrium, and she didn't like it. She'd drifted off at work thinking about her, about how she held herself when she sang, and the pureness of her singing tone, and now she knew more about her, Cam wouldn't be able to stop thinking about her. She'd never daydreamed before and had always been judgemental of those who didn't focus. In the past, she'd been attracted to women with a yearning that was never fulfilled and had never expected her desires to be reciprocated. The only time she'd had the courage to try, attempting to impress Mary with her singing, it had all been for nothing. If she had no expectations, she couldn't be disappointed. She just needed to rebalance and remind herself of her rules that had served her well: look, but don't touch, and admire from afar.

This could be no different. Yet Cam watched the way Gloria's lips moved when she talked and saw how her eyes sparkled when she was passionate about her point. A speck of hope blossomed in her heart, and she couldn't help wondering if she was about to break her own rules.

Chapter Eleven

Gloria entered the small kitchen of their lodgings. Bea sat in her usual seat at the cramped table next to the range, wrapped up in a blanket and writing neatly on blue paper. Gloria stepped towards her and caught sight of the salutation, "Dearest M." She hadn't intended to pry, but a thrill of glee shot through her. Bea had a secret lover. Well, it might not be a secret, but Bea had never spoken about him. "Cuppa?"

Bea's head shot up. "Good morning, Gloria. I didn't hear you come in. Yes, please."

Gloria turned and in the corner of her eye, saw Bea placing the letter below some other papers. So she didn't want Gloria to know she had a lover. *How intriguing.* Perhaps he was married, like her da having a not-so-secret affair with Nancy Ramsbottom. She couldn't imagine Bea being a mistress. Despite them working in secrets all day long, Bea struck her as being honest and open. Gloria grinned as she took down the cups and set them in the matching saucers. "I assume Mrs Jones has gone to church?"

"Yes, and she can't believe she has two heathens billeted with her. She's probably going to demand a refund from the Park."

"The Park?"

"What they call Bletchley Park. I'm surprised you haven't heard it called that. Or we Wrens call it HMS Pembroke, because everything is named after a ship."

"To be honest, I haven't heard anything. All I do is sit and type slowly. Agnes Black keeps stressing 'Accuracy is key.'"

Bea tilted her head to one side. "You don't seem very happy here."

Gloria deflated and flopped into the kitchen chair closest to her. "Honestly? I'm feeling a little overwhelmed by some of the people and underwhelmed by what I'm expected to do."

"The latter I can understand, but the people?"

"Don't get me wrong, most people seem friendly enough, especially in the choir, but either people seem to be super bright, or like the group I work with, they've been established for years and have their own in-jokes. They share a dorm and socialise together, and a couple of them play pranks because they're bored. I'm not sure where I fit in."

"Do you want to? I always thought of fitting in as having to adopt the same looks and attitudes of people around you, and that doesn't seem authentic. Being accepted and valued for who you are is more important, even if you're different...*especially* because we're different. One of the things I love about the Park is that people are completely individual, and that's perfectly fine. And we have people from all walks of life here. But perhaps I was selfish in inviting you to my lodgings. I wonder if you'd be better off in a dorm with the others, so you'd feel more part of it. Sorry, I didn't think of that."

"No, that's not what I meant." Gloria took the whistling kettle off the hob and poured it into the teapot. She gave it a good stir, then replaced the lid. "I may be young, but I've never been interested in talking about men and fashion. I haven't found my niche yet, where I belong. Perhaps the singing will help with that. I thought I might ask Mrs Jones about the church choir. It's strange not to go, and I feel very guilty."

"You'd be her favourite for life if you did. And you seem to be a hit with the singing."

Gloria closed her eyes briefly and remembered the moment she shared with Cam as they held the extended note, when something seemed to pass between them. A recognition maybe, or a frisson of something she didn't understand. Perhaps because Cam dressed in such a dramatic—although appealing—way, they were both outsiders, and there was a kinship in that.

"And with the singers. Jamie in particular seems smitten."

Bea's statement was a cold rain burst that trickled down her neck. Of course that's what Bea meant, so why had she thought of Cam? That was something to ponder in the long dull days of typing and pasting snippets. "Yes. Jamie, Archie, and I finished first in the crossword puzzle test." She couldn't hide the pride in her tone, even though it seemed that might be the pinnacle of her achievement, and everything would be downhill from here.

Bea frowned. "Yet Jamie and Archie are in the codebreaking sections. You mentioned that before. I'll check with administration to see if there's been an error."

"Oh, Bea, you don't have to do that. You've already done so much for me, and I'm very grateful—"

"But it's probably rather boring for you, lodging with me when I'm either working, rehearsing, or writing letters."

Gloria grinned. "I saw you were writing. Do you have a lover?"

Bea raised her eyebrow. "I'd forgotten how direct you are in the north."

"Is that rude?"

"No."

Bea seemed slightly uncomfortable, but Gloria couldn't help pushing a little harder. "Is he away fighting?"

"No. Not fighting. Reserved occupation."

Gloria couldn't see Bea being with a miner or dockworker. She was too posh. "Doctor or teacher?"

Bea laughed. "You don't give up do you?"

Gloria grinned. "No. I'm like a dog with a bone, my da says." Her grin faded at the thought of him. Would they ever build bridges again? And did she want to? That was the more uncomfortable question she didn't want to address. She stirred the tea more briskly than she would normally, squashing down her regret.

"Land Army."

The Land Army? Weren't they all women, plus some prisoners of war and conscientious objectors? "So he's a conscientious objector then?"

The twinkle in Bea's eyes dimmed a little. "Something like that. Now are you going to pour that tea?"

Gloria grinned as she poured. "I'm a Yorkshire lass. We like our tea strong."

"I noticed." Bea added milk and sugar to both cups and pushed one across the table.

Gloria sipped at her tea and idly checked her watch. She clattered her teacup in the saucer and jumped up. "Flippin' 'eck, is that the time? I need to go. I promised to have lunch with Jamie. I'll see you at the rehearsal before my shift starts."

"See you later. I'll sort out your cup. Have fun."

"Thanks." Gloria grabbed her bag, rushed outside and wheeled her bicycle to the front gate. The shifts seemed to come around so quickly. She had barely time to eat, rehearse, and sleep before the numbing tedium came again. All the more reason to grasp the spare hours and stuff them with joy and companionship. Now she was beginning to feel she had friends here: Bea, and Jamie, and Cam. And maybe even Archie, although he always seemed wary of her, though for what reason she couldn't fathom. She felt like a mouse being watched by a cat about to pounce, but he was Jamie's constant companion, so they had to get along. She could almost imagine Archie wiggling his furry cat bottom in preparation to attack, like Bea's stray, Lovelace, and it made her smile. Gloria wheeled her bike to the cycle racks by the old manor house. It really was a beautiful place to come to work, even if the work was as dull as dishwater.

Gloria entered the ladies bathroom and stared at herself in the mirror. Thankfully, her bruise had faded completely, and she could revert to her simple make-up of lipstick, eyeliner, and a touch of rouge. Her mam had written to say her da only came home for meals now, and a rush of guilt smacked her head on that she had abandoned her family. But her mam had encouraged her to escape.

She used the lipstick to accentuate her Cupid's bow, then pressed her lips together on a piece of hand towel stamped with a crown to show it was government property. She ought to have a crown printed on her forehead to show she was government property too, doing her duty as required, even if it was tedious. She rolled her shoulders and stiffened her back. *You made your bed, lass. Now you've got to lie in it.*

When she emerged and made her way to the dining hall, Jamie stood near the entrance smoking a cigarette, the sole of his foot resting against the wall. Her da would not have approved of such a casual attitude. But he wasn't there. She smiled.

"Well, that's a nice welcome, Bradford." He dropped his cigarette and ground it into the dirt, amongst all the other cigarette butts.

Given this area was cleared daily, it showed how many people must have used the hall over the last twenty-four hours. Gloria calculated it must be hundreds if not thousands. She didn't bother to set him straight that her glee was because of her newfound freedom rather than anything else. "Ay up. I hope you haven't been waiting long."

"You're here now. Let's go in. I have a bet going that it will be spam fritters today."

He punched the air when he realised it was on the menu. Gloria took her plate more sedately and headed for a table away from everyone else. She nodded to a group of women from her shift, but they didn't invite her to join them. In all fairness, they probably thought she was having lunch with her beau, but nothing was further from her mind. Jamie was nice enough, but for all his charm, he was full of himself and teased her like Ben did.

Gloria observed Jamie as he settled himself down. He was handsome in a rather boyish way. He had a cheeky way about him that seemed to charm everyone but Cam. Thinking of Cam made her smile. What suit would she wear today? Doubtless it would be impeccable with a neat crease down her trouser leg. They must take ages to iron. Cam always cut a fine figure. The thought of Cam stirred something within Gloria, but she didn't want to examine what that might mean for who she might be. And if her pulse increased and she needed to swallow when she saw Cam, that was just normal, wasn't it?

"Away with the fairies?" Jamie asked as he picked up his knife and fork.

Because he was a gentleman, he would wait until she took her first bite before he ate. She appreciated his gallantry but didn't need it. "What? No, just daydreaming." Heat rose up her neck. She should give Jamie her attention. He would grab it even if she didn't offer it, so better she steered the conversation by asking questions. "How is your solo coming along? Are you still practising?"

He pouted like a little boy. "I wish I was doing a duet with you instead of just the quartet."

"But sopranos normally duet with tenors, and you're definitely a bass. It's amazing how deep you can go. It sends shivers down my spine." She picked up her cutlery and carefully cut up her fritter.

"Good shivers, I hope. I'd love to send other shivers down your spine too."

"Jamie Gordon, are you being forward with me?"

He grinned. "Can't blame a guy for trying. So what will work? Telling you how beautiful you look, although I'm sure you get told that all the time. Or maybe if I tell you I know why you were put in with the machine pool in Block C rather than with the codebreakers."

She pointed her fork at him. "Keep your nose out of my business."

He leaned back in his chair still grinning. "Even if I'm helping?"

Now she was intrigued and despite trying to affect nonchalance she had to force herself to set her knife and fork down. "Really?"

He grinned. "I spoke to admin—"

"They're not supposed to talk about anything that's private to anyone else." She snatched up her cutlery again and attacked the fritter.

"I can if I'm requesting you to join my section."

She paused with her fork halfway to her mouth. "You what?"

"I have formally requested you join my section as a codebreaker. I told them you finished the quiz first."

This was some sort of prank, and Gloria wasn't going to fall for it. "But it's not your section, you're the deputy—"

"Thanks for making me feel *so* important. I've spoken to Keith, and he agrees. We're at least one down now Nigel has signed up for the Navy."

She ignored his sarcasm. "Are you sure you aren't baiting me for your amusement?"

"I wouldn't do that, Bradford. I've too much respect for you."

Did she want to work with Jamie? He was lively, but it might be exhausting. But she couldn't turn down a chance to use her brain. And wasn't Cam on the same shift as Jamie? Her breathing quickened a little, though she put it down to the excitement of doing something interesting and useful. Or maybe it was the thrill of working with Cam. "Yes, okay. That's fantastic."

"I think so too." He polished an imaginary medal on his non-existent uniform.

"So why was I put in admin in Block C even though I can't type?"

Jamie shuffled in his seat and wouldn't quite meet her eye.

"Well?"

"The reference from your place of work said you weren't suitable for anything but the most basic of tasks. Not that there's anything wrong with those tasks, but—"

"My bloody father and his reference." Blood rushed in her ears.

Jamie jumped back. "Doesn't he approve?"

Gloria huffed. "No. He didn't want me to waste my time here when I could be doing important war work in his factory, be under his thumb, and marry his appointed heir to take over. He didn't even want to give me a reference, but I thought I'd persuaded him to do so. This is his revenge. He probably thinks I'd get bored and return home, the sly old fox. He'll hear what I think about that."

She rose, but Jamie grabbed her forearm. "Stay and have your lunch. We can't waste even this mediocre food. Don't respond when you're angry. Though I have to admit you look extremely sexy when you're all riled up."

Gloria yanked her arm away. "You did *not* just say that."

"Sit down, Bradford. You're clearly upset. Sorry I angered you."

She flopped onto the seat, gracefulness be damned, and put her head in her hands. So much for escaping her da's influence. Did he really hate her that much, or was he just trying to manipulate her? She swallowed back the bile. "I can't believe he did that out of sheer spite."

"It sounds like it. That must be hard to hear."

She caught his gaze and held it. "Thank you for saying that, and thanks for asking to transfer me into your section. I'll do whatever I can to show your confidence in me is justified."

He smiled and laid a hand on hers. "I'm sure you will. Now I was going to ask if you would like to accompany me to London, and perhaps to stay a little longer in the Savoy this time. There are frequent trains to London from Bletchley station, so we could be there and back in a day."

Something about the way he asked made her think he had an ulterior motive. Just because she was grateful didn't give him the right to anything else. "I'll think about it." She checked her watch again. "I need to go. I don't want to be late for rehearsal."

"But you've left your cabbage."

"You have it. See you later." Gloria rose and hurried to make it to rehearsal on time. She couldn't wait to tell Cam that she would be transferring to their codebreaking section soon. Curious, though, that she was more thrilled to tell Cam than Bea, whom she knew better. She almost skip-walked out of the dining hall, but then slowed. A codebreaker would need to behave with more decorum. She swallowed hard, hoping she'd live up to the trust placed in her. Stiffening her spine, she marched to the rehearsal room.

Chapter Twelve

CAM RUBBED HER EYES and checked the clock on the wall. The eight-hour shift had clicked round to thirteen hours as she dealt with an urgent assignment. They were all urgent, but this was ultra-urgent, and Jamie had requested she stay until they had an answer one way or another. She kept thinking it was just out of reach. She closed her eyes for a second to imagine the patterns and leaned on her rickety desk. It wobbled. She wouldn't be able to concentrate until it was level, so she took a clean piece of paper and folded it three times to put under the table leg. That sorted it for now.

Cam rolled her shoulders and focused on the middle distance to give her eyes a break. Archie and Richard were puffing away on their pipes, which didn't help the stinging grittiness in her eyes. She started again. She took the German words for weather forecast and lined them up with a message. There was probably an error in the receiving because the operator couldn't hear it clearly. Maybe the crib word wasn't weather forecast but something else? She stood and paced across the room to warm her hands by the old iron stove belching out smoke. With that, and damp wood from the dilapidated huts, the atmosphere was clogged and cloying. Not great for thinking hard or making a breakthrough. "How are you getting on?" she asked Richard.

"I'm stuck."

He shared the code he was working on, and she suggested a couple of different ideas before returning to her desk.

"Bingo!" he shouted, a couple of minutes later. "Thanks, Cam. That's it. Let me pass this on."

He sent the message on to be translated into plain text before being re-encrypted and passed on to the admiralty or other relevant departments. Cam smiled, thrilled at having provided the catalyst for someone else in the ever-increasing pile of incoming messages. Now she just needed to go back to hers.

The buzz of pride was enough to give her an adrenaline boost. She would never get the credit or the wages the men got, but she was the person most people consulted if they had a problem, even Jamie. It gave her respect and acceptance, and knowing she'd found her place in the world made her brim with satisfaction. Perhaps it was the confidence of making a break for someone else that gave her the inspiration to try a different key— one key out of the 16 million million million combinations. A partial word came out in German, and the error was now obvious. She corrected for it, and the rest of the message followed with a flow of high-level intelligence. She whooped and did a little jig before sending it on.

Although it would have been great to bask in the glory of the break, she picked up another of the unsolved messages from the pile. She'd try one more then get home to sort out supper for Aunty Florrie.

Her mind drifted back to the duet rehearsal from the other night and the closeness of Gloria. Cam watched her intensely to match her breathing and phrasing and they'd both leaned into each other as they sang. Gloria had smelled of Pears soap, and her eyes had lit up when they harmonised perfectly. Then Cam had blown it when they departed. Gloria said she had something to tell her after rehearsal, but the slimy Jamie said he'd accompany Gloria home, and they didn't get the opportunity to talk properly.

Gloria looked back at Cam as she headed towards the bike shed with Jamie. "Thanks for the rehearsal. It was wonderful to sing with you."

"Thanks. And you. To sing together I mean. You have perfect

pitch and a pure soprano voice, and the emotion you manage to convey..." Cam sounded like a babbling idiot.

Gloria laughed and waved her hand. "I'll see you soon."

Cam turned and almost tripped on the pavement, and she was never clumsy. She just hoped Gloria didn't see. And even more so, Jamie, as he would laugh at her.

Even now the memory caused Cam to burn up. She checked her clock again. Another fourteen-hour shift. Her back was stiff, and she rolled her shoulders. She would definitely need a session at the punching bag when she got home. The door to the large office banged open, and Jamie came in looking very smug with himself.

Cam did a double take as a woman entered behind Jamie and her eyes must be deceiving her because it looked like Gloria. Cam's cheeks flushed—but it wasn't from the heat coming off the iron stove.

"Everyone, can I have your attention? We're swamped with work, so I've managed to snag us another codebreaker. Some of you may know her already. This is Gloria, and she'll be joining us from the next shift. I hope you'll make her very welcome."

Jamie puffed up with pride as if he'd solved all of the keys at once. Cam bowed her head, caught up with the rush of conflicting emotions: delight, jealousy, excitement, chagrin, and professional pride all intertwined in a tight ball that settled in her stomach. When Cam was a child and couldn't express her emotions, Aunty Florrie had suggested to look inside at the different threads of her emotions and see them as different colours that needed untangling, so red was anger and blue was upset. As she got older, the range of colours had expanded, but she still had to unthread the knot, name them, and let them free.

She tugged at the first emotional thread. She was delighted for Gloria, whose whole demeanour was lighter and brighter, and she glowed. Her eyes were such a contrast to the dull, sunken expressions of her hut mates. To see Gloria everyday would be a joy: to get to know her better, to help her with her work, to guide her, to get closer to her. Cam's pulse quickened and to wipe away the sudden clamminess of her palms, she ran her hands down the creases in her trousers. Yet she was also conflicted. This was her sacred space, where she got to shine, and she didn't want to lose any of the hard-earned respect she'd won from the men. The men all buzzed around Gloria, including Richard, which surprised her. She was about to lose her novelty factor in the hut, and that was fine if she kept her unacknowledged, top codebreaker status. No, that didn't matter either. It was deeper than that, more raw and complicated. Beneath the surface, fear coiled in her stomach as she pulled at the threads of understanding. She was afraid she wouldn't be able to hide her desire around Gloria.

Chapter Thirteen

ON HER WAY INTO the hut on Gloria's first shift, Jamie pointed to the six-foot-high brick walls about three feet from the hut which formed an alleyway. It reminded her of the ginnels, the narrow passageways between the residential homes of their factory workers.

"Against stray bombs," he said.

"That'd be as useful as a chocolate teapot," Gloria said, then let her smile fade at Jamie's scowl, and meekly followed him inside. The smell of damp and creosote hit her nostrils, and the hut itself seemed flimsy after the solidity of the blast proof walls in Block C. A long dark corridor had various doors leading from it. Through the thin walls, sounds of people moving and talking and the constant clicking of typewriters evidenced people hard at work. Jamie gestured to the powder room. He strode past it and marched towards the door at the far end, which he opened with a flourish.

"You met all the chaps the other day," Jamie said as they entered.

Gloria greeted them all: Drew, the sporty Oxford Don; Richard, the older Cambridge Don; Acidic Archie; and finally, closest to the door and in the coldest part of the room was Cam, fascinating, enchanting, dangerous Cam. She waved to them all, and her smile broadened when she caught Cam's eye.

These men in tweeds and spectacles with slicked hair, gripping pencils or pipes, had an earnest exhaustion about them. Their excessive brain power was daunting. She just hoped she could live up to the confidence Jamie had shown by transferring her into this elite group. Somehow, she didn't think they would spend their breaks discussing the latest dance or how to secure nylons, like her previous work colleagues.

"Welcome to the Duddery. We deal with the messages that fail the machines." Jamie pointed for her to sit at the desk beside his.

He reminded her of a fluffed-up peacock strutting around his domain. Gloria perched on the chair and placed her handbag on the desk like a barricade. It would probably offer as little protection as the brick walls beside the hut. She shuffled in her seat. Was her arrogance about to be exposed? But she *had* come first in the crossword puzzle test, beating both Jamie and Archie, and they belonged here. She adjusted her posture and sat up straighter. She had a right to be here, whatever her da said, and she'd do what she could to serve her country.

"All the Axis powers use variations of the Enigma machine to encrypt their messages. It's about the size of a typewriter with three or, with the U Boats, four wheels, each with twenty-six letters. Each day, they choose a new setting for those wheels, out of a possible eight wheels, making it almost impossible to decrypt unless you have the key to which settings are to be used."

Richard coughed and pointed his pipe at the large notice on the wall with SECRECY in capitals.

Jamie shrugged. "So? To be effective, Gloria needs some context."

"If she's bright, she'll pick it up as she goes along," Richard said. "Like we did."

Gloria's smile slipped a little. She'd warmed to Richard the other day when they'd met, but now she felt like a reluctant student who hadn't done her homework for her formidable tutor.

Jamie twisted away from Richard's gaze. "The operator sets the start position for each of the wheels depending on the key for the day and presses a letter from the message, say A, on the keyboard. A corresponding letter is lit up on the top, say J, which he will record. To complicate it, a wheel may move forward with each depression of the key, so A no longer corresponds to J but another letter. With me so far?"

Gloria nodded her head, ignoring the glare from Richard at the edge of the room.

"The cypher is then transmitted by Morse and is intercepted by our listening stations all over the world. Thousands of messages come in by teleprinter or despatch rider every day, which can be anything from a movement of troops, the weather report, or an order to attack. All information is useful, and a high volume of information will often indicate that something's about to happen."

Richard puffed on his pipe, and Gloria swore she could hear his teeth clenching the stem.

"What your friend is not saying is that the enemy must never know we've broken Enigma, which is why nothing of this may be repeated. Ever," Richard said.

Gloria cast a glance at Cam, who looked down hurriedly as if she'd been caught staring. Had she been listening in on the conversation? She had an urge to impress Cam and wanted to elicit the same warmth she saw in Cam's eyes when they sang. Here, her eyes were hooded in a neutral mask, and Gloria couldn't read her.

"The receiver will press the encrypted letter, and the plain text letter will light up. The message is transcribed and passed on to the relevant field officer."

She must have missed some of what Jamie was saying, but hopefully she'd pick it up. "How do they know what settings to use?"

"Good question."

Jamie puffed up, and Gloria was glad to have earned his approval, although she hoped it wasn't at the expense of the goodwill of the rest of her hut.

"They have a book of keys, but they change them regularly. So even if the books are captured by spies, they're only useful for a while. More often than not, we have to work backwards from what we're expecting in a message from the identification of the unit, or the weather report, or key phrases to produce a crib. They also spell out numbers which can help. One flaw with the Enigma machines is that one letter cannot be coded onto itself, so if we come across say, an A being coded as an A, when we're trying to work out the cribs, we can eliminate that solution."

Gloria tried to make sense of what he was saying and hoped Richard was right that it would become more obvious in practice.

"The crib is used to choose the start settings for the Bombes, which are the big noisy machines you'll hear operating in Hut 11. They mechanically brute force a start position until they get a suggested solution which can be passed on to different departments to decrypt the message, translate it to English, re-encrypt it, and send on to the admiralty for analysis and decisions." Jamie ran his fingers through his hair, disturbing a lock that didn't seem to sit smoothly.

She remembered he had the same issue when they first met. Maybe it was something he did when he was thinking or nervous. She'd learned more in a few minutes than she had in the previous weeks working in Block C. Now she could understand the security risk. If the enemy ever discovered the Allies had broken Enigma, they would change their system, and lives would be lost. It might even affect the outcome of the war. This was the important work she'd always hoped to be involved in and she couldn't wait to challenge herself.

"Our job is to take those messages that can't be solved by the Bombes and try every trick in the book to solve them." He picked up a message and pulled his seat across to her desk.

His knees almost touched her legs, and he was so close, she caught the whiff of cigarettes and soap. Gloria's gaze lifted and caught Cam's disapproving expression, her brows furrowed, and a frown thinned her lips. Gloria sent her a reassuring wink, hoping to ease her nerves, but Cam blushed and glanced down, pretending to be engrossed in her work. It was almost as if Cam was jealous of Jamie getting too close, or maybe she was just unimpressed by having her work disturbed.

Some hours later, Gloria raised her head when a shadow passed in front of the circle of light on her desk.

Jamie smiled down at her, with a glint in his eyes. "Bradford, how's your first shift going? I thought I'd escort you to lunch."

Gloria slid open her desk drawer to reveal a package wrapped in greaseproof paper. "I've got my sandwiches, thanks. I might take a walk round the lake and get a bit of fresh air."

His shoulders drooped a little, and he stared out of the window. She followed his gaze. Heavy rain raced down the glass. He might have thought he'd caught her out, but in the previous windowless bunkers, she had escaped even in the pouring rain, just so she wasn't living like a troglodyte.

"It's a bit wet to walk today, unless you want to shiver in wet clothes for another four hours until your shift ends. Come on. It'll be a complete break and I'd like to get to know you better."

Gloria didn't want to be included as one of the boys or have it assumed she would just comply. She called it independence; her da said she was stubborn. She carefully unfolded the package, and the paper crinkled in a satisfying way. It was like Pavlov's bell, the harbinger of food and a few minutes' respite. "No, thank you. I'll just eat my sandwiches here then take a brisk walk."

Jamie looked so disappointed with his pouting bottom lip and doleful eyes that she almost laughed. He was probably used to charming most of the girls to his will, but she wasn't like most of the girls. She wanted to make her own way in the world. "Enjoy your lunch," she said.

"Okay, chaps. Let's go." Jamie strode to the door, and the other men followed him out.

In the corner of the room Cam was perched at a trestle table staring at Gloria, with her mouth slightly agape.

She smiled, a genuine one for Cam. "Don't you go to lunch in the canteen?"

"I bring my own sandwiches too," Cam said, before she pulled a package out of the leather briefcase at her feet.

"May I join you?" Gloria asked.

Cam blushed and nodded. Was Cam shy? This was a side that Gloria hadn't seen before. To date, she had heard her wonderful tenor voice and observed her brilliant mind at work. Gloria was captivated by Cam's sharp clothing and her neatly cropped hair, with the small strands in front of her ears that added a touch of intriguing femininity.

"Of course."

She was so confident around the men, but this timidity was endearing.

"Thanks." Gloria took a chair from another desk and set it opposite Cam. "I might freshen up and put the kettle on. Would you like a cuppa?"

"I'm sorted." Cam raised her flask and liquid sloshed around inside.

Gloria withdrew to the tiled bathroom and washed her hands and face. She reapplied her lipstick, wondering why she was trying to make herself more appealing to Cam. The realisation hit like a hammer blow, and the repercussions reverberated throughout her body. There was no sense in that, but she found the vulnerable knight so attractive. She wrinkled her nose at herself in the mirror. What was happening to her? She didn't have time for this now, or ever.

With only twenty minutes to have tea and eat her lunch, she hurried out to the kitchen and tried to reason with herself as she waited for the kettle to boil. It was absurd to be so stirred up. The shrill sound of the whistle jerked her out of her chiding. She looked at her reflection in the glass, unnerved by her visceral reaction to seeing Cam. The throbbing parts of her she'd forgotten about was disturbing. Needing a distraction, she attempted to clean out the brown stain in the teacup. No wonder Cam brought her own flask.

What was happening to her? She'd been attracted to a couple of men before, but she'd never been aroused at the sight of a woman. It must just be the novelty and the excitement of her first day in her new role. Finally, her pulse slowed, and she could breathe evenly again. Failing to have made any progress in removing the grime from the china cup, she opted for the enamel mug and poured her tea, still willing her body to calm down. She took up her mug and courage and swept into their workroom.

"I can see why you have your own mug, unless you want food poisoning as a side effect of drinking from their teacups." Gloria avoided meeting Cam's eyes, fearing that Cam would read in her expression that she was attracted to her. There was no other way to describe it, but that was ridiculous.

"Yes, I have my flask and egg sandwiches." Cam held up her half-eaten food.

"Flippin 'eck, you have real eggs?"

"Yes. We have seven chickens. Number Three is my favourite because she produces an average of 4.75 eggs per week and a total of 247 eggs a year."

Cam went red, whether from embarrassment or because she was rambling, Gloria didn't know. But it was adorable. The precise calculation made her smile. It was so typical of Cam. Gloria could imagine her recording all the details in a little notebook. The mundanity of the act was a tiny sliver of normal life.

"Does your landlady mind you using all the eggs?" Gloria's mouth watered at the thought of something other than the powdered variety.

"No landlady. I'm lucky enough to live with my Aunty Florrie, and she's more than happy that I eat the eggs. If we have any spare, would you like some?"

Gloria sipped her tea and shook her head. "Oh, no. I couldn't ask you to do that."

"Why not? I'll square it with Aunty Florrie. I know she won't mind. She'll be glad I'm making friends."

A look of sadness crossed Cam's face that made Gloria's heart ache. "Don't you have any friends? I thought you'd been here ages."

Cam placed her sandwich down onto the wax paper. "Since the beginning of the war. I don't get on with people very well. Most people think I'm odd."

"Honestly? I thought being odd was a prerequisite to work here. Maybe we can be friends?"

"I'd like that. Do you play chess? I have a set, but no one wants to play at lunchtime. They're all members of the chess club, but I go home when my shift ends, unless I'm rehearsing our singing."

Gloria caught Cam's gaze, and a strange excitement fizzed below her belly. She was sure it wasn't hunger for those eggs. She cleared her throat. "Are you sure it's not because you're brilliant, and they can't bear to be beaten by you?"

Cam laughed, a low, deep rumble that caused Gloria to tingle. "No."

"I'd love to play chess. I haven't really played since our Ben..." The familiar knife of grief stabbed and gouged her heart. She'd almost forgotten her brother, she'd been so caught up in the conversation, but now the overwhelming tide of sadness crashed into her.

"Ben is your brother who died?"

Gloria gave the smallest incline of her head.

"Sorry," Cam said. "If it brings up bad memories, we don't need to play—"

"No, it's okay. It will be good to associate the game with something positive. Let's play then. Can we leave the board out if we don't finish our game?"

"Yes." Cam moved to the filing cabinet behind her, where Gloria hadn't noticed a chessboard already set up.

Cam rearranged the pieces until they were precisely in the

centre of the squares. Then she took up two pawns of different colours and hid them in each hand for Gloria to pick. Cam's fingers were long and delicate, like a musician's, with neatly manicured nails. She wore no polish, as expected. Gloria tapped the back of Cam's left hand, sending a gentle jolt through her fingertips. As Cam upturned her palm, revealing the white pawn, Gloria felt compelled to place her own hand there but stopped herself in time. She blinked to bring herself back to reality. What was she thinking? It seemed like some magic spell Cam was weaving over her, like Prospero from *The Tempest*. Bea had talked about that play the other night, and the parallels with its remote island and Bletchley Park struck Gloria as remarkable. The Park, as she was told to call it, was remote from the war and yet it was the place where strange sorcery was afoot, to uphold and challenge corruption and the unjust usurping of power. She just hoped they would emerge into a brave new world at some time too.

"Your turn," Cam said, her head tilted to the side as though she was appraising her.

Gloria confidently moved her pawn, entering the battleground. They had only completed seven moves when Jamie and the rest of the men returned in a wave of testosterone and boisterousness, breaking their quiet contemplation. Cam flinched.

Gloria shot a look of disappointment at Cam and rose, carefully balancing the board on top of the filing cabinet and lining up the taken pieces behind. "We can continue tomorrow."

"Who's winning?" Jamie asked and surveyed the board. Gloria really hoped he wouldn't offer them tips. "It's early days yet." She stretched her back and returned to her desk next to Jamie's. Hers was a proper desk with lockable drawers, and she had more floorspace than Cam, who was cramped on a trestle table with her long legs stretched out in front of her. It didn't seem fair, given Cam had been here much longer. "Cam, do you want to swap desks?"

"No. I need you beside me so I can show you what to do. It used to be Nigel's desk before he signed up to the Navy. Damn shame to lose him; he was great at cricket and rounders. Do you play rounders? We're always looking for new people for our team. We play on the lawn in front of the house, using different trees as bases. The arguments about whether someone has reached the base can be quite entertaining and heated." He grinned. "So what do you say? We play in the summer and on nice days in spring and autumn."

Gloria smiled. All these invitations. Somehow, she had to balance working her new job with having some sort of social life without giving any false encouragement. She wanted to live life to the full while she was here and experience everything, and this sounded like a group exercise that gave them some fresh air. "Why not?"

They settled down to work, and the sounds of puffing pipes and pencils scratching surrounded her as she sunk deeper into the patterns and logic. "I think I've got it," she said. Jamie leaned over to check her work. It was definitely German that came through. Jamie placed his hand on her shoulder too precisely to be casual, and she resisted the urge to shake it off.

"Well done, Bradford. I knew you'd be a great addition to the team."

She basked in the acceptance for a few seconds and glanced at Cam, who bobbed her head slightly. Gloria's heart did a little skip at the approval. She suspected Cam's respect needed to be earned and was doled out sparingly. She held Cam's gaze. Gloria had no idea what it might portend, but it was like when they sang, when they anticipated each other's breath and phrasing, and they seemed to communicate without words. She smiled, until a body blocked her view—Jamie's body.

"Right, let's get this off. We put it in the container and send them off. Here's your next code—just pick them off the table when you're done. See what you can do with this."

He traded papers, and Gloria settled her mind into the next dud cypher.

Despite trying her hardest, she was disappointed not to decode another cypher before the end of her shift, while Cam had done another five. She must be a real expert. It was wonderful to see her in her own domain, having solved probably twice as many as each of the men. Cam was impressive, and tantalising, and very much her own person, and also adorably sweet when talking about her Aunty Florrie and her chickens. The overhead pendant lamp made her dark hair gleam, and deep shadows emerged where the light didn't reach.

Gloria jumped when Jamie clapped his hands together. "Okay, time for a celebratory drink. You up for a bevvy, Bradford?"

He cast those puppy dog eyes at her again, but she shook her head. "Not tonight, Jamie, but thanks for the invitation." Gloria gathered up her belongings, said a quick goodnight, and hurried to the bike sheds, suddenly needing to escape. She was glad for the ride back to her lodgings, even though it was difficult to make out the road with hooded headlights and no moonlight.

An owl hooted, and the rain had slowed to nothing more than drizzle. Cam had seemed so pleased, proud almost, when Gloria had broken the dud code, and that approval had warmed her to her bones. But if she dug a little deeper, the other feelings it stirred terrified her. Why was she so drawn to Cam? Why couldn't she just be charmed by Jamie, who was patently keen on her? She didn't quite believe his excessive bonhomie. He reminded her of a magician she'd seen at Scarborough who pulled a threepenny bit from the ear of a child and guessed the card of an unsuspecting patron at a music hall. Jamie was all flash and no substance, whereas Cam was all substance with no need to be flash. Gloria knew which option was more appealing, and that was exciting and unsettling in equal measure.

Chapter Fourteen

CAM STRUGGLED TO CONCENTRATE that morning not because of the fug of cigarette smoke hanging in the air, or the constant rain on the roof and the slapping of water cascading from the broken gutter, but because Gloria looked, well, glorious this morning. The way she'd shed her coat with a shimmy of her shoulders and tossed her hair out of the scarf she'd worn to cycle in the rain gave Cam the urge to rush up to her and twirl her around. Gloria was such a breath of life, and joy, and intrigue, and ... *Stop it*.

She forced herself to stare at the random letters in groups of five on the page of yet another dud message. This infatuation was messing with her ability to do her job. Since Gloria had arrived two weeks ago, Cam's average break rate had dropped by more than one full break a day to an average of nine. That was appalling. She still had the highest break rate in her shift, though.

Jamie stepped back into the room and stood beside Gloria. "I've checked all the lockers in the corridor are empty. Now I need to inspect your drawers."

Gloria laughed and pulled back the drawer slowly, as if she was seductively revealing her clothes. Cam ducked her head and groaned softly. That image was not one she wanted in her brain. At least not with Jamie included. This ridiculous infatuation could go nowhere, and the last thing she wanted was for Gloria to be uncomfortable around her. The most they could ever share was their tranquillity and settled calm when singing or playing chess.

Cam smiled. Gloria beat her in chess yesterday, much to Cam's surprise and delight. Gloria must have been observing her strategy and adjusted accordingly. Cam had been distracted by watching Gloria nibble her bottom lip when she concentrated, but she couldn't use that excuse. She'd been beaten fair and square, and her respect for Gloria increased threefold. Intelligence in a woman was such a turn-on.

If she had to describe her ideal woman, it would be Gloria. Her lively manner, being friendly and at ease with everyone, and the way she spoke her mind in her northern accent, not caring what people thought about her, was intoxicating. This was more than just lust; she really liked Gloria for who she was. And so did all the men who buzzed around her, particularly Jamie. He was obviously as smitten with Gloria as she was. He had the right to talk to her, to approach her, to invite her out for tea or a meal, or take her to a dance or to London. Cam had none. And yet, their connection felt real. When they harmonised in the duet and clashed over chess, they were so focused and intense, with a warmth and energy that Cam couldn't describe. If only Gloria was interested in women, specifically in *her*.

This was getting Cam nowhere. She would never get to dance with Gloria, or kiss her, or share a bed. Cam picked up her paper to reset herself and concentrate on the job she was paid to do.

As the rain stopped, and the constant drumming on the roof ceased it was easier to absorb herself in her work. She was following a particular path and mapping out the logical possibilities when the door behind her crashed open, making her jump.

Three military policemen rushed in with their rifles raised, accompanied by a man in a mac who looked like the archetypal spy in the movies.

"No one move. This is a security spot check."

The MPs pulled out desk drawers and tipped the contents on the floor, where pens, coins, and tobacco tins rolled around. The noise was too loud, and Cam ducked and held her head in her hands, wishing to escape and willing the men to stop.

"Carter, this is a surprise," Jamie said to the man in the mac. "How have you been? I haven't seen you on the golf course recently."

Carter gave a quick smile. "No time. We've been tasked with tightening security."

Why did the man have to make such a din? Every word boomed in her head.

"Present your identification papers to my men and empty your desks, lockers, and bags."

Gloria stood up, her eyes wild. "You can't just waltz in here and ask to see inside a lady's handbag."

She'd gone an interesting shade of purple. Cam admired her courage, or was it stupidity? Riling the authorities was never a good idea.

Jamie turned and gestured for her to sit down. "It's okay, Gloria. Carter here is from MI5. He's just doing his job to keep us safe from traitors and to check there are no breaches in protocol."

"Too many reds and queers in this place," Carter practically shouted. "Don't trust any of them."

He glowered at Cam, and she lowered her gaze, trying to keep her headache at bay. Why did he have to hover here, snooping over her shoulder?

"Selling our secrets to the Russians."

Gloria closed the distance across the room to him. "The Russians are our allies."

"Doesn't mean you're allowed to send them any classified information. Is that what you've been doing, Miss...?"

"Gloria Edwards. I'd say it's a pleasure to meet you, but that would be a lie."

All three of them loomed over Cam's desk. She wanted to shrivel and lie in a darkened room. Her heart beat a fast tattoo, her breaths became shallow and rapid, and her vision shrunk to the size of the spotlight illuminating her desk. She gripped onto the rickety desk to stop herself from toppling over.

The MPs extracted the drawers of Drew's desk and upended the contents with a clatter. Then he shone his torch into the carcass of the desk.

Carter moved to the bank of small cupboards just outside the door in the hallway. "Open this cupboard," Carter shouted.

Cam staggered to her feet and knelt by the cupboard she used as her locker every day. She entered the code in the padlock that she changed daily. It was always based on the number of eggs Number Three had laid, plus one random digit at the front. It wasn't foolproof, but it kept out the casual nosey parker. The MP grunted as he got down on his hands and knees to rifle through her possessions: her sandwiches and flask, sheet music for the duet, and her bicycle clips. He tossed them back into the space, and she gritted her teeth at his rough treatment of her possessions. They must hope people were stupid enough to keep incriminating evidence in their lockers.

"We'll get you next time," he whispered, then he stood and kicked the cupboard door closed with unnecessary force.

Cam's head throbbed, and after resetting the combination, she slumped onto her chair. They knew about her. They were watching her.

At Richard's desk, one MP gave a shout. He withdrew a *Picture Post* magazine with a handsome man on the front from behind the drawer.

"Fucking fairy, hiding pictures in your desk," Carter said.

Cam glanced across to see how they were treating her one-time tutor and now friend.

Richard's eyes were wild, and he held up his hands. "I didn't know it was there. It must have slipped behind the drawer."

Carter towered over him. "Yeah? You're coming with us for questioning. Queers are too ripe for blackmail. If we find a shred of evidence, you'll lose your security clearance quicker than you can say fucking queer."

Two of the MPs manhandled Richard away. Cam tried to give him a smile in solidarity. Lose security clearance? He couldn't do his job if he didn't have clearance. Nausea rose. She had to swallow hard to keep it down and wiped at a bead of sweat on her brow. *That could be me.*

Gloria blocked the door. "You can't just accuse someone with no evidence. What happened to innocent until proven guilty?"

Carter scowled at her. "You're new here, aren't you? Don't you understand the consequences? If this person has been passing over secrets, he'll hang by the neck. Personally, I'd hang him by his goolies. Fucking queers. Now if you'll excuse me, Miss Righteous Busybody, we need to get on."

"Come away, Gloria." Jamie pulled her away from the door. "Fancy that round of golf when you're free next?"

"Sunday?"

"Perfect. Call me at my lodgings, and we'll arrange a time."

"Great."

Carter left with a door slam, as if he was determined to make a dramatic exit.

Cam held her head, and she trembled uncontrollably.

"Hey," Gloria whispered. "Are you okay?"

Cam peered up through the cage of her fingers to see Gloria kneeling beside her, concern etched on her face. The noise and the attitude took her straight back to school, being beaten up for her looks, for being a tomboy. "What are they doing to Richard?"

"I don't know. They're bullies in uniform. Let me make you a cup of tea. I know you've got your flask but let me help you. You probably need some sugar too; you seem quite shocked."

"No, I'm fine. It's just a headache," Cam said, embarrassment curling around inside her. Her heartbeat was gradually returning to normal. There but for the grace of... They would snatch away her security clearance, and she would be nothing. She'd have no job, no status or respect, nothing. Her quaking became so great, the paper keeping the desk level worked its way out. She leaned down to fix it.

"Let me do that." Gloria pushed the paper until it caught under the leg.

Jamie frowned. "Okay, everyone, let's get back to work. We've got more to do, and now we're a person down."

"Thank you," Cam said.

"You're welcome. Are you sure you don't want some tea?"

Cam shook her head, and Gloria returned to her desk.

It took Cam fifteen minutes until she was steady enough to focus. She'd just about settled down when the door opened again.

Richard slunk in, looking grey. He stopped by Cam's desk. "They said they're watching me. Any misstep, and I'll lose my security clearance," he whispered.

"Sorry you got targeted," she said.

He gave a wan smile. "We have to stick together."

As he trudged to his desk, panic struck her again. She couldn't lose everything. Without Bletchley Park, she was just a misfit. The threads of her emotions tangled into a huge ball. It would take a long session on the punch bag this evening to clear her head and loosen her warring emotions. She wanted Gloria more than ever, but there was no way she could take the risk. Bletchley Park was who she was: her entire identity and sense of worth was wrapped in it.

Yet Gloria was kind, friendly, and vivacious, and today, she'd shown she was brave by standing up to Carter and being protective. Cam melted a little more inside and wondered how she was going to maintain her platonic admiration from developing into something dangerous for them both. That might be the most difficult puzzle she'd had to decipher yet.

Chapter Fifteen

Gloria pulled the dinner plates out of the oven, still shaken by the raid earlier. All she had achieved by standing up for Richard was drawing attention to herself. That was reckless, and her place in the hut was too new to be secure, yet. She placed the plates on the bare kitchen table. Her mam would never have had a meal without a tablecloth, but Mrs Jones had no such sensitivities. It probably saved her an extra amount of washing each week. "It's all burnt and congealed. Mrs Jones had to do an evening shift at the factory, so she left our supper for us."

"She works so hard," Bea said as she extracted the cutlery from the drawer and set it out. The cat, Lovelace, wound herself around Bea's legs begging for a scrap, following every move she made. "It's food, and I'm famished and exhausted. And I'm so grateful it's prepared for us. Today has been a particularly frustrating one, but never mind that. How was your day?"

Gloria told her about the MI5 raid. "I saw a different side of what we're doing today, and I didn't like it one bit. I can't believe Richard would betray his country. He's so gifted and bright. They all are. I'm in awe, really. I've always been the brightest person in a room, and now I'm not. That's dented my pride, but I'm thrilled to be using my brain at last. I'm very grateful to Jamie for arranging the transfer to the Duddery."

Bea raised her eyebrow.

Gloria sensed something was amiss. "Didn't he get me the transfer?"

Bea swallowed her food slowly, as though taking her time to decide how to respond. "I'm sure an additional request didn't harm."

"But he was so adamant he'd sorted it out. Is that not true?"

"He seems very sweet on you."

"I know, but I don't feel the same way, not like..." The heat in her cheeks could have burned the food to a cinder. "He's nice enough."

Bea's eyes glinted. "You're not interested?"

Gloria shook her head. "He's been very helpful, and he's funny, and he reminds me of my brother. But at the moment, I just want to settle into my work."

Bea sipped her water then replaced the glass on the table. "If not Jamie, is there anyone else?"

Suddenly, the cottage pie seemed fascinating. Gloria cut off the charcoal bits of potato and fed them to Lovelace who had no qualms about scoffing the food. There was no way she was going to admit what was churning around in her head or confess to Bea how she felt when she and Cam sang together. It was all too confusing, and disturbing, and didn't mean anything. It was just the joy of singing, nothing more. She replaced her knife and fork on the plate between mouthfuls, as she'd read somewhere that made the food seem to last longer.

Bea laughed, pulling her from her reverie. "Given by your reaction, I suspect the answer is yes. Who else is in your shift? Archie? No, I can't see that; he's too besotted with Jamie. Richard? He's a lovely man, but you'd be barking up the wrong tree with him. Drew? No, he's too obsessed with sports to notice women. Besides, he's married. Wait." Bea's whole face seemed to light up from within. "Is it Cam? I've seen how you look at each other when you sing together. It's like you're two parts of the same organism."

Gloria groaned and dropped her head in her hands. "I feel so protective of Cam. She's a bright, powerful woman, but I can see her vulnerable side, and I don't want anyone to hurt her."

She rubbed her palms over her face. Bea had exposed her

feelings and read her so easily, and Gloria was confused with the stirrings inside her. They didn't make sense. But if she had to trust anyone, it would be Bea. Slowly, she met Bea's eyes, but there was no judgement there, only glee. "I think I like her, but it's wrong. It's against the Bible. My da would go ballistic."

Bea snorted. "I don't believe in all that. The Bible was written by men who had a particular goal in mind. Can you imagine how different it would be if women had written it? There'd be a much more fascinating set of rules. More love and less damnation. Anyway, I digress. From what you've said about your father, he's not exactly sticking to the Ten Commandments."

"What about honour thy father and thy mother?"

"You've done that for many years, looking after house and home, supporting your mother as well as the full-time role at your father's factory. You've done your duty to them, you've honoured them. What's all that compared to love?"

Gloria's hand shot up to stop her before Bea went too far in her enthusiasm. "I didn't say it was love. She's fascinating: the way she dresses and carries herself, slightly apart and confident in her abilities. She must have a brass neck to wear those clothes in the face of such judgement and opposition. And it's dangerous, if today is anything to go by. Although it's a very attractive look, but that's too shallow. She's clearly highly intelligent, like everyone else I've met here, but she's also kind, looking after her aunt, whom she speaks of very fondly."

Bea smiled. "And that's wonderful."

Now Gloria was building up a head of steam, and all her concerns flooded out. "Isn't it wicked or unnatural?"

Lovelace jumped onto Bea's lap and she stroked the kitten who sounded like a sawmill. Bea turned to Gloria. "Wicked is a moral judgement imposed by culture. If it was unnatural, it wouldn't be seen in nature, but it is. And if your infatuation leads to love, how natural and fulfilling is that? We all need love and connection."

"You make it seem so simple. I'm not sure if it's just fascination because she's unique and accomplished, and I've never met anyone like her before."

"The only way to find out is to get to know her better. 'Our doubts are traitors and make us lose the good we oft might win by fearing to attempt,' as Shakespeare said. Get to know her as a real person, as a friend. She's a lovely soul and you need to discover that for yourself."

"I don't want to mither her. You think I should?"

Bea grinned. "Mither? Is that some Yorkshire idiom I don't know?"

"I don't want to bother her, then."

"Why not? Of course in society and at the Park, discretion is needed, but we all have secrets."

"Like the secret letters you write to the mysterious M?" Gloria hoped she hadn't pushed too far, but Bea threw her head back and laughed.

"Maybe. You remind me of Miranda in *The Tempest*, staring around in wonder as you come out of sleep and see the world through different eyes."

Bea was right. Her understanding had shifted as if she'd changed perspective since coming to Bletchley. She would explore this strange new land and find out more about herself and Cam along the way.

Chapter Sixteen

DREW ENTERED THE HUT one day, excited in a way Gloria had never seen before.

"The Yanks have challenged us to a game of rounders, only they call it baseball, so I'm trying to get up a team. It's next Saturday afternoon before our evening shift. Anyone up for it?"

Gloria observed the dynamic as all the men agreed to play, including Richard. No one asked Cam, and she didn't volunteer.

Drew looked at Gloria. "Would you girls like to play?"

Cam scowled and bowed her head close enough to the desk to rub her nose in her work.

"If I was a *girl*, I wouldn't be able to play. As a bairn, I played cricket with my brother, and he taught me to catch." The sharp pain of grief at Ben's death stabbed at Gloria's heart, but she tried to cover for it by smiling at Drew.

"You catch? That'll do."

There was an awkward pause. Gloria tried to meet Cam's eye, but she was assiduously avoiding everyone. Gloria's heart went out to her. Cam wasn't quite one of the girls or one of the boys; she was just Cam. She didn't belong with the rest of the hut, despite them respecting her work. If there was something Gloria could do to break down those barriers, and get them to accept Cam, she would. She grinned. "I'll play if Cam plays."

Cam's head whipped up. "No, I can't. I have things to do on Saturday afternoon."

"That sounds like an excuse so you don't have to mix with your hut mates," Gloria said. Given the acidic look Cam gave her, perhaps her challenge was a little much, but beneath that rather alluring exterior, she was sure there resided a lonely soul. And, selfishly, she wanted to spend more time with Cam. The connection between them had grown over more rehearsals and chess games, and she wanted to develop that further.

Cam continued to scowl at her, but Gloria simply smiled sweetly, willing her to relent.

Richard glanced between the two of them staring from different ends of the hut like the showdown at the O.K. Corral. "Cam, you're fit. I bet you can run."

"Yes," Cam said without removing her glare from Gloria.

Gloria revelled in her honesty. Cam didn't hide her skill behind the false modesty that seemed to be the modus operandi of most southerners.

"And don't you do some form of callisthenics or something?"

"Boxing." Cam's expression softened a little.

"In which case, you'll be a much better addition to the team than I am. I know I'll only be there to make up the numbers. I'm all fingers and thumbs." He laughed and danced his hands in the air, and his middle-aged spread wobbled a little.

Jamie muttered something under his breath which Gloria was sure included the word homo. She didn't care for the tone, so she glared at Jamie, who held his hands up.

Gloria turned back to Cam. "Please come. It would be good to have the whole hut there. We need some fun after the last few hard days." That was an understatement. The Enigma machines must have been altered again as the tried and tested cribs no longer worked for the naval section, which meant more urgent dud messages had been passed onto their hut. Every unsolved message could make the difference to the mariners sailing in convoys across the Atlantic, as vulnerable as bath ducks easily taken out by the submarine wolf packs. They didn't wait to pick up survivors either. All those lives, all those desperately needed provisions sunk in the bottom of the ocean. Jamie in particular was jittery about it. He had snapped more and smoked more of his strong cigarettes.

Gloria had asked him why he smoked the French Gitanes that were impossible to get.

"I like them. They set me apart from the crowd. A friend of mine can still get them, and we do a trade when we meet in the Savoy."

"So you *were* meeting someone there. I thought you were being mysterious when you disappeared for so long. I assumed you'd forgotten me."

Jamie flashed his warmest smile. "I could never forget you, Bradford. Who else butchers the King's English like you do? Or stands up for lost causes." He glanced at Cam and Richard.

"You're only jealous because you don't come from God's own country."

"I thought that was Kerala in India?" Jamie put on a mock innocent expression.

"Yorkshire. It's Yorkshire, as if you didn't know—"

"Never heard that." Jamie grinned, and she felt like pummelling his solid chest with her hands.

"All right," Cam said, "I'll play."

Richard clapped his hands together. "Great. Now we have a chance of winning."

Cam didn't quite maintain her neutral expression, and her eyes twinkled. *Well done, Richard, for including her.* Gloria decided to make sure Cam was made to feel part of the team in the future. She wanted the rest of the men to like Cam as well as respect her work. If they got to know her a bit better, maybe they would see her as Gloria was beginning to see her.

Saturday was surprisingly warm for spring. Or maybe Gloria was used to the bitter winds on the moors; this was balmy in comparison. It was probably why *Wuthering Heights* was her favourite book: all those wild moors and wilder passion. Not that she'd had much passion. But she could dream. She glanced across at Cam, who was stretching and flexing.

Drew had set himself up as umpire and liaison. A group of six men and one woman dressed in various US uniforms came over, and Drew made introductions.

One of the Americans, Chuck, shook and held Gloria's hand. "What's a beautiful doll like you doing with all these boffins?"

Jamie turned on him. "Keep your mitts off."

Chuck shaped up to Jamie. They were the same height, but Chuck had more muscle.

"Stop being such tossers. I'm quite capable of speaking for me sen, thank you. We're all doing the same job, and we've come here to have a bit of fun on a lovely spring day, so let's just do that, shall we?" She turned to see Cam roll her eyes. Gloria laughed.

"You've got a different accent," Chuck said.

This was getting old very fast. "So have you. We don't all speak like the king."

Drew cleared his throat. "We need seven players in each team, including one woman, and thank you, Edmund, for being an honorary member of our hut today. To stop the arguments that almost turned into a fight in our last game, this is a mix of baseball and rounders that I'm calling raseball. The bases are those four trees." He pointed out the relevant trees on the main lawn in front of the house. "Throws can be over or underhand. We're playing with rounders bats and balls because that's all we've got. There are no stealing bases and no tagging while running to first base—"

He continued to outline the rules, and Gloria surreptitiously watched Cam rolling her shoulders as if limbering up for a major tournament. Her tight-fitting vest showed off the muscles in her arms, and Gloria was very tempted to squeeze her biceps, just to check how hard they were.

"Let's get on with it. We've only got a couple of hours until we're due on shift, and all we'll have done is talked about the rules," Jamie said, and they laughed.

Drew puckered his lips, then nodded.

The Brits were made to bat first, and Cam and Gloria stood

near the back of the line. There were no runs when the men had all played. Richard and Jamie had both been caught out.

"He's wearing a great big glove. How's that fair, Drew? They should have to catch it with their hands like we do." Jamie thrust both his hands in a pocket, looking like a boy who'd lost his ball.

Drew gritted his teeth. "Ask if you can bloody wear them when we're fielding if it's so unfair."

"Good luck," Cam whispered before Gloria lined up against the pitcher.

It was reminiscent of facing her brother bowling at her in the back garden; he always tried to trick her with a spin. She tried to anticipate what the pitcher would do. It was weird there was no run up, just a leg lift before the ball came hurtling towards her. She wasn't quite ready, but she clipped it with her bat.

"Run, run," Drew shouted.

She hurtled towards first base and touched the tree with her bat before the fielder got to her. She grinned back at Cam, who was lining up to face the pitch, but the look of concentration on her face was similar to the one she wore when she was working on a complex cypher.

Cam smashed the pitch, and it sailed between the branches of the second base tree and beyond. The fielders had no chance of catching it, and Cam ran so fast, she could have overtaken Gloria.

"Home run!" Drew called, jumping up and down.

Even Jamie shouted as Cam touched the fourth base and raised her bat in triumph. She shone with delight, and Gloria gave her a hug as the remaining batters lined up. As if that wasn't good enough, Cam repeated almost the same hit the next time round.

As they made their way back to their hut later, having declared a draw, Richard and Drew chatted to Cam about how much she'd played before. Gloria tried to listen in on the conversation, but Jamie was badgering her.

"I was robbed. I would have scored a rounder if the Yank hadn't used that ridiculous glove!"

"Don't be such a mardy arse, Jamie. We would've been trounced if it hadn't been for Cam with her two runs and two catches."

Jamie offered her a cigarette, but she shook her head. He took a second to light up and inhale deeply. "You did a great catch too, even without the glove." He grinned in that cheeky manner that reminded her so much of Ben.

"You aren't forced to play cricket all your childhood and not learn how to catch—if you value your fingers anyway. But I was so chuffed, I almost shouted howzat." Although the achievement she was proudest of was getting Cam to play at all, and it warmed her heart to see Cam chatting to Richard and Drew.

"Come for a quick cuppa before we start work?"

"I want to freshen up first." She sighed when he gave her a pleading look, his bottom lip all but pouting. "All right, I'll have a cup to take away."

"We'll come with you," Jamie said and clapped Archie on the back.

When they arrived at the hut, Jamie took her cup into their office, and Gloria disappeared into the ladies' bathroom, where she discovered Cam stood at the sink, shirtless and washing herself.

She gasped at Cam's taut arms, the slight swell of her breasts under her bra, and the hard muscles of her stomach. "Marvellous," she whispered.

"Pardon?" Cam paused her ablutions and blinked as she turned.

Oh, she must have said that aloud. "Your playing today was marvellous."

"Thanks."

The slight quirk to Cam's eyebrow indicated she knew exactly what Gloria had been thinking. As if she could tell Gloria's mouth was dry, and it wasn't just her heart that was throbbing. "You're very sporty." How banal. What was happening to her that her brain couldn't come up with a more coherent thought?

"I used to row at Cambridge."

Gloria could imagine it: the creak of a boat and small splash on a slow river, with a slight mist rising, diffusing the dawn light. She would have loved to have that life and that opportunity. "If you rowed as well as you played today, you must have been very popular with the men on your team."

Cam raised her eyebrow even higher. "I went to an all-women's college."

"With the women then."

There was a silence between them, charged like the air before a storm. Gloria was sure they weren't talking about sport anymore, and the thought thrilled her. As Gloria stared into Cam's dark eyes, she was tongue-tied, and a strong pulse of arousal rippled through her body. Her view of herself and who she was in the world shifted perspective, like discovering what she thought was a flat square was a whole cube of possibility.

The sounds of the men coming down the corridor on the other side of the thin-partitioned wall after their cigarette break brought Gloria to her senses. She smiled and moved towards a cubicle, then caught a whiff of Cam's scent. Not perfume, it was something more woodsy and masculine, and it suited Cam. "You smell nice. What is it?"

Cam grinned. "Tabarome. If it's good enough for Churchill, it's good enough for me."

"I'm sure it smells much nicer on you."

Cam's response was a gaze so dark and intense it stirred desire deep in Gloria's gut. Not for the first time she sensed she was playing with an unexploded bomb that could blow her life apart. And she wasn't sure if she wanted to light the fuse or not. Heat crept up her neck and face and she clutched her bag close to her chest. "I thought I'd freshen up too, before we start work." She closed the door and sat on the toilet trying to get her breathing and heart rate back to normal. What was happening to her? It was terrifying and thrilling in equal measure.

Chapter Seventeen

"Okay, we need a break," Reggie said. "I need a cigarette. Archie, are you coming?"

Two seconds later, the door swung closed behind them.

Jamie turned to Gloria. "Hey, Bradford, can I talk to you in private, please?"

Gloria threw a puzzled glance at Cam, who tried to keep the scowl off her face. Cam shrugged as if she was nonchalant about such things, that she had no proprietorial claim over Gloria.

Gloria strode forward without taking his proffered elbow. "Sure. I hope you won't try to entice me with those disgusting foreign cigarettes you like. Smoking isn't good for my throat."

Bea gently touched Cam's hand. Only then did Cam realise she'd been gripping the music stand so hard, she was surprised it hadn't collapsed.

"Let's make a pot of tea and talk about it." Bea made her way to the kitchen in their rehearsal space.

Cam followed without thought, unable to express what was churning inside. "I don't know what's going on in the rehearsal. None of us seem focused." She pulled down the institutional green cups and saucers from the shelf marked for educational hut use only and placed them onto the work surface.

Bea switched the kettle on then turned to Cam. "We can talk about the rehearsal, but I'm sure Reggie will want to tell us what we're doing wrong when he returns. I'm more concerned with you. You're clearly angry and upset. What's going on?"

"Jamie is going on. I feel so foolish. I hate the way he hangs around Gloria, taking up her time and energy. I hate the way he can make her laugh. I hate feeling jealous, and I've no right to feel that way. How farcical is it we're singing an aria about jealousy, and I'm caught up in it."

"Have you spoken to her?" Bea asked as she took down the tin of tea leaves.

Cam gave her best withering stare. It was only when Bea looked up from unclipping the tea tin that she saw.

She simply laughed. "I'll take that as a no."

"How can I talk to her? She's not into women, and he's watching me like a hawk. So is his bully dog, Carter. They're just waiting for one wrong move from me, and they'll remove my security clearance. I have to work." Her sentences came out in gasps and jerks. Her life was smooth, structured, and simple, but these feelings were turning her around and agitating everything.

"Get to know her better. Invite her to the play readings. There are some great performances in that." Bea grinned.

Being a Shakespeare aficionado, she was of course appearing, doing Portia's speech from *The Merchant of Venice*, and Cam had seen her mouthing the words to herself in their rehearsals while she was waiting for her turn to sing.

Bea pointed toward the noticeboard that advertised a concert by the lake that Sunday. "What about the chamber orchestra concert?"

"Won't it be cold this weekend?"

"They'll have it in here if that's the case."

Cam looked around the wooden floored hall that served as a dance hall, cinema, and orchestra venue. Something tight clamped around her heart. "What if she says no?"

"Just ask her, Cam. I know she likes you."

"As more than a friend?"

Bea shrugged. "I can't say that. You need to discover that for yourselves, while being discreet, of course."

"But what about Jamie? She's completely bewitched by him. Can't she see him for the fraud he is?"

"She thinks of him like a brother."

The tight ball of emotions in her stomach loosened a little. "Really?"

"That's what she told me." Bea poured the tea. "But you'll only be certain if you get to know her better and talk to her."

"What if she says no?" Cam asked again, tapping her fingers on the table.

Bea stretched over to still them. "Will you be any worse off than you are now, eating yourself up with anxiety and jealousy? Do you really think she would stop your friendship? I can't see it."

Cam got slightly distracted by the visual of being eaten up but caught the gist of what Bea was advising. She would ask Gloria to the concert on Sunday. Cam particularly liked the Schubert quintet piece they were playing anyway, and Gloria said she loved classical concerts. They would go together, and she could bask in Gloria's proximity, and maybe they would share a moment when energy and understanding seemed to pass between them like when they were singing their duet or playing chess.

She was besotted, and she knew it.

Reggie and Archie re-entered in a miasma of smoke and accepted the tea that Bea offered them. Within seconds, Jamie returned too, looking triumphant. Gloria followed, and she smiled across at Cam. Delight glowed below her skin. Jamie stepped in front of her eye line, blotting out her view of Gloria. His chest was puffed up like a cockerel. Cam almost expected him to crow.

"I've asked Gloria out, and she said yes," Jamie said to no one in particular.

Cam dropped the saucer she was holding. Fortunately, her quick reactions resulted in her grabbing it before it smashed on the floor, but not before tea slopped over the side of the cup and filled the saucer. She swung around to the sink, giving herself time to compose herself while Bea sorted out the teas. A hollow sensation gouged out her stomach. *Too late.* She should have known it was inevitable. Had Gloria's smile been to placate her, or was it just the afterglow of being asked out by Jamie? The thought stuck in her craw, and she blinked a couple of times. She was not going to cry about this. Or vomit.

When she was courageous enough to turn around, Bea and Jamie had joined Archie and Reggie. Gloria waited by the counter for her refreshments. Cam flashed a smile in her direction but avoided catching Gloria's eye as she handed over the replenished tea.

"Cam, look at me," Gloria whispered.

Slowly, Cam raised her head and saw only kindness in Gloria's eyes.

"He asked me to go to the Shakespeare play readings, which I agreed to because I was already going to support Bea. That's all."

Hope nestled in her heart. Gloria wouldn't say anything unless she thought Cam would be upset. What did that mean? There was only one way to find out. "I was going to ask if you'd like to go to the chamber orchestra concert by the lake on Sunday, unless it's pouring, in which case, it'll be in here."

Gloria's smile broadened into one of true joy and lifted Cam's spirits.

"I'd love to, thank you. I really look forward to it."

Cam's stomach tingled, and she made a little squeak of excitement. How articulate. This infatuation had stolen her tongue and dulled her brains. "Great. I'll reserve seats."

The connection between them seemed to hum with anticipation, and Cam was so tempted to reach out and touch her.

"I'm looking forward to it too."

Now the thrill of exhilaration hit her, and she needed to see her again, before the weekend. Cam turned her head and Gloria was so close she had to refocus. "Also, my Aunty Florrie said she'd like to meet you. Would you like to come to my place after work for supper one day?"

Gloria held her gaze. "That's champion. I look forward to meeting your Aunty Florrie, and the chickens, of course. Especially Number Three."

Cam thought her heart would burst. "Can you make Thursday?"

"Aye. Thank you."

From behind them, a baton tapped on the music stand. "Can we start again? I want to focus on the phrasing and the timing of the entrances in particular."

Cam put aside her glee and became absorbed in the performance of the scandalous duke in the *Rigoletto* quartet. By the end of the rehearsal, she was exhausted and had to depart quickly to get back to Aunty Florrie. As she left, Jamie was hanging around Gloria. She shut her eyes to that and concentrated on getting home as quickly as possible. She had two social occasions lined up, and that was more than she'd had in months, if not years. And that was an opening of possibility. The first unfurling of hope blossomed in Cam's heart. She was sure she hadn't imagined the connection between them. Thursday couldn't come soon enough.

Chapter Eighteen

Gloria followed Cam on her cycle, committing the turns to memory so she could find her way home in the dark later. She was anxious enough meeting Cam's Aunty Florrie, never mind cycling down unlit, unfamiliar lanes with the hooded lights. Although there was little risk of invasion now, the road signs had still not been replaced.

Cam cycled at a fast lick the whole way, and her gear changes were smooth and efficient, unlike Gloria's, which were accompanied by an irritating click before the chain finally settled on its proper cog. Despite it being mainly flat around this part of Buckinghamshire, Gloria was puffing slightly when Cam finally swung her leg over her crossbar and leapt off her bike. She pushed open the gate leading to a quaint red brick cottage. To the front was a large garden stuffed with vegetables that Gloria struggled to identify. Gloria closed the gate behind her and hurried to catch up with Cam, who was disappearing around the side of the house, where a large yard was enclosed by various outbuildings. Set apart in a fenced off orchard was a wooden hen house. When Cam opened the outbuilding filled with tools and wheeled her bike inside, the hen house erupted in a wall of clucking and crowing.

"Okay, okay, chucky chicks, I'm coming," Cam said, then spun around to Gloria, her face turning scarlet. "Sorry, do you mind if I feed the chickens and shut them up first? Then you can meet Aunty Florrie."

Gloria hid her smile at this adorable side of Cam. "Of course. I'm looking forward to meeting them all. Where can I leave my bike?"

Cam's colour deepened. "I'm so sorry. I'm being a terrible host. Let's leave it inside the tool shed." She pointed to the brick outbuilding but took the bike herself.

Gloria snatched her bag from the basket before it disappeared.

Cam leaned the bike against hers and fastened the door with a simple wooden lever. "Aunty Florrie can't manage keys with her arthritis, so I have to take the risk that no one will steal from it. Wait here, and I'll just grab us some overalls and wellies."

Cam seemed discombobulated, as if her routine had been put out. Gloria wanted to hold her, to calm her down. "Just do what you normally do, Cam. Don't mind me. I'm happy to fit in."

Cam flashed her a grateful smile. "Thank you. I've never brought anyone home before, and it's blurring different parts of my life, which feels uncomfortable. But I'm very glad you're here."

Cam turned and disappeared so fast she could have drilled a hole in the ground.

Gloria looked around. A brick path led to the hen house, bordered with rosemary, sage, and possibly thyme.

Cam returned and handed over a brown canvas overall coat, not unlike what people wore in her da's factory. "You're much taller than Aunty Florrie, so you can have my overall." She held it up like a matador's cape.

She was such a gentlewoman. The coat had the faint scent of Cam. Gloria inhaled deeply and coughed as it also reeked of chickens.

Cam blushed again. "Sorry, it's workwear. I should have washed it before you came."

Now Gloria was embarrassed that she'd made Cam uncomfortable. "Not at all. It's just a tickle in my throat."

Cam knelt before her like Prince Charming with a glass slipper. Gloria slipped off her shoes and wobbled slightly as she slid her feet into the wellington boots, thankful for Cam's shoulder to lean on.

Cam led her into the hen house carrying a small jug of water, which she poured into a tin trough. "I don't like to think of them not having anything to drink. I also check they have some food in the feeders in here, but they graze during the day, so shouldn't need much at night. This is Three."

One bird cocked its head to one side and seemed to purr low in its belly.

"She's happy to meet you, if that's not too anthropomorphic," Cam said. She quickly cast her eyes over the laying boxes. "No eggs tonight, but we had four this morning. Chickens are fascinating. Do you know if you pick one up and move them around, their head stays in the same position?"

She scooped Three under her arm, which Three didn't seem to mind at all, and demonstrated. Gloria laughed, but the sound must have startled the birds, as one hen gave an irritated cluck and rattle and ruffled her feathers.

"Settle down, girls. Okay, should we leave them to it?" Cam gestured to the door, and she scrambled after her, ensuring none of the hens escaped. Again, she fixed the door with a simple wooden latch. "I used to lock them up at night, but Aunty Florrie can't let them in or out if I'm on the night shifts. Careful, the path is a little uneven here. I'd use a torch, but the wardens are strict around here."

Gloria smiled at Cam's chivalry as she held the kitchen door for Gloria to enter and indicated the sink to wash her hands. Cam hung up the overalls and placed the boots neatly in the porch before handing Gloria a towel and washing her own hands.

Cam bit her lower lip. "Come and meet Aunty Florrie."

Again, she allowed Gloria to enter the room first and pulled a heavy burgundy coloured velvet curtain behind them, presumably to keep out the draught. It took Gloria a couple of seconds to adjust to the light. A fire roared in the grate, and a standard lamp shone at the back of a wing-backed chair. In pride of place beside the chair was a tall wireless radio cabinet, currently silent. The tuning dial was in easy reach of the chair, out of which a stooped woman struggled to stand. Cam hovered, ready to help.

"Don't get up," Gloria said.

"Of course I want to stand, dear. I want to look you over," she gave a delightful chuckle, "to see if you're good enough for my Camilla."

Cam jerked her head up. "Aunty Florrie!"

"Keep your knickers on, I'm only joking."

Florrie held out her gnarled hand for Gloria to shake. The strength of the old lady's grip and the steadiness of her gaze surprised her. Florrie's face had more lines than the London Underground, and she had deep creases around her eyes as if she had spent her lifetime laughing. Her brown eyes, which were remarkably similar to Cam's, glinted as if she was about to cause mischief.

"Call me Florrie. Lovely to meet you, Gloria, dear. Cam speaks a lot about you. She told me how lovely your singing voice is and how fascinating and interesting you are—"

"Pot of tea, Aunty?"

Florrie winked at Gloria. "I don't mind if I do."

"You're a fan of *It's That Man Again*?" Gloria asked, conscious of Cam's discomfort. "I try and get my mam to listen to that."

"Gloria, if you take that seat in front of the fire, I'll get the tea."

Gloria sat, and Cam slipped out of the room.

"I love that show. 'It's being so cheerful that keeps me going,'" Florrie said, quoting another of the catchphrases from the radio programme. "With all the doom and gloom of the war and rationing, we need something to make us laugh."

"That's true," Gloria said.

"I do want Cam to have more friends. She said you're going to a concert together on Sunday."

"Aye, that's right."

"She's such a kind soul. She never complains about looking after an old biddy like me, and she's so thoughtful and clever, and I'm sure you are too, dear, otherwise you wouldn't be at that secret place that we're not supposed to know about. Do you know they said it was for a shooting party before the war? Well, you don't get thousands of people at a shooting party. It's hard to miss all the buses going in and out of there three times a day. It's a secret factory." She tapped her nose and winked.

"I couldn't possibly comment on that."

"Anyway, I'm so glad Cam's friend Bea persuaded her to do the singing. She's a lovely tenor, but you know that, don't you? I'd like to hear you both sing together, because she said you have a pure soprano voice. I wish I could come to the concert, but it's difficult to get out. Bea sings too, doesn't she? Do you know her well?"

Gloria had to laugh at the wall of questions cascading around her. "Yes, I share lodgings with her."

"She was supposed to come around here for supper one day, but the shifts haven't worked out yet. You all work so hard. Sometimes Cam is all but asleep on the bicycle when she gets home. I worry about her falling in a ditch one night, she's so exhausted. Now I haven't asked about you at all. How rude of me. Do you have family?"

Gloria's delight faded as the familiar grief washed over her. "I had a brother, but he was killed in the Battle of Britain."

Florrie leaned forward to pat Gloria's hand. "I'm so sorry to hear that. It's through his sacrifice that we can live in a free country, and we owe them all our gratitude. Let's pray for an early and successful end to the war. It's been going on too long. How about your parents? Are they still around?"

Cam entered with a tray and a teapot and crockery. "Aunty Florrie, you can't ask that."

"Why not? I hope they're being nicer to you than Cam's parents have been—"

"Aunty, please—"

"I can't believe my own sister would turn out her child because she doesn't dress and act like she expects. It's ridiculous. Well, her loss is my gain. Although I don't want to be reliant on Cam, because she'll be back to Cambridge after the war, no doubt. Did she tell you she was a mathematics tutor there? Of course, it's ludicrous they won't allow women to graduate. Perhaps she should go to one of the more enlightened universities—"

"Aunty Florrie, I'm sure Gloria doesn't want to hear all about my sorry past. And I love living with you."

Although Cam had blushed again, the genuine affection between them was obvious. It was lovely to watch, and she was a teeny bit envious too. "I'm glad you have each other, and it's fascinating to hear anything about Cam; she doesn't talk about herself very much," Gloria said, accepting a cup of tea from Cam. Their eyes met, and Gloria smiled to reassure Cam everything was fine. "Thank you."

Cam handed Florrie her tea. Florrie poured some of the tea into the saucer and slurped from it.

"Aunty Florrie, please. We have a guest."

"Oh, fiddle faddle, Gloria won't mind. I prefer my tea from a saucer, so it doesn't scald me. Like a cat, I'd be purring now if I could. Close your mouth, Cam, dear. You're catching flies. Now, where was I? Ah, yes. Family. Do tell me about them."

"My mam hasn't been the same since our Ben died. And Ben's wife and baby son went back to live with her mother in the Midlands, so she can't even be a nan. My da spends more and more time at the factory he owns that makes tank tracks, belts, and chains, so he's never home." Gloria paused a second to take a sip of tea, debating how much to reveal. "He wasn't thrilled when I came here though." *That was an understatement*. She was tempted to touch her cheek even though the physical mark had long since gone. The emotional scar would take much longer to heal.

Cam looked perplexed. Gloria hadn't told her that because it wasn't important, but Cam looked distinctly upset about it.

"I'm sure you're much better off doing your secret work." Florrie took another slurp of tea and smacked her lips.

"Not according to my da. He wants me to stay close to home and marry his successor."

The fear emanating from Cam was startling. What was that about? "Don't worry, I have no intention of marrying for anything but love. Call me a romantic, but I'm not into dynasties. Now I'm earning my own salary, I'm becoming independent. But I feel guilty about the whole honour thy father and mother thing."

Florrie poured more of the tea into her saucer with a trembling hand. "Honour is a strange word. I think it means to cherish and respect your family, and that goes both ways. I don't believe it means blind obedience to the detriment of everything else. The slanted interpretation of the teachings of the Bible has probably caused more grief and heartache than anything else. If you stick with God is love, I don't think you can go far wrong."

"I agree, Aunty, but not everybody will—"

"It's all right, I won't say that at church or if the vicar comes round. But we black sheep of the family have to stick together. Now, how long is it until supper, Cam? I'm sure Gloria is hungry after her busy day."

"It will be another ten minutes. I'll just put the leeks on to boil. Excuse me."

"Can I help you, Cam?"

"No, I'm fine. Talk to Aunty Florrie, as long as she doesn't tell any more stories about me." She gave her aunt a hard glare, but Florrie just waved her hand dismissively.

"But those are the most interesting ones. Like the time you climbed a tree and refused to come down because your mother wanted you to wear a dress." Florrie turned to Gloria. "She stayed up there three hours. She must have been tired and hungry, but she only came down when her parents relented."

Cam shook her head and hurried out.

Although Gloria loved these snippets of her early life, she preferred Cam to tell her if she wanted, so diverted them back to safer topics. "Are the leeks from the garden?"

"Yes, we try and grow everything for ourselves. We even had a pig last year, but it escaped and caused havoc in the garden, so we agreed we wouldn't do that again. It was my fault; I hadn't latched the pen properly, but Cam didn't get angry. Cam does most of the heavy work, but I can potter in the garden on my good days, and it gives me so much joy. When the primroses are out and the bluebells are in bloom, it shows nature prevails even through war. It feels like they are the first signs that winter is over and spring is on the way, politically as well as in the garden."

"I hope you're right."

"Would you like to take some leeks and potatoes to your landlady? I presume you've given her your ration books?"

Gloria nodded. "That's very kind of you, but can you spare them?"

"Of course. I'll ask Cam to look some out for you afterwards."

"That's so kind of you. Have you finished your tea? Shall I take the tray through?"

"Thank you, dear."

Gloria collected the crockery and carried the tray through to the kitchen. Water boiled in pans on the stove, and Cam was sitting at the kitchen table with her head in her hands.

"Cam, what's wrong?"

Cam lifted her head. "This is harder than I thought. All the separate parts of my life mingling together."

"But I love Florrie. She's an absolute delight."

"You do?"

"Of course. She's a joy to be around, and she clearly adores you."

Cam smiled, but it looked reluctant. "I adore her too."

She moved to the stove to stir the gravy. A spiky, uncomfortable energy seemed to surround Cam, as if she regretted inviting Gloria.

"Thank you for inviting me to your home."

Cam shrugged and glanced up. "I feel so exposed."

Gloria stepped forward but restrained herself from touching Cam. "I'm honoured you're letting me in, for trusting me with your real life outside work. Trust is letting me see your vulnerabilities, playing with the hens, helping your aunt."

Cam spared a glance. "Thank you for being so good with her."

"Oh, it's my pleasure. I think she'd like us to do our duet afterwards, if you're up for it?"

"Sure, why not? If you're happy. Nothing like an impromptu recital. Would you mind laying the table in the dining room?"

"Show me where everything is."

Supper passed quickly, and it wasn't long until they were back in the sitting room with Florrie settled in her chair by the fire.

"Gloria says you wanted to hear us sing," Cam said.

Florrie clapped her hands together. "Oh, yes, please."

Cam strode to the upright piano against the far wall and lifted the lid. Beside it stood a cello in a canvas cover.

"Do you play?"

"Occasionally. Not that I have much time now."

"She plays beautifully," Florrie said, and Cam rolled her eyes.

"Flattery won't get me to indulge you."

"But will you indulge me?" Gloria wasn't sure why she'd asked. They shared a look. It was like when they were singing, that communication without words that made her body flutter in a way she couldn't fathom.

"I would indulge you with everything I could," Cam whispered so Florrie couldn't hear. "Shall we start with 'As Steals the Morn?'" she asked, louder.

Cam settled her fingers on the keys. There had been truth in Cam's comment: raw, clear, and unsettling. And Gloria wanted to share in that truth, to explore it and hold it to the light, even while she knew she should run screaming from the room. Cam turned back and her look was so intense and focused, it made Gloria feel as though she were the most important person in the world.

With men, it had always been admiration and a desire to possess, to display her, to show her off to their mates. And that could be fun—they could be fun. With Cam, it was different. Cam's gaze cracked open her soul; she saw behind the mirror and wanted to connect on a real, deeper level. What she was feeling for Cam—affection and attraction—was much more than friendship. Cam was opening Gloria's heart, and that was simultaneously exciting and terrifying.

They didn't have the sheet music for the piano arrangement Archie had been using, so Cam replicated the introduction. It was brilliant. *She* was brilliant. When they started singing, the accompaniment became simpler but underlined the richness of their harmonies and counterpoint. They synchronised their breath and phrasing and became enveloped in the aria. There was just the two of them, Gloria taking cues from Cam, becoming part of the music, their voices blending and interweaving to produce a rich, complex sound. They had never sung better or more intimately. As the piece ended, Gloria's whole body pulsed with a life force energy, swirling around her, lifting her up. Singing about waking from a drug-induced dream seemed to inspire that haze of semiconsciousness that categorised the limbo between sleep and wake, where anything was possible. Thoughts fluttered and stirred the truth that dared not be spoken as they stared into each other's eyes. She searched Cam's face. Beneath a mask of indifference, hidden desire sparkled in Cam's eyes. Gloria recognised it because it resonated with her own.

Gloria was so tempted to press her lips to Cam's, to capture the feeling and express it differently and she leaned forward. The fear in Cam's eyes stopped her short. Of course, her aunt was here, observing them.

"That's beautiful," Florrie said softly.

She clapped gently as if she didn't want to disturb a rare bird perching within touching distance in case it fluttered away. Gloria blinked. That was close. What was she thinking?

"Shall I play the cello now?" Cam asked, avoiding Gloria's eye.

Without waiting for a reply, she removed her cello cover and settled the instrument on her shoulder. She plucked the strings and tweaked the knobs to tune it perfectly before settling into the opening strains of "The Swan" by Saint-Saëns. She didn't look at Gloria once. Still without acknowledging her, Cam modulated into Bach's "Cello Suite No. 1."

Gloria tried to unscramble what was happening between them. Cam had been as invested as she was but had now pulled back. It seemed the shift was more than the presence of her aunt, that Cam was having second thoughts about inviting her here and showing her softer side. Gloria would not betray that trust or openness, as she revelled in it. Not that she could say that. With the revealing of Cam's home life Gloria wanted to dip closer and inhale the sweet fragrance of attraction blossoming between them, even as it scared her. The emotions defied logic, and the puzzle eluded her.

Chapter Nineteen

THE NEXT FEW DAYS they worked flat out, with a series of midnight to eight a.m. shifts that stretched into the early evening and kept them all busy. The concert was scheduled for five p.m. after the first day shift had ended and Cam prayed she wouldn't fall asleep.

"Let's have a picnic by the lake before the concert," Gloria had said, and so Cam had provided egg sandwiches, cake, and a blanket for them to sit on.

With the wartime double daylight-saving time, it was still light in the early evening, and the spring sun was bright. Daffodils bowed in the breeze and primroses dotted yellow on the banks. Magnolia and pink cherry blossoms scattered in the breeze.

"This isn't like the picnics we used to have before the war," Cam said as she handed the bread to Gloria, feeling like a stingy host.

"It's a feast. And having real eggs is such a treat. Did you have picnics as a child?"

"Not really; my parents were too busy on the diplomatic circle. When I stayed with Aunty Florrie, we walked everywhere and she would make whatever we were doing seem interesting, and she'd tell me stories of her childhood with my mother in Belfast."

"Ah, that's what her accent is. It reminds me of my sister-in-law, Ailish's accent. Why did they leave Belfast?"

"My mother married my father, who was a low-level diplomat she met at work. When women marry, they have to leave work in Northern Ireland. She was already expecting me, so Aunty Florrie left with them to help look after me when I came along. I've always been closer to Aunty Florrie."

Gloria pulled at a blade of grass and rolled it between her fingers, before raising her eyes to Cam. "You never talk about your parents."

Cam inhaled deeply, wondering how much to reveal, but she felt she could trust Gloria with her secrets and her vulnerability. "No. They couldn't cope with having an odd child who didn't behave as they expected. I almost caused a diplomatic incident when I accused the daughter of the French ambassador of lying about not having a biscuit."

"Had she stolen the biscuit?"

"Yes."

Gloria picked another blade of grass. "So you did the right thing."

"They didn't see it that way. I was supposed to know that I shouldn't have said anything. It was the last diplomatic event I went to."

"Do you still see them?"

"No. They don't approve of me or the way I dress and behave. Aunty Florrie is my only family now."

"She's lovely." Gloria blew on the blade of grass between her fingers, making an owl noise.

"Ah, nearly, but not quite right. The male owl makes the too-woo sound, the female the too-wit call."

Gloria pulled her hands away. "Really?" She smiled after Cam nodded. "You know such fascinating facts."

Cam shrugged. "I just remember things I find interesting."

Unsure what to say next, Cam took a bite of her sandwich. Gloria was the most fascinating person she'd ever come across, and she'd like nothing more than to lie down on the blanket with her. That Gloria was even passing the time of day with her and seemed genuinely curious was a balm to her nerves. But that was not something to be expressed.

Cam cleared her throat. "Did you go on picnics as a child?"

"Aye, we all walked up to the top of the moors and had cheese and tomato sandwiches. At one time, my da would do anything for us. Ben said I wrapped Da around my little finger. It wasn't true, but he'd tease me about me being Da's favourite. He was always closer to my mam. They were both quieter and less feisty than I am. But after Ben died, everything changed. We pretended we were still a family for a while, but that's all gone now." As if she'd regretted saying as much, Gloria threw down the grass and rose. "This has been lovely, but shall we take our seats before the concert starts?"

Cam was still folding the blanket when Gloria walked towards the chairs that faced a makeshift stage area. Had she upset Gloria? Cam hurried to catch up, wanting to rekindle the closeness and openness they had shared earlier.

When Cam came alongside Gloria, she pretended she didn't see Gloria brush at her cheek. They walked in silence to the concert area. Cam so wanted to reach out and squeeze her hand, to comfort her, to connect on a physical level without the need for words, but she withdrew her outstretched hand.

Gloria settled into her allotted seat close to the aisle. "Tell me about the pieces we're about to hear."

Cam told her about the music, although she suspected Gloria already knew but needed a distraction while she steadied her emotions. The strains of the instruments tuning up caused the audience to settle into eager anticipation. Everyone needed something that wasn't just war and work to lift their spirits. As the music played, Gloria seemed to lose herself, and Cam leaned towards her, equally enthralled.

The sounds of the cellos and violins carried on the wind, and Cam couldn't be any happier than she was now. She caught Gloria's glance and smiled shyly. Gloria's lips trembled.

"Are you cold?" Cam asked.

"A little."

Cam removed her overcoat and placed it over Gloria's shoulders in a protective cloak, then spread the blanket over their knees. Their fingers touched as Cam adjusted it, and goosebumps that had nothing to do with the cold shot up her arm.

"Huddle up. Don't get cold yourself," Gloria said in the short break in the music.

Without waiting for a response, she snuggled close to Cam. Instead of the normal jitteriness with physical contact, Cam leaned into the touch, wanting to be close with Gloria. She was happy, and she absorbed it all. The warmth of Gloria's body, her hair flipping in the wind, and her light perfume clung around her like a cloak. Cam's senses were full of the sweetness that was Gloria. She needed to focus on the music so she didn't make a fool of herself. The Schubert *String Quintet in C Major* was haunting and beautiful, and Cam followed the cello line. The cellist was good, especially as their fingers were probably numb with the biting cold.

Gloria snuggled in even closer and, under the canopy of the coat, she trailed her fingers down Cam's arm. But when Cam whipped her head around, Gloria was staring forwards as if she was entranced in the music. Cam reached across with her other arm and tentatively placed a finger on Gloria's hand. Gloria didn't pull away. If anything, her stroking became more intense. The hairs on Cam's forearm rose under Gloria's touch, and nerve endings tingled throughout her body.

Gloria was so daring under the semi cover of the blanket, and it stirred hope in Cam. At the next gap in the music, Gloria removed her hand, and Cam felt bereft without the touch.

"When can I see you next outside work?" Gloria whispered.

"I'm not sure. Whenever we can arrange it."

"Would you like to come over next Friday for supper at my lodgings? Bea is working the evening shift, and my landlady is out at the factory."

"I'd love to. What can I bring?"

"Just yoursen."

The music started up again, and Gloria faced the front. Cam couldn't concentrate. It was really happening. Gloria was asking her to her place when they would be alone. The way she'd invited her made Cam shiver all over. For the first time ever, the crack of hope opened up. And she wanted to see what lay within.

The round of applause indicated the end of the concert, startling Cam. She could have stayed there all evening, surrounded by music, in physical contact with Gloria, and enjoying her company.

Gloria leaned into Cam. "Thank you. I enjoyed this."

"I did too." Even with the cold, it had been almost the perfect evening because it had given her an excuse to get close to Gloria. "This means so much—"

"Hello, Bradford, did you enjoy the concert? I saw you from over the other side. We're just going for a drink. Would you care to join us?" Jamie gripped Gloria's shoulders.

Cam was tempted to swipe at him and tell him to get his grubby hands off her, but Gloria smiled as if she was unconcerned.

"I didn't see you, Jamie. I can't, sorry. I said I'd go straight back after the concert and phone my mam to see how she is."

"Such a shame," he said. "I was hoping we could get all warm and cosy in the Eight Bells. It's gone chilly, hasn't it?"

"Aye. Have a lovely evening. See you at work tomorrow, bright and early."

He bowed and withdrew.

Gloria turned to Cam. "Sorry about that. What were you going to say?"

The moment had broken, and reality trampled over the frail hope, in the form of Jamie. "It doesn't matter. How's your mam doing?"

"Much better, thank you. Mrs Henderson has been a godsend, keeping the house together and making sure Mam eats every day."

"I'm so glad."

Gloria handed the blanket and coat back to Cam. "Thanks for the loan of this and thank you for a wonderful concert. It was a great treat away from the grind and stress of work. Now I must get going. See you tomorrow. Unless you want to cycle some of the way home?"

Oh, she would so love to cycle side by side in the twilight until their paths separated, and maybe in the shadows, out of the way of all these people, she could say what she really wanted, that she wanted to spend more time with Gloria, and she couldn't stop thinking about her, that she had shaken her whole world. But she shook her head. "I promised I'd help sort out the chairs."

Part of her hoped Gloria would offer to stay behind too, but she'd already said she was leaving to call her mam.

Gloria stretched forward but then stopped herself. Had she been coming in for a kiss and then remembered where they were? "Tomorrow, then."

Cam watched Gloria walk towards the bike sheds, then refolded the blanket. She was so tempted to sniff it to see if it had retained any of Gloria's scent. Helpers were stacking the chairs to return to the hall, and she was getting in their way, so she reluctantly turned her back on the departing Gloria and fulfilled on her promise. If it hadn't been for Jamie's interruption, which was little more than staking a claim on Gloria, it had been a perfect evening. And maybe Gloria liked her a little more than she would a friend. A boundless energy bounced her along as she carried back a stack of chairs, all her earlier exhaustion vanished. She and Gloria were having supper next Friday, and they were going to be alone in the house. If she allowed herself, perhaps she could dream. Her footsteps around the lake were lighter than they had ever been.

Chapter Twenty

Gloria wetted her finger and dabbed it on the plate to make sure she got every last crumb of the Victoria sponge made with real eggs. "Please thank your Aunty Florrie for the fabulous cake. It rounded off the meal delightfully."

"I will. She hoped it would be sweet enough; she was worried because she had to reduce the sugar and thought it might change the texture too much."

"It was perfect." Much like this meal had been. Gloria settled beside Cam, and she thrilled in the novelty and frisson of taboo. The food may have been cobbled together from leftover stew and stale bread, but it was washed down with a pitcher of delight. The same connection they'd shared when singing strengthened as they talked.

Cam sipped her tea and leaned back in her chair. "Let me do the washing up for you."

"No, no. You're my guest. There are only these cups and saucers to do, and it won't take me five minutes. I did everything else as I went along. Let's go into the sitting room; the fire should be nice and warm now. Mrs Jones made it up before she left after I'd told her I was having a visitor. She said it was fine as long as it wasn't a gentleman. I said it was a female friend from work. I didn't say you were a gentlewoman, even though you are."

Cam coloured. Surely she realised Gloria was complimenting her. Perhaps she wasn't very good at taking praise or didn't like approval based on such trivial things as looks, and that was fair. It was shallow, and it wasn't just Cam's looks that intrigued and attracted Gloria. "I'm so glad you came around. I can't tell you how excited I am that you're here. I love spending time with you." She needed to be the one to open up and make a move, if she could. Her heart thumped and her hand trembled, but Bea had encouraged her to follow her feelings. "I can't stop thinking about you. I'm sure you can feel this connection between us, even if you are being the perfect gentlewoman. But it scares me too, because I don't know what it is or what it means."

Cam paused, her cup on the way to her mouth, her eyes and mouth had formed a perfect O.

"Or is it just me?"

Cam replaced the cup on the saucer with an uncharacteristic clatter. "No, it's not just you. I've admired you since the day I met you, and I'd like nothing more than to treat you the way you deserve, but we can't. The Park is the only place where I'm respected for what I do, where I can be me, where it doesn't matter if I'm odd—too much. Now I'm in Carter's sights I have to be doubly careful. I can't risk losing my job, and I'm sure you can't either."

A thrill ran through Gloria at Cam's first sentence, so she paid little attention to the rest. So it *was* mutual. "True. But I also don't want to hide how I feel about you. Even though I've felt nothing like this before."

Cam gripped her hands around the cup so hard, Gloria was concerned it might crack into a thousand pieces.

She had gone too far, and her food settled in a lump in her stomach. "Don't fret about it. Forget I opened my big mouth. I can see I've unsettled you. Let's just practice our duet." There were only a couple of official rehearsals until the concert, and Cam had seemed anxious for it be perfect. Their last rehearsal had been technically correct, but it lacked their usual emotion. Reggie had asked them to work out what had gone wrong and fix it. Now seemed a good time to explore that.

The look of relief on Cam's face was enough to make Gloria weep. She couldn't take this further. She'd already said too much.

Gloria led them to the sitting room where the fire burned brightly. Lovelace was sprawled on the rug and didn't even lift her head when they entered.

"Nice cat," Cam said and knelt to stroke her.

"She likes you. She doesn't let strangers fuss her like that. I think she's a good judge of character." Cam's face flushed, and Gloria needed a distraction, so she approached the piano at the other side of the bay window. "I don't know when this was last tuned."

Cam crossed the room to join her and lifted its lid. With a barely audible tut, she took out her handkerchief from her waistcoat pocket and dusted off the leather stool before sitting on it.

"Or when it was played last." Gloria grimaced, hoping Cam wasn't judging her for the state of the housekeeping. Poor Mrs Jones worked every bit as hard as they did, and although she and Bea did what they could to help, the coal dust formed a fine film on the top of every surface moments after it had been cleaned.

Cam laid her fingers on the keys and played a couple of scales, wincing at the tinny tone that sounded like a honky-tonk piano in a sleazy bar. Not that Gloria had ever been to such a place, but she'd seen them in the movies.

Lovelace jumped up and rushed from the room, making them laugh. "Not an aficionado then," Cam said and patted the stool, and Gloria sat beside her. With a mischievous grin, Cam launched into the "Maple Leaf Rag." It was so unexpected in its jaunty syncopation that Gloria stifled a laugh, then she had to lean back so that Cam could stretch across her to reach the high notes.

"Well, that wasn't Handel," Gloria said. "You are a constant surprise—in a good way," she added as a flash of hurt crossed Cam's expression.

"Too upbeat? You prefer something like this?"

She modulated into the Marlene Dietrich number, "Falling

in Love Again," and mimicked her sultry half-spoken, half-sung style. Was there something significant in the choice of song? Probably not, as Cam began to croon the words of "Lili Marlene."

Gloria clapped when Cam played the final notes. "I can see you as Marlene Dietrich; you've definitely got that look about you."

"Thanks." Hardly breaking a beat, Cam dropped into the introduction to their Handel number with simpler accompaniment.

Gloria nestled against Cam as they sang. Cam's chest expanded in a quick breath before she formed the last few notes in the aria. Gloria was mesmerised by the rise and fall of her chest, the delectable incongruity of Cam's breasts in male clothing, and the movement of her hardly pronounced Adam's apple in her long, graceful throat. She longed to run her fingers along it. The rich tenor tones came from her soft lips, plump for the kissing. When Cam exhaled the last few notes and their eyes met, they were so full of longing, Gloria inhaled sharply. Cam's eyes were so expressive, a tiny ring of brown haloing dark pupils in which Gloria could see herself.

For weeks, the energy between them had whirled when they sang, when they played chess, or they worked, like tuning forks resonating at the same frequency. It seemed Cam would never act on it; she was too controlled, too much a gentlewoman to impose on Gloria and unfurl the desire shining in her eyes.

By contrast, Gloria was all fire and passion. She would have to be the one to push for this. Gloria gulped. Almost without thought, she caressed the sharp angles of Cam's jaw, giving her ample scope to withdraw if she wanted. Cam's skin was smooth and warm, and Cam angled her face to give Gloria easier access. Gloria curled the longer piece of Cam's hair dangling in front of her ear and looped it around. Cam pulled her even closer. Their breaths united as the significance of what they were about to do rolled over Gloria. A tiny bead of sweat formed on

Cam's forehead as if she was struggling to maintain control.

"May I?" Gloria asked, surprised at her temerity, but her brain was still floating on their musical high.

Cam swallowed and an almost imperceptible nod gave Gloria the permission to gently press their lips together. Cam's warm hand cupped the back of her neck, pulling her closer, and Gloria obliged, releasing the fear, the doubt, and the judgement as she slipped into the kiss. Waves of excitement cascaded through her body. Cam trailed her tongue along Gloria's bottom lip, which she lowered, welcoming her in. Their tongues touched and explored each other, and all the weeks of unacknowledged lust, longing, and denial dropped away.

She was kissing a woman, and every cell in her body vibrated with the thrill of it. Gloria had been kissed before, but they had been all stubbly scratches and slobbering drool, as if a kiss was only a stepping stone to other things. But this was luxurious intoxication, and she was drunk on desire. Cam tasted of cake and tea, and Gloria lost her mind, until she had to pull away to catch her breath.

They both panted hard, and Cam's eyes were wild, as though the kiss had unleashed a tiger within, one which Gloria wished to be devoured by. They kissed again, leaning in until they almost toppled from the piano stool. Cam caught them before they fell over, and they giggled. She had such strong arms from her boxing, something Gloria would love to watch her do. She wanted this intimacy, this closeness, this outpouring of wanting, even though she couldn't allow her mind to articulate it. Once spoken, it couldn't be unsaid, and she didn't want this dream to shatter and reality to come screaming in.

"Should we move to the sofa?" Gloria asked between shallow breaths.

As if not wishing to break the spell by speaking, Cam pulled her up from the piano stool and took her across to the sofa, sitting beside her, half facing her. If Gloria could capture this moment, she would take a photograph with Cam's eyes shining, her expression full of yearning, just for her. She traced Cam's jaw, the action mirrored by Cam. Her fingers were slightly calloused and cool, or maybe Gloria was burning up.

"May I?" Gloria asked, her hands tracing down Cam's neck.

"Please," Cam said through a long breathy exhale.

Gloria wasn't the only one being affected by this. She unfastened Cam's tie and loosened her top button, then she pulled her shirt from out of her trousers and slid her hand below Cam's shirt and up her stomach and higher, savouring the sensation of Cam's smooth skin under her fingertips.

Cam arched her back giving her more access and unbuttoned her shirt.

Gloria pushed it back to reveal a plain cotton bra. "Oh." The sight of Cam's breasts constrained by the cloth made her want to rip it off her body. "Is this okay?"

"Yes. I trust you. I..." Cam slipped her hand from Gloria's neck and undid her own bra, revealing small breasts.

Gloria swiped her thumb over her nipple, and it hardened, making Gloria exclaim with delight. Cam's body—another woman's body—was a joy to behold; firm and muscled around her stomach, soft in the swell of her breast. She was the epitome of contrasts, and Gloria revelled in it all, wanting to absorb everything about her, to hold her, to devour her.

Cam writhed beneath her touch. "Oh it's so much more arousing when they're touched by someone else."

Gloria pulled back. "Has no one else touched your breasts, or admired them before?"

Cam shook her head, her face glowing red.

"Well, I'm honoured to be the first. Thank you. They're beautiful. *You're* beautiful...or maybe handsome is a better word."

"Thank you." Cam wriggled down the sofa and gently tugged at the zipper holding Gloria's dress together.

To have it removed with such reverence and delicacy was

delightful and caused her pulse to quicken. Gloria shrugged the dress from her shoulders, and it slowly slipped down her body. Her bra soon followed, and she pressed her body to Cam's, breast to breast, her nipples hardening at the touch. The pulse between her thighs seemed stronger than elsewhere, and Gloria was a whisker away from removing the rest of her clothes when the doorbell rang. She felt Cam stiffen in her arms.

"We haven't got a light showing. Maybe they're got the wrong house in the dark and hopefully they'll go away," Gloria whispered, but Cam was already fastening her shirt.

Gloria sighed. "Can you help me with my zip?" She pulled her bra away from where it had ruckled above the cascade of fabric and let Cam draw the cool zipper against her naked skin.

The doorbell rang again, and a boy's voice called out, "Telegram."

Her mind rushed back to the night when they received the telegram to say Ben's plane had been shot down. Panic flooded her, and her heart raced as she rushed to the door and flung it open.

"Miss Gloria Edwards?"

"That's me." She virtually snatched the envelope from the young boy and ripped it to read the message inside. It was from her Da. *Not Mam, please not Mam. She's just getting herself together again.* She scanned the telegram.

Come home immediately, you are needed. Da.

She was needed? She wouldn't be surprised if this was just a ploy to force her home.

"Is everything okay?" Cam asked.

"I don't know. I have to call. Thank you, no reply," Gloria said to the young boy who looked relieved, then he scampered down the path to pick up his bike and race off, presumably for his next errand.

Gloria's hands trembled as she picked up the telephone receiver and asked to be put through. She hoped Mrs Jones wouldn't mind her using it as this was an emergency. "Mam? It's Gloria. I just received Da's telegram. What's going on?"

"Oh, Gloria, we've just heard that our Ben's wife Ailish and her mam have been in a car accident in the blackout and are in hospital, so we've agreed to take Benjy for a while. Ailish's da is bringing him up tomorrow. We need you here to help."

"But, Mam, I'm doing important war work. Are they going to be all right? Is Benjy going to be with you for good?"

"No, hopefully just for a few weeks until they're back on their feet. Surely your work can't be that important that they can't spare you for a fortnight or so?"

With a sick feeling Gloria said, "It is. Can't you manage a child on your own? You used to do it for our Ben and me."

"Oh, Gloria, I was younger then, and well..."

"You have Mrs Henderson helping you—"

"We can't ask her to take on any more."

Gloria could hear her father saying something. It must be serious if he was home for the evening.

"Your da has already informed your bosses where you work that you're needed."

"He can't do that."

"It's done," her da bellowed. "There's a train tomorrow at 8:13. Change at Birmingham and Leeds."

The phone went dead, and Gloria slumped onto the floor, her entire world crumbling. So much for independence.

"What's happening?" Cam wrapped her arms around her.

"I have to go home to look after my nephew until my sister-in-law is out of hospital, but I don't know how long that will be. Part of me thinks this is just a scheme for my da to get me back home. I'll go back so I can work out what's happening, but I'll return as soon as I can." Gloria shook her head when Cam looked so bereft, as if Gloria had just snatched the last banana before they were rationed. She knew how she felt. "Don't look like that. I'll sort out what Da needs, and I promise I'll be back when I can.

Please wait for me."

"I've waited this long. But what about our rehearsals? It's only three weeks until the performance."

"I know. I hope I'll be back by then. We've also got to finish that chess game. I'm on a winning streak now, I can sense it."

Cam's lips turned upwards. "Nonsense. I've worked out your strategy now."

"In that case, I'll love to prove you wrong." She sighed, wishing the evening hadn't ended like this. "I'd better pack now if I'm going to catch the early train."

"Please keep in contact. I feel like I've just found you and don't want to lose you again."

"Oh, Cam."

Gloria pulled Cam into another kiss, passionate and fierce, trying to burn the sensation into her memory.

Cam pulled away and swiped at her eyes. "I have to go." She pulled together her clothes and sniffed surreptitiously. When she turned to face Gloria, her eyes shone with misery. "Let me know how you get on. Safe travels."

With no further physical contact, she left, and Gloria heard Cam's bicycle as she wheeled it out of the gate. The sound of the catch echoed a final click on a wonderful evening. Gloria hoped that wouldn't be the last time she'd see Cam or get to touch her. Dread and nausea clogged her throat, and her hands trembled when she cleared up the plates before going upstairs to pack. She just hoped this wasn't the last time she'd be in this house. She was finally beginning to thrive in this new life, and she wasn't prepared to give it up—family responsibilities or not.

Chapter Twenty-One

HALF AN HOUR OF punching the bag hadn't provided Cam with an answer. Physically, she was exhausted, and emotionally, she was a tangled mess. The kiss had been wonderful. Gloria had taken control, and Cam had let her, willing to release the tight grip she held at all times to keep herself safe and her life ordered. There was no precedent for this, and it thrilled her.

She had to decipher what was going on with Gloria. She had guided Cam and opened up a part of her she never knew existed. Now Cam was in a place where the longing had been allayed, though she craved more. She wasn't convinced she should expect it. The heat, the goosebumps, and the electrical impulse flared under her skin like one of the Bombe machines had been shorted and had clicked through the myriad options and landed on Gloria. Gloria, Gloria, Gloria.

That kiss—her body still buzzed, and to have her breasts kissed and sucked; she'd always wished she didn't have any, but it had been so arousing, which was both surprising and intoxicating. She volleyed a series of hooks, jabs and uppercuts while her mind flipped between thrill and fear.

"Cam!"

She caught the bag before it gave her a full body check and twisted around. "Bea? What are you doing here?"

"Sorry to surprise you. I've been here a couple of minutes. Florrie said I'd find you here. We're on opposite shifts this week, and Gloria asked me to give you this letter. I also wanted to check you're okay."

Cam pulled at her training gloves and bindings but in her

fluster, the knot pulled tighter. She huffed out in exasperation.

"Let me help."

Cam obediently proffered up her hands as meekly as a scolded child.

"Are you all right?"

"Yes. No. I don't know. Don't get too close; I probably smell like a pig."

Bea handed back the unknotted bindings and gloves. "As long as you don't squeal like one. There you go."

"Thank you." How humiliating to need help, as though she was some rookie. What must Bea think of her? Slowly, she raised her head and all she saw was concern on Bea's face. To give herself time, Cam carefully replaced her gloves in the old travel chest that she used to store her equipment, then closed the lid and slumped on it. She patted it for Bea to join her. "I can't believe it. I think I'm falling for Gloria. We've only kissed once, but I wanted her to touch me, I wanted to touch her, to be held, to be with her. I think about her all the time; it's affecting my concentration. Now she's gone back home, and I don't know what to do, and I always know what to do. My life is simple, straightforward, and safe. This feels the opposite of that." She leaned her head back against the cool wall and closed her eyes trying to hold onto tears.

"May I?" Bea asked, hovering her hand over Cam's forearm.

"Uh-huh."

Bea lowered her hand. "If I can offer anything, I'd say take one step at a time. Why don't you read your letter? I'll go and check your garden and acquaint myself with your chickens. We'll talk when you've had time to think about it." She slipped out of the stables and left the door ajar.

Cam's fingers fumbled with the envelope and she pulled out a single piece of paper.

Dear Cam,
This must be in haste as I'm packing to leave in the morning.

Thank you for a wonderful evening together, and I'm so sorry it was cut short. I want to do that again (and dare I say, more). You've captivated me completely. I want to spend more time with you when I return, and I will do everything I can to make sure I come back. We have a concert to sing, and I can't wait to harmonise with you again...in every way.
Yours truly,
Gloria
X

Cam traced her finger over the paper, reverently absorbing the implications of wanting to do more. She so wanted to explore that now that her heart had been opened.

When Bea returned a few minutes later, Cam handed her the letter.

"Well, that's lovely," she said after reading it.

Cam tucked it into her waistcoat pocket. "I don't know what to do or how to feel. I loved kissing her. I never thought I would ever get to kiss a girl."

Bea squeezed her forearm.

"But she kissed me. It was wonderful... Everything I thought... and," Cam felt her neck burning, "a little bit more than that. Now I'm torn. I would love to do more. I think I love her, but I've never been in love before, never had this mix of anxiety and euphoria at the same time. I'm petrified of being caught. They threatened to take away Richard's security clearance if they could prove he was queer. They'd do the same to me. My whole life is the Park. It's where I'm respected for my work and have a place, and we're making a difference to the war. But we're more vulnerable to blackmail. I'm not sure I can take that risk."

"What if you're discreet? We can all keep secrets here. Surely you can do that too?"

Cam shook her head. "But what if she doesn't come back? Her father will doubtless put pressure on her to stay. I know she's strong, but is she strong enough to stand up to him? She said he got physical when she left, and I hate that. And I can't bear the thought of not seeing her again."

She leaned her elbows on her knees and tears dripped onto her forearms. She wiped them away roughly, and her breathing became fast and shallow.

"Okay. Breathe slowly and think about this logically one step at a time. You're a brilliant chess player; think of it like a chess game and aim for the win. If you cannot act now, you may need to wait until after the war." Bea gave a small sigh and then refocused as if she was pulling herself together. "The first step is for her to come back and you have no control over that. The second is to have an open conversation. Tell her how you feel, then you can make a joint decision on how you proceed. She certainly seems keen, but if you need to wait, then you'll have to wait."

"It could be years and the outcome of the war is uncertain. You see the same things we do at work; the ships lost in the Atlantic, the pushback and ferocity on every front."

"In which case you might decide you can't wait, and you'll take the risk, and that's something you need to do together after really communicating how you feel. If saying it out loud is hard for you, write it down. You like lists; do a summary of pros and cons and talk her through it."

Cam scrubbed her face, then slapped her hands on her knees. "Thanks, Bea. I'll think about it. Would you like that cup of tea?"

Bea grinned. "Florrie has already promised me cake made with real eggs. I'm not turning that down." She wrinkled her nose. "In the meantime, you're right about the piggy smell; you might consider a bath."

"Cheeky." Cam pushed Bea off the trunk, and she squealed and jumped away, laughing.

She could strategise all she wanted, but it was Gloria's move. In Gloria's letter, she'd said she intended to come back for the concert. Cam would readily take the paved road to hell and the hope it promised.

Chapter Twenty-Two

GLORIA PAUSED A SECOND before the front door to give her strength to deal with whatever waited behind there. A toddler and a depressed woman were not a good combination. A blackbird sang in the still air, but there was no sound coming from inside.

She knocked before entering. It seemed like the polite way to establish she was a visitor to this house, but she could already feel her father's net closing around her. This was his revenge. He hated it when he didn't get his way.

Gloria placed her suitcase on the hall tiles and looked around. Everything was in its place and gleamed.

"You can put that suitcase upstairs in your bedroom, young lady, and not leave it cluttering my hallway," a voice came from upstairs.

"Hello, Mrs Henderson. Of course. Lovely to see you again." She obediently untied her laces and placed her shoes into the polished walnut shoe stand and her coat on the hat stand. The floor was cold underfoot; she needed to retrieve her slippers from her suitcase upstairs rather than gather the wrath of Mrs Henderson by opening it downstairs. She tiptoed up, avoiding the creaky stairs in case her nephew, Benjy, was sleeping. And where was her mam?

Mrs Henderson was attacking the corners of the landing ceiling with a feather duster. To Gloria's knowledge, it was the first time it had been touched for months. When she'd been running the household, there never seemed to be the time.

"Hello, Mrs Henderson, lovely to see you again," Gloria repeated, addressing a pair of thick calves. Mrs Henderson didn't step down from her perch on the stool and glared down at Gloria through her half-moon glasses.

"Aye, well, I'm just getting the house back together again after the state it was in."

Gloria gripped her suitcase handle harder, but she needed to be polite. "Well, I'm very grateful you're here, cleaning the house and cooking for my parents."

"Someone had to, your Mam was all over the place."

She didn't need this not-so-veiled criticism, so she smiled. "Where are my mam and nephew?"

"She's taken him for a walk in the park. I told her to get out from under my feet while I'm trying to clean."

Gloria shut her mouth with a snap. Her mam had hardly left the house since Ben's death. That was a miracle in itself. And everything seemed ordered under Mrs Henderson's well-scrubbed hands "Thank you. I'll make a cup of tea. Would you like one?"

"Aye, I don't mind if I do."

That popular catchphrase again. Gloria grinned as she paused on the landing. "You like *It's That Man Again* then?"

The steps creaked as Mrs Henderson heaved herself down to floor level. "Aye."

Her face was still etched with the deep perpetual frown marks Gloria had been terrified of when she was a child. "It's being so cheerful that keeps you going?" The ITMA catchphrase slipped out before Gloria could stop herself, and she hoped Mrs Henderson didn't think she was mocking her.

"Did you say 'owt about a cup of tea?"

"I'll just get my slippers and go down."

Gloria entered her bedroom. Her knick-knacks had been scooped into a bowl, and all the surfaces gleamed with polish and smelled of lavender. Her bed had been made with pink floral sheets, clearly Mrs Henderson's preferred choice of acceptable decoration for a girl. The structure reminded her of her childhood. That ordered life seemed a long time ago.

She sniffed and dabbed at her eyes carefully with a handkerchief so she didn't smudge her mascara. There was a cough from the landing, prompting her to click open the locks on her case and retrieve her slippers. Not wishing to earn further disfavour, she hurried downstairs to the kitchen, where everything was ordered and neatly tidied away.

There was no evidence of chaos or distress. Gloria swallowed hard, feeling her da's net strangling her. As she suspected, his telegram had been nothing more than a ploy to get her to return home where she would be under his control. Perhaps looking after Benjy was a problem though. He could be a maelstrom, difficult and upset while his mother was in hospital. Maybe her mam wasn't coping, but that had never prompted action from her da before.

She waited for Mrs Henderson to come into the kitchen for her tea. "How is everything? It seems very organised."

Mrs Henderson gave her a withering look.

"Obviously, I expected the house to be to your usual impeccable standard. I meant, how is Mam coping with Benjy."

Mrs Henderson's expression softened, and she sat down in the comfy chair reserved for Gloria's da. "It's doing your mam good to have someone to think about instead of moping around feeling sorry for hersen. We've all lost someone, or know someone who's gone, but we just keep calm and carry on. It's the only way we'll win the war."

She sipped her tea with much relish and smacking of lips.

"So do you know why I've been called back from important war work?"

Mrs Henderson lifted her cup part way to her lips, as though thinking and drinking required too much attention. "Your da's got plans for you to marry some high-up in his factory."

Gloria groaned and put her head in her hands. "I knew it. I won't be manipulated. Not now. I can't."

"There's someone else who's taken your fancy where you're working then?"

"I—I... Yes, there's someone I'd like to be with, and I think it's mutual." She shouldn't have gone down this path because Mrs Henderson wouldn't let up on sniffing out the gossip. Time for some distraction and obfuscation. "There's a chap, Jamie, who is very keen on me. He's very bright and is comfortably off. He's always going down to London on the train, and he took me to the Savoy."

"Aye? He must have more money than sense then, wasting brass on pretty surroundings."

"They were lovely surroundings though, on the side of the Thames, and lots of interesting people are staying there at the moment. They have their own bomb shelter."

"So they don't have to mix with the riff raff? How typical. Anyway, this backsiding about isn't getting my work done. When you've unpacked, you can peel the onions and potatoes for tea."

Gloria grinned and stood up. "Right you are, then." She wished she could dismiss her da's machinations just as easily. Now she needed to extricate herself and return to the Park without destroying her family relationship, if that was possible.

A few minutes later when she was preparing the vegetables, the back door opened to a wall of sound with a three-year-old's constant chatter and an echo of prompting to remove coats and boots. Gloria almost didn't recognise her mam in the responses she made. It reminded her of her own childhood when her mam had been warm and interested. It was both poignant and comforting. Maybe this time with Benjy would do her good.

"Do you know who's here today?"

Her mam's voice buzzed with enthusiasm and warmed Gloria, even if she thought it may not be genuine.

"Father Christmas?"

Oh dear, anything less would be a letdown for the poor boy. She set down her knife as her nephew barrelled into the kitchen.

They stared at each other. He had the same blue eyes as Ben, but the shy smile was Ailish's.

"Daddy?" he asked.

If Gloria had tears in her eyes, it was the onions she was chopping. She wiped her hands on her apron, knelt down to his height, and held out her hand to shake his. "I'm your Aunty Gloria. Pleased to meet you."

He took her hand very sombrely in his rather sticky palm. "I'm Benjamin William Edwards, and I'm nearly four. Are there any biscuits?"

He ran off to Mrs Henderson who was holding out the biscuit tin.

Her mam laughed and the sound, rusty and unfamiliar through disuse, cut through years of grief. Gloria took a sharp intake of breath.

"Come on, Benjamin, you and I will go into the dining room and have our juice and biscuit there." Mrs Henderson swept up the tin and a glass of juice in one hand and caught Benjy in the other.

Gloria studied her mam, whose eyes gleamed with a spark she hadn't seen since Ben was alive. "Have you been having fun with Benjy?"

Her mam put the kettle on the hob. "We have. We've been to the park and fed the ducks and played on the swings. He's so like our Ben was at that age."

"Remarkable. And how is Ailish getting on?"

"She's recovering slowly, but I'm dreading him going home."

Gloria picked up her knife again and began to scrape the carrots. "Could you ask to see him regularly? Maybe for them to come closer to here."

"She won't leave her mam."

"Could you go there?"

Mam blinked. "I couldn't." But possibility slipped across her features. "Or maybe I could help when they come out of hospital.

I'll not be missed here, will I?"

The question didn't need a response.

Her mam nodded. "I'll write a letter this evening and see what they say."

"Goodie. You seem to have it all in hand. So Da's telegram requesting my presence had nothing to do with needing help with Benjy?"

Her mam shook her head and stared at the pile of vegetables. "No. Your da wants you to spend some time with Stanley. He's invited him here for supper this evening."

She picked up the carrots and placed them in the boiling water. Gloria hadn't seen her mam do anything in the house for the last couple of years. She scraped the peelings into the bin for Mrs Henderson to take back for her pig. "I won't go out with him or marry him." She swallowed. "I'm seeing someone." The moment she said it, she regretted it and sent up a prayer to apologise to Cam. She couldn't betray her trust.

Her mam's head shot up. "Really? Who? What does he do?"

She couldn't tell her about Cam, even though she would love to talk about her. Her parents would never understand or approve. It wouldn't matter that her da was the biggest hypocrite there was, going to church on Sunday with a fancy woman on the side. No. Better to lie, a lie that had morphed with each telling. "Jamie works with me. He's my boss on our shift. He's clever and wealthy, and he reminds me of our Ben."

All of that was true, but the juxtaposition hid the truth, implying something that wasn't accurate.

"Why isn't he in uniform? Is he sick?"

"No. Not all war work is in uniform. We work with the Foreign Office, I told you, but I can't say anything else."

"Is he a spy?"

She couldn't see Jamie as a spy; he was too open and friendly with everyone. "I can't say anything, Mam. Don't ask me."

"So he's a spy then. Is it safe? Wouldn't you want a safe bet, rather than risk him getting killed like our Ben?"

"No, Mam. It doesn't work like that. If by safe, you mean Stanley, then no, I don't want safe. I have no interest in him and frankly don't care if I never see him again. He's dull and stupid. Why would he interest me?"

Cam wasn't safe. Cam had turned her thoughts about herself and who she was on her head. And there was no denying it, however much she had tried.

"So this Jamie, is he good to you? Is he serious or just after a good time? You can't trust men's motives."

This interrogation was becoming more uncomfortable by the second. "I think Jamie's serious." That was the problem. He'd been more insistent that she go out with him, and she couldn't put him off much longer. "So I need you to help me put off Da."

"Like he listens to me."

"He might. You seem so much better now."

"I've something to live for now."

That sliced through Gloria's complacency. "Wasn't I something to live for?"

"Oh, Gloria, you were always self-sufficient and assured. And feisty, even as a little girl. You never needed anyone and wouldn't let people close to you. You didn't need me, but Benjy does."

Gloria had always been so proud of her independence but hadn't realised it would put others off. But everyone wants their mam. "I needed you too. But I'm glad you've found a purpose. You seem more like your old self."

"I do feel more like my old self. I have to do things for Benjy, and he's such a sweet, serious little boy."

The sharp sting of grief and jealousy hit her, along with relief and joy that her mam was more engaged. Not wanting to examine the turmoil of emotions, in case they all spilled over, Gloria said, "I'll go and lay the table. Does Benjy eat with you?"

"No. Mrs Henderson feeds and bathes him, and I read to him before he goes to sleep."

"Mrs Henderson is a godsend."

"She is. Don't forget to put out the best Sheffield cutlery."

Gloria left the kitchen, glad for a short respite and an excuse to busy herself.

Thirty-five minutes later, she was mashing the potatoes, adding lots of milk to make it go further, when the front door rattled open and the sound of male voices drifted in. Her heart sunk. She'd hoped Stanley wouldn't come.

She took his coat and hung it up in the hall. She couldn't see him and his partially bald head and obsequious manner without thinking about Uriah Heep.

"Nice to see the'sen again, Gloria, it's not the same in t'factory since you left."

She nodded, not wishing to lie. "I'm sure they're all managing in the cash office. Anne Coggins is a very able person."

Her da enveloped her in a hug. "Gloria, it's so good to have you back home."

She stiffened in his arms. So he was going to play happy families. Well, she wouldn't put up with that nonsense. She shrugged him off and stepped back. "Under false pretences. Mam is doing much better than I've seen her in years and I'll be returning to work as soon as I can."

"We'll talk about that later. Now, how's the food coming along?"

"If you wash your hands and sit down, we'll bring it through in a couple of minutes."

"I'll open a bottle of wine then."

After the procession of their best china serving dishes being laid with a flourish on the table by the women, there was the awkward shuffling as Stanley held Gloria's chair for her to sit down, before settling himself in prime position opposite her father.

After seemingly endless factory talk that Gloria ignored, she checked her watch. What would Cam be doing now?

Putting away the hens and making a cup of tea for her Aunt Florrie no doubt, followed by her twenty-seven-minute nap before preparing herself for the midnight shift. She had to smile. Of course Cam had tested and calculated the precise time to optimise being fresh for the start of the shift when the new codes came in and revised priorities were established.

"Can you ask your Masonic friends if they can supply the hard coal rather than the lignite? It isn't hot enough to fire the furnaces without clogging the chimneys." Stanley continued to ingratiate himself with her da and ignore her completely.

She ought to try to make polite conversation. "Do you sing?" she asked and sipped at the wine.

He turned to her, his eyes wide as if he'd forgotten she was there. "Nay, waste of time. Can't be doing with all that namby pamby stuff."

"How about chess?"

He looked genuinely puzzled. "Why would I want to strategise war when business is much more important—and profitable?"

"What about reading?"

"If you mean fiction, no. Why would I stay up all night reading what other folks have stayed up all night to write?"

"So you're only interested in business?"

"Aye, you could say that. I can't be doing with all this arty stuff—"

"Don't tell me; you think it's a waste of time."

"Aye, lass, you've got it."

"Stanley's made a couple of suggestions to improve the factory systems." Her father looked fondly at him.

She'd had enough of this. "As did I in the cash office."

"Did that affect the bottom line?"

"And that's all that matters to you, isn't it? Maybe you two should marry each other; you're a perfect match."

"Don't be ridiculous. Stanley's come around to ask you. He's already sought my permission, and I said yes."

"The answer is no. I don't care how convenient it may be for both of you. I'm not interested. And never will be." She threw down her napkin. "Excuse me, I need to write some letters this evening." She hurried upstairs and paced her room, trying to calm her racing heart. A few minutes later, her mam came up, flushed and flustered. Her da had probably sent her up.

"Will you come and say goodbye to Stanley? I didn't raise you to be rude to our guests."

It would have been so easy to reply that her mam hadn't raised her at all in the last few years, but didn't want an argument, so she bit her tongue and followed her downstairs.

Stanley leaned forward and made to kiss her. She shuddered and held out her hand. He placed a clammy hand in hers and shook enthusiastically.

"I'm sure we can come to some mutually beneficial arrangement."

Like she was a business deal being completed. "I know we won't." Her jaw ached with holding it tight.

He frowned and turned towards the door. She deliberately wiped her hand on her dress trying to erase all his bodily contact from her skin and shivered. It was like the oil he slicked on the hair covering his bald patch was seeping out of his pores. As he said goodbye to her da and opened the door, she sidled past the cabinet in the hallway towards the stairs.

As soon as the door clicked shut, her da turned on her. "You were rude, and you won't get a better offer."

Too late. She spun around on the bottom step. "Except I have. I told Mam earlier about someone I'm seeing."

All remnants of the smile he'd worn all evening had been replaced by a glittering stare. She glared back, squashing down the agitation in her stomach.

"You've only just met him. How serious is he?"

Now she'd put her foot in it. If only she'd learn not to leap in. She cleared her throat. There was no way she'd marry the obnoxious Stanley. She'd prefer the tedium of the typing role forever than subject herself to that.

"Gloria says he's very serious. I think we should let her choose who she wants to be with. It's important to marry for love."

Her mam fixed Da with a glare, and he had the decency to look a little sheepish. Hopefully he was reflecting that he'd always vowed to love her mam until death did them part, and yet he was having an affair. She was being naïve. He probably thought it was his right as a red-blooded man to take his comfort wherever he wanted.

His fists clenched. "If you don't get engaged to this man in six months, you have to marry Stanley."

Gloria looked him in the eye. Being on the first step put her on the same level as he was. Idly, she noticed his hair was thinning on top. He'd always been so proud of his thick hair, thinking it made him look good for his age and powerful. Now the power was shifting. She was twenty-one, she was working and making her own way in the world, and he wasn't responsible for her anymore. Once she had worshipped the ground he walked on. Not now. She straightened herself to face him. "I don't accept that. Whatever happens in the war, I won't be marrying that reptile of a man."

He raised his hand as if he was about to strike her again but thought better of it. "You listen to me."

"I've listened to you all my life, but you've nothing to say that's worth hearing." She wasn't entirely sure where the courage came from, except perhaps from the quiet rage borne of all the injustices and hypocrisy she had faced from him.

"In that case, you won't be allowed back under my roof. You'll break up the family. Think what that'll do to your mam."

She almost laughed at his crude manipulation. "The family's already broken, and I don't mean by our Ben's death. That's at *your* door. Goodnight." She fled upstairs, not daring to look back. So much for hoping to solve this with minimum impact to their relationship. But she couldn't live under his rules or control anymore. The door clicked behind her, and she shut out her filial submission, her childhood, and everything that made her what she'd been until now, until the Park, until Cam. Life had changed irrevocably. She checked her watch again. If she packed now, she could probably catch an early train tomorrow morning and be back at work the day after. Then she'd see Cam again. Her heart picked up pace at the thought. As she lifted her suitcase from the floor, she couldn't help the smile blooming. She had a duet to sing and Cam to impress. And maybe they could continue where they left off before they were rudely interrupted.

Chapter Twenty-Three

AFTER COMING OFF A bank of nightshifts, everyone in the hut seemed more cranky than normal. No more than a few grunts of acknowledgment were passed around. Cam locked her sandwiches in her small cupboard in the long hall and took her seat. As she leaned on the desk, it wobbled, and she let out a huff of exasperation. The folded paper she had put under the leg had been removed. "Who moved my paper?"

She received a couple of shrugs in response. Had they done it deliberately to annoy her? She wouldn't put it past them. Jamie looked smug at the other end of the room in the hut, but then he always looked smug. "Don't let it get to you." She remembered what Aunty Florrie had said when she'd complained about her work colleagues earlier in the week.

She retrieved a clean scrap of paper and folded it into a tiny wedge to go under the leg and hold the desk stable. In fact, it seemed sturdier than before. Satisfied, she went to the middle table to pick a priority dud message and returned to her desk to puzzle it out. Given how easy it would be to mishear Morse being transmitted over airwaves fading in and out, Cam was always impressed how few they were left to deal with.

Cam stared at the paper but saw only gibberish. She gasped. She was so used to seeing the patterns, but not today.

Richard looked across from his desk. "You okay, Cam?"

Embarrassed that he'd noticed, she stood up and stretched. She could say that her stomach was cramping rather than the truth that she was anxious about Gloria. Cam hadn't received a letter since Gloria's meeting with the chap her father wanted her to marry. Did that mean her father had forced Gloria to agree?

Richard observed her with a frown.

She rubbed her hand over her face. "Thanks, Richard. I'm just tired, and nothing seems to be working today."

Jamie raised his head from his work. "Not up to the job, Cam?"

His smile was as false as the message she was trying to decipher.

"Don't mind him," Richard whispered and puffed at his pipe, causing smoke to billow.

Recently, Jamie had made more snide comments about her and to her. She suspected it was because he had noticed how close she and Gloria were becoming, and he didn't like it. She glanced at the empty desk next to his: Gloria's desk.

Jamie quirked an eyebrow as if challenging her to say something. She scowled at him. This man had all the arrogance of wealth and status and was blessed with all the anointments of society, and he was using his position as the deputy hut leader to make life difficult for her and for Richard.

Cam closed her eyes to centre herself. She didn't want an argument. Gloria was very fond of him, and Cam didn't want to cause a schism between them, or for Gloria to have to choose. Part of her worried Gloria would choose Jamie, because that was what society expected. She still couldn't quite believe that Gloria had kissed her, but she knew it couldn't last, and inevitably, she would be bereft and alone once more.

Snatching the unsolved message from her desk, she held aloft the piece of paper. "I'll leave this on the pile and start a new one."

Very rarely did she place unsolved codes onto the discard pile. Like a game of cards, another codebreaker could pick it up and play with it. A different set of eyes could often see the solution. Normally, Cam prided herself on being the one to choose and solve the discarded messages. But today, she was struggling to focus.

Cam sat down with the new code and smiled at Richard. She

sharpened her pencil, as if honing her mind to be as precise and pointed. The letters remained a jumble, and her thoughts strayed to Gloria again. Would she be able to defy her father again? Her knuckles on her pencil were so white, she had to consciously relax and stretch her fingers. Being cramped like that wouldn't be helpful for playing the piano. It was only seventeen days until their concert, and she'd missed singing with Gloria. It was too late to practice with someone else, and she didn't want to. After dreading singing in public, she was now looking forward to performing. More correctly, she lived for six short minutes of being at one with Gloria in an exultant blend of joy and harmony. It was the closest she would probably ever get to feeling ecstasy with a woman.

She burned at the thought of having sex with Gloria and raised her head to be confronted with the empty desk, and next to it, seemingly even closer than before, a glowering Jamie.

Cam flashed a false smile, determined he wouldn't catch her out again. She tested a couple of letters that seemed suspect, working back from the output dud message attached to the original sequence of codes. If the letter was a W rather than a J (as they were similar in Morse code) that might work. She followed through the thread of possibilities, unkinking the code.

Sometime later the door sprung open and snapped her out of her concentration. Her heart leaped in joy, and the mood in the hut seemed to shift and lighten.

"Hello, you tykes, the bad penny's back again." Gloria grinned and placed her handbag beside her desk.

She tugged at the fingers of her gloves one at a time in a manner that was mesmerising.

Jamie leapt up and strode over to give her a kiss on her cheek. "Bradford, great to have you back again. It's boring without you."

His familiarity and closeness rankled, and she half rose but Richard shook his head at her. Had he worked out how she felt about Gloria? She sunk down into her seat.

"Hi, Gloria, lovely to see you here. We seem to be struggling today," Richard said with his arms open in a welcoming gesture.

Drew and Archie echoed his welcome.

After she'd shucked off her outer layer and greeted everyone individually, Gloria's gaze alighted on Cam. Her heart beat a little faster, and she didn't bother keeping the smile off her face. Gloria was back, and her whole life lit up.

Gloria paused by Cam on her way to the hall to secure her bag in her locker. With Jamie out of eyesight, Cam's gaze connected with Gloria.

"Is everything okay?" Cam whispered.

"Short answer, yes. Long answer, I'll tell you later. I must get on." Gloria departed. Cam really shouldn't be looking at Gloria as she walked away, so she stared at the message.

Gloria returned to the room holding up a letter. "What's this?"

She snuck a glance at Cam and raised her eyebrows, but Cam shook her head. She didn't go into anyone else's locker ever, and they were supposed to be locked anyway, but for some reason, Gloria always left hers unlocked.

Gloria blushed as she read the contents, but her mouth was a thin line. Jamie jumped up and down like a puppy dog, so Cam suspected it was from him.

"Thanks, Jamie. I'll think about it. Maybe we can talk about it later?"

Cam uncrumpled the coded message in front of her and had to smooth it out to read the letters. What was he plotting?

Jamie beamed at Gloria with his typical self-assured charm. "I know you're probably tired, but it would be so much fun to come to London with me on Sunday. The Savoy has a cocktail with your name on it. Do say you'll come."

"I've only just come back from leave."

"Yes, but it's officially our day off. They can't stop you from having that."

"I always practice my duet with Cam—"

He waved his hand in dismissal. "You can do that on one of the mornings before shift. You sound perfect as it is."

The look was even more smarmy. Couldn't Gloria see he was a conniving flatterer?

Gloria flashed an apologetic look at Cam. "Do you mind if I go on Sunday? Could we practice every other day?"

Yes. Yes, I mind very much. Why are you so taken with him? Cam sighed. Gloria clearly wanted to go, and how could Cam deny her that? "Starting tomorrow?"

"You're on. It's a date."

If only it were a date. It was nothing as fancy as a trip to London. They were just rehearsing. The excitement from when Gloria came in dissipated, and Cam turned back to her code, trying to ignore the sick feeling in her stomach.

Jamie leaned over from his desk, placed a hand on Gloria's wrist and whispered something in her ear. She laughed and tapped him on his forearm, flicking her hair back as if she was really enjoying his company. Richard coughed beside Cam and frowned at her; he had to know about her infatuation for Gloria. She must have been staring.

She couldn't understand how Gloria could enjoy Jamie's attention and touches. Cam would never understand Gloria and could never compete with Jamie and his trips to the Savoy. She had none of his charisma. Jamie could offer her stability, marriage, and a family if that's the way Gloria wanted to go. Cam could offer none of those things. They would always have to be hidden and secret, and Gloria might resent it all eventually. It could go nowhere. No. Instead of yearning and hoping, she should just keep calm and carry on decoding.

Chapter Twenty-Four

A FEW DAYS LATER, the only sounds in the hut were the puffing of pipes, chairs creaking, and the tapping of pencils on paper. Sunlight shafted in from above the blast wall, highlighting the smoke swirling around and making the dust motes glisten.

Gloria looked up at the pile of dud messages, which was growing exponentially. She was unsure if there were more messages as the war progressed or whether the listening stations were picking up more. Whatever it was, they were never quite on top of everything, and if she let go she felt she would drown. By the door, Cam looked up and smiled with a dark intensity to her eyes that seemed to invite her to share her secrets. She wore a full three-piece suit and looked particularly dapper. There was something about the way she wore her clothes that seemed so authentic. And Gloria found her bewitching. She crossed her legs to stave off an inappropriate reaction at work.

"Hey, Bradford. How are you getting on?" Jamie frowned.

Had he seen her smiling at Cam? "Just thinking. You know, doing that thing we get paid to do for two thirds of what you men get." She grinned, knowing that would rile him up.

"We've discussed that. Men have to provide for families."

"You don't have a family." She could almost feel the trap shut as she said it.

He leaned over her desk, and she could smell his strong cologne and stale cigarette breath.

"If you went out with me, we could remedy that." He grinned that cocky grin that he used to charm all girls.

"I've already told you, I don't have time to date," she whispered, conscious of Cam trying to listen in. "Only Drew has a family at home." She was saved by the door opening and Helen, one of the messenger girls, came in.

The others groaned. "Not more duds?" Jamie asked.

Helen pulled a telegram out of her sack and handed it to him. She bit her bottom lip as he split open the envelope. Telegrams were never good news. Jamie released a low moan and covered his mouth.

"No reply," he said to Helen, who scurried out.

Jamie tried to hide a sniff with a cough. He was obviously struggling with whatever he'd read. Was nobody going to say anything?

"Cup of tea?" Gloria asked, rising from her seat.

Jamie shook his head and after a second, when he looked as if he was controlling himself, he said in a hoarse voice, "Come for a walk around the lake with me."

That was unprecedented. While people strolled around the lake during their break, they never went during work hours. They were always too conscious that the messages they were working on might be critical, warning of an imminent strike. Jamie was the supervisor of their shift, so she assumed it was okay. "All right. I'll just put this message back onto the table and get my coat."

Jamie locked his desk drawer and avoided meeting the gaze of anyone as he almost staggered out of the door. Cam flashed her a puzzled look, but she shrugged. She knew no more than anyone else.

As she left the hut, Jamie was close to the lake, and she had to hurry to catch him up. He looked so bereft. It could only be his brother, Duncan, who had recently transferred to the Navy from the Foreign Office. The convoys were still being torpedoed by the submarine wolf packs, and there were very few survivors when they did.

Gloria tucked her hand within the crook of his elbow. "Want to talk about it?"

Jamie kicked at a tuft of grass. "I told him not to go. He was safe in England but was fed up with being accosted in the pubs, being called a coward and told to fight. He drowned when his ship was torpedoed. I should've intercepted a message. We could have got it through to the admiralty before it happened."

Gloria squeezed his arm tight. "You know it doesn't work like that. Even if we'd solved the cypher, you know they don't act on everything. They have to keep the secret that we've broken their Enigma machines. There's nowt you could have done. You didn't know. I'm really sorry."

"You're sorry? How would you know what it's like..."

In an instant, she was back to receiving the news of Ben and that life-gouging denial that there must be a mistake. Her nostrils flared as she tried to swallow the grief. "I do know. And you can't help but split life in two: before they died and afterwards. Everything gets twisted and distorted, and you find a way to continue life, but it's never quite as radiant or carefree as before."

They paused by the old stone bridge leading from the lawns to the house.

Jamie picked at some moss from the stonework and tossed it into the water. "I don't know how I'll continue without him. Duncan had been my idol ever since we were little. He taught me to play cricket and football and set me maths puzzles. He was always brainier than me. What a waste. And all because he hated being called a coward."

He turned to face her and in full view of anyone who might be looking out of the windows of the house, he sank into her arms, having to duck his head quite low to reach her shoulder. She held him as he sobbed.

Eventually, the sobs slowed to a hiccupping gasp. "Sorry," he said.

"Don't be." Before she could pull away, he drew her close and pressed his lips against hers. But she didn't want to be kissed by him and jerked away. "No, Jamie. Now is not the time, and this is not the place." *I never want to kiss you, because you're not Cam.* But she couldn't say that. "Please don't. I'm not interested in dating or kissing. You're just upset and seeking comfort. I can give you that but no more. I'm sorry."

He gave her a watery smile, and she didn't want to disabuse him when he was clearly so distraught.

His smile widened into a grin as his confidence seemed to return. "Maybe not now, Bradford, but maybe after the concert, you'll have more time."

They continued walking again, doing another circuit of the lake, and he seemed to marshal his emotions.

"Are you ready to go back to work now?"

He sighed. "Yes, boss. But promise me you'll think about it?"

They turned towards their hut, and Gloria inhaled the fresh smell of spring and absorbed the yellow of the daffodils and primroses, their last view before returning to the haze of the smoky atmosphere. "I'll think about it, but I can't promise anything."

There was no way she wanted to be with him. She ought to like him, and he would make a great husband. He was funny, and clever, and charming, and she was sure her da would eventually accept him. But he wasn't Cam. Not that Jamie would ever understand that.

There was something about Cam, the way her confident, impressive exterior hid a vulnerability that made Gloria want to protect her, to get to know her better...to *love* her. What was she thinking? She couldn't love Cam. They hadn't known each other long enough, but there was something between them she couldn't explain, an understanding so strong, they vibrated at the same wavelength, humming in synchrony. She checked her watch again. Less than half an hour before the end of their shift.

The time passed quickly, and Gloria shifted in her seat as she couldn't concentrate on the message. Cam had solved the one she had been working on previously. Of course she had. She and

Cam were going to rehearse their piece together after work, and she was anxious that Jamie's affections wouldn't come between them. She hoped they hadn't lost that sense of togetherness because a lot had happened since the last time they sang.

As they strode across to the hall, Cam was fidgety. They disturbed a duck, and it flew off the lake with a flurry of wing beats. Cam cleared her throat and stared straight ahead. This awkwardness was killing Gloria and she had to tell her. "Jamie tried to kiss me when we walked around the lake."

Cam's face tightened and closed off. Gloria could almost see her withdrawing. She picked up her pace, and Gloria had to hurry to keep up.

"I didn't want him to and told him so. I like you, Cam, but I'm confused because I've never felt anything for a woman before, and it isn't what society or the Bible accepts as normal. And I'm conflicted because I like Jamie but only because he reminds me of Ben. And he's just lost his brother, and I feel for him because it's a horrible place to be. But I don't yearn for him like I do for you. I don't wonder what he's up to. My heart doesn't pick up pace when he's close, like it does with you. I've tried to brush it away, this attraction I have for you, because it's so...so inconvenient."

That didn't sound like her. Normally she was sure, determined, and would go for something she had set her heart on, but her common sense held her back. "I'm not sure we can do anything or go anywhere with what we have."

Cam stopped not far from the stone bridge where she'd been with Jamie and swung around to face Gloria. The hurt in her eyes made Gloria want to draw her in her arms and hug her. "Sorry, this is coming out all wrong. I'm just in a muddle. I feel sorry for him, that's all, and he's pressuring me to go out with him, and it would be so much easier. But it's not what I want. Surely you can see that?"

Cam shook her head and stiffened. Her eyes glittered, revealing what? Pain, anger, or resignation? Perhaps a mixture of all three.

"I don't know what to believe, except you say it's 'inconvenient' for you."

Gloria tugged at Cam's arms, but she pulled away. "I'm sorry I've hurt you. Can we just pretend we haven't had this conversation? I know you're vexed and we're both overwrought. Maybe we should just get on to rehearsal and sleep on it. Trust me, the last thing I want to do is hurt you. I'm drawn to you. You intoxicate me, and I want to get to know you better. Cam, please don't close up on me. We need to sing together now."

Cam said nothing as she marched to the rehearsal hall. Gloria raced after her. She'd blown it and hurt Cam in the process. Cam busied herself with her score and didn't look at her as Archie and Reggie came in to sort out their music.

"Let's get started," Reggie said and raised his baton.

Archie stretched his fingers before placing them on the keys.

"Sorry," Gloria whispered as they stood by the music stands, waiting for Archie to play the introduction.

Cam shrugged and stared at her music as if she was studying a new piece, even though she knew it off by heart.

When they sang, both of them seemed flat, not musically but emotionally. Torn apart, boiling with rage and regret on one side and completely closed off on the other. The six minutes seemed endless. It didn't help that Bea and Jamie entered the hall halfway through.

Reggie stared at them. "What's up with you two? You've never sung with so little feeling. It's as if you've had a lovers' tiff!" He laughed. "No point rehashing it now. Sort it between you, and we'll go on to the quartet."

He was much closer than he realised, and Gloria wasn't sure what she could do. Instead of singing about being awoken from a dream, it felt like she was waking from a nightmare.

Chapter Twenty-Five

GLORIA HURRIED OFF AT the end of rehearsal with hardly a goodbye, and all Cam could do was to stare at her retreating back. Jamie and Archie disappeared too, whether to catch her or not, Cam didn't know and didn't want to know. That left Bea, Cam, and Reggie to clear up.

Reggie gathered his music. "I don't know what's going on between you and Gloria, but you need to sort it out. You've lost your joy at singing together, and it shows."

Cam couldn't deny it. A brutal truth cuts deeper when it's justified; she'd lost her joy in her life too. And she had known it was coming. It hadn't been the same since Gloria had gone home, and now she seemed to have reconsidered everything about them and withdrawn. Cam was being hypocritical, as she'd decided they should wait, and hated herself for being weak. Despite logic and reason, a little part of her had held out a candle of hope they could be together. The tiny crack of possibility had snapped shut, and she wasn't sure Gloria would even be there for her even if they did wait. Doubtless she would be swept off her feet by Jamie. She tried to form a smile, but it felt false. "I'll work on it."

Bea clasped her music to her chest and caught Cam's eye. "Shall we go for a cuppa at the dining hall? I'm on the midnight shift, so I planned to write letters and read before my shift started."

Cam didn't want to have to examine her emotions and behaviour, to confess her jealousy and uncertainty, as she didn't like what they meant. Nor did she want to vocalise to anyone that she had feelings she couldn't tame, however much she tried.

"I need to get back to shut up the chickens and see to Aunty Florrie."

Bea raised one eyebrow. "I thought you'd said you'd rigged up a door catch so Aunty Florrie could lock up at night or release them in the morning?"

"I have, but—"

"And Aunty Florrie knows you're at rehearsal tonight, so she'll be settling down for her programme. Oh, good night, Reggie."

Reggie hovered, obviously keen to return home. "I've closed all the windows. Can you lock up, Bea? Goodnight, ladies."

The door clicked shut behind him, and Cam stacked her chair with the others to give herself a distraction and time to think.

"Stop. Cam. Look at me. What's going on?"

Cam leaned heavily against the chairs. "I hate it. I'm wracked with jealousy, and I have no right, and I hate myself for it. Gloria's father wants her to marry one of his factory managers, and Jamie is pushing for her to go out with him, and why shouldn't she? She's beautiful, and smart, and funny, and she would be a wonderful catch for anyone, and I can't stand it. She said she's confused and conflicted, and that what we have is inconvenient. I feel so ashamed. I hate who I'm becoming. It's not logical. I've always hidden my crushes in the past, kept them sealed up so even the object of my desire doesn't know I feel anything for them." Cam smoothed a crease on the leather of the chair, not daring to look at Bea. "She kissed me, and it was wonderful. I can't stop thinking about it, wanting to do it again and again, and to do more. I feel so exposed and jealous of anyone else's attention, and that's not fair on her. She's so friendly with everyone, and I'm not sure if this is just a trifle to her. It feels like I can't let go around her anymore. I can't let her see how much she means to me, in case she doesn't feel the same. So I've been holding back, even in the singing, and then she responds to my passionless singing. The quartet is fine, but the duet..."

"Okay, there's a lot in there. If I can summarise, you're saying you like her a lot, and she likes you. She must do, or she wouldn't have kissed you."

Cam nodded. "True."

"Hold onto that. Unfortunately, society doesn't welcome people like us, so we have to grasp what happiness we can, when we can."

"You always seem so sanguine about it all. I can't imagine you being jealous."

Bea laughed. "I quote a lot of Shakespeare to calm me down. Come on. Let's lock up here, and I'll buy you a cuppa and tell you all about it. Then we can work out what we can do for you."

Cam was grateful for Bea's support and relieved to be able to talk to a friend about it all. They closed the door and locked it in the darkness.

"We need to drop off the key at the admin offices," Bea said, and they walked side by side towards the main house. Although the sun had gone down, it wasn't too chilly. The moon reflected off the lake and the trees became hulking shapes. Cam was so honed to the war that instead of thinking it as being romantic, she immediately thought it was a bomber's moon. Though there hadn't been many air raids over Britain for a long time now.

She glanced across at Bea, who always seemed so happy and serene, extracting joy from every moment. Yet Cam hardly knew anything about her other than she'd had an affair with a woman in Cambridge all those years ago. "Are you saying you've been jealous? I didn't know you were seeing anyone; you never said."

Bea skipped a little. "I'm in love with a woman called Maud. She's been in the Land Army since the beginning of the war. When her family found out about us, she had to agree to marry a man. She intended to have a very long engagement until we could be together. It took a long time before she called that off."

"Weren't you jealous?"

"Yes. I was angry and upset at first. But I love Maud, and she was in a bind, and we had to put up with the short-term difficulty so that we can be together in the long term. She couldn't afford to support herself so we agreed to the farce until she becomes financially independent, and after the war, we'll finally be together. I can't wait, but I must; we all have to do our duty."

"How do you cope?"

"Like everybody else who's been separated by the war; we write letters every day and hope that we'll be together soon. But I couldn't be jealous all the time. She needed my support and reassurance that I would wait. I did get cross when she delayed longer than I thought was necessary, but she had to do it in her own way and at her own speed. Love is not forcing our will onto another. It's about letting them come to their own conclusions, even when it's hard."

Cam didn't say she loved Gloria; she wasn't sure what it was. If she wasn't there yet, she felt very close. When did admiration and infatuation become love? Did it stealthily grow when she wasn't paying attention? What was the difference between that and close friendship? She looked across at Bea, whom she was very fond of but had none of the heart-skipping, toe-curling delight she felt around Gloria. "Do you manage to see each other?"

"It's hard. Even if our leave days coincide, Maud is expected to go back to her family, which I find galling as they don't accept who she is." Bea sighed, and a sadness washed over her normally smiling expression. "I write lots of letters and treasure those I receive, and I keep very busy with singing, and the Shakespeare theatre group, and working longer hours than I'm contracted for."

Cam hesitated but then took Bea's hand. "I'm sorry, I didn't know."

Bea's smile returned. "I don't talk about it, so you wouldn't, but it's such a relief to be open about Maud, and I can do that now." She jangled the keys. "Let's deal with this, and then we can talk about what you can do."

After Bea had dropped off the keys, they turned towards the dining hall, still open for the evening shift workers.

"Do you think I should accept that Gloria may have to go out with Jamie?"

"I think you need to have a conversation with her. How does she feel about you? She seems interested in more than just a bit of fun with you. If that's the case, what do you need to do to be together in the long term?"

Cam kicked a stone and watched it disappear into the shadows. "I'm guessing I need to find out what she wants, even though it's scary."

"I think so."

"That might be easier said than done." Cam felt more comfortable than she had for days. It would be worth it to be with Gloria, to wait for her, and she was luckier than most because she saw her love every workday. Love? With nothing to compare it to and no evidence to collect, it was difficult to assert. She thought she'd loved Mary, but Mary had just wanted adoration. She could see that now, and Cam had been happy to think it was mutual, but it had been no more than craving that wouldn't be returned. Infatuation with an unobtainable woman was very different from the joy of being around someone who understood her, someone she was getting to know as a friend. No, Gloria meant more than that. Cam's world was brighter and sped faster. When Gloria entered a room, Cam wanted to dance and sing opera, to laugh at nothing and everything, and soak up her presence. It had to be love. She just had to tell Gloria and find out how she felt.

Just as her eyes became accustomed to the darkness in the blackout, so she thought she had a way through. Now she just needed to find the opportunity to talk to Gloria alone.

Bea held open the door to the dining hall so Cam could pass through. "Talk to her. What's the worst that can happen? Clarity has to be good, doesn't it?"

Cam gave her a wry smile. "As long as I hear what I want to hear."

Chapter Twenty-Six

ABOUT TEN DAYS LATER, Gloria cycled home just after midnight. This was when the night seemed blackest, when the hooded light barely showed the road ahead, and she had to judge her distance to the left turn by time alone. A cough came from behind a hedge, and she jumped, then laughed. It was only a cow, even though it sounded like an old man. An owl hooted, and its mate replied. She hadn't known the refrain was two separate birds until Cam spouted one of her quirky facts.

She smiled at the thought. It had been easier at work the last couple of days, although they hadn't managed to speak alone and work had been particularly busy. There was none of the usual banter, and they'd all taken their meals at their desks. The tension had been building as it seemed that maybe, just maybe, the war was finally turning in their favour. If they could just break a few more codes. She didn't dare hope.

A noise behind her made her jump.

"Gloria."

She jerked up and must have twisted her handlebars as she careered into a ditch.

"Oh, God. Gloria, are you all right?"

Jamie. She had been trying to avoid a private conversation with him and had succeeded until now. Her knee stung, and she trailed her hand down and caught the snagged silk. "Damn. My stockings."

"Sorry, I didn't mean to scare you. I thought you knew I was there."

"Why would I know you were there?" Warm blood trickled

from her scrape, and she swung around. "What the hell are you doing following me around in the middle of the night?"

In their dimmed headlights, she could now see his face.

"I've been trying to get hold of you on your own, but you always have your creepy shadow around."

She poked a finger at his chest. "You're a fine one to talk about creepy shadows, and don't speak about Cam like that. We're very close friends. What do you want to say to me? You've ruined my stockings and insulted my friend, and now my chain's come off."

"Let me help you—"

"No. I don't need your help. Stop trying to take over. It's so annoying." She dabbed her knee with a handkerchief. The graze stung but at least it had stopped bleeding.

"Sorry, I was only trying to help."

She ignored him as she stooped by the bike to set it right. The chain wasn't broken, so she carefully fed it over the smaller cog and got it to run smoothly. Jamie held out a fresh handkerchief.

"That's impressive. I'll get you some new stockings. It's the least I can do."

She could see he looked contrite as she wiped her oily hands on the hanky. "What did you want that had you chasing me home?"

"I'm sorry, Bradford. This is all going wrong. I just wanted to speak to you alone."

"Why didn't you talk to me at work?"

Jamie looked down. "Like I said, I can't get hold of you on your own."

"Fine. You can ride with me and make sure the chain doesn't come off again." She swooped to pick up her bag and tuck the hankies inside. Not waiting to see if he followed, she pushed off. Her knee stung as she pedalled, but she wasn't going to let him see that. She let her anger power her through.

She supposed she should be nice to him. He'd just lost his brother, and that was probably what he wanted to talk about.

Shame had a bitter taste, but like a medicine, it had to be ingested if it was to effect change.

Gloria glanced over as he rode beside her. "What did you want to talk about? Is it about Duncan?"

In the reflected light, his smile dropped and his cycling slowed. "No, I...I wanted to talk to you about going out with me. I know you said before about it not being right, but I'm serious, Bradford. I have never seen such a beautiful, bright, feisty woman like you before. I think about you when you're not here. When I say I'm serious, I mean it. I'm not talking about just a fling. I know your father wants you to marry a local man, but I'm happy to step in. I'd *like* to step in as I think I'm a pretty good catch."

Gloria screeched to a halt and almost fell off again. She slipped off the saddle and straddled the frame. "You're like my brother, and I couldn't."

"What do you mean? I wanted to ask you nicely and get an expensive ring from London, and I'd still like to do that—"

"No, Jamie. I really like you, and I'm sorry about your brother, but I can never feel for you that way."

"Why? Is it about the man in Bradford?"

"God, no! I've already told my family I'll never marry him, which probably means my da will never speak to me again. I can't, and I won't, marry for anything but love. It's not fair on you to lead you on. And I don't want to be your chattel. For the first time in my life, I have real freedom." She pushed off again with a little wobble, and he hurried to catch up.

"I wouldn't stop you from doing what you want. I love that you use your brain and challenge me. I'd like to date you and get to know you better outside work."

"I can't. I don't think of you that way. I've already told you, you're like my brother."

"What do you mean? Please, just stop."

Gloria applied her brakes and freewheeled to a stop so he could close the gap.

"Is there someone else? Someone here? Archie? No. Drew or Reggie? No, they're both married. And we all know Richard's queer."

She turned her head away but felt the heat rising up her cheeks. She hoped he didn't notice. There was an awkward pause, and she glanced back up at him.

Jamie stared at her, then as if realisation washed over his features, his face contorted into a sneer. "Is it because of Cam? That's disgusting. No, no, no. It's not true."

She pushed her bike forward. She couldn't deny it. To deny it was to reject Cam, and she wasn't going to do that to her love. There was no avoiding the truth. She loved Cam. "I'm not having this conversation with you."

"You damn well will. I'm not having my position usurped by some perverted invert—"

"Don't talk about Cam like that. And it's not your position, and you haven't earned that right. Go away." She realised she had been trapped into confirming what he had guessed. How stupid. She would have to warn Cam and hope he didn't exact retribution on her.

"It's true."

"Leave me alone, Jamie." She pushed hard on her pedals and cycled away.

"But I love you."

As if that would make any difference. How could he love her when he didn't even know her? And she loved Cam. "I don't love you in that way." Perhaps it wasn't a sensible parting shot. It was bound to hurt him, especially as he was still reeling from his brother's death. But she couldn't tell a lie or pretend. She was done with pretending. She just hoped the truth wouldn't come back to haunt her.

Chapter Twenty-Seven

THE DAY OF THE concert was going from bad to worse. At three that morning, Cam had shot out of bed after being woken by the noise of her aunt falling off the last step.

"Will you help me up, dear?"

"Aunty, I've told you before, if you want to go downstairs in the night, give me a shout."

"I'm okay. Just winded. I couldn't sleep with my arthritis, and I just fancied a cup of tea. But you've got a big day tomorrow. Just help me to get into my chair, and I'll be comfortable, then you can go back to bed."

Trying to get her stiff bones to move was obviously a struggle, and Cam wished she wasn't so proud and would use a wheelchair, or at least a walking stick, when she was like this. Finally, her aunt flopped into her wingback chair. Cam rearranged the cushion behind her back. "I'll go and get you a duvet and a glass of water. Would you like me to stay up with you?"

"No, dear, I'll be fine. And I'll sort the hens out today so you don't have to worry about them when you get back from your concert. Go back to bed now. Goodnight, and thank you."

Cam kissed her aunt on the forehead. "If you need anything, just shout." She hurried off to bed, but sleep was neither swift nor easy, and when her alarm clock rang, it was like she hadn't slept at all. Her throat felt rough, and her eyes were gritty. She gargled with salt water, but it didn't help much. *Great.* Just what she needed for the concert. And she still hadn't resolved her quandary with Gloria. She had to let it go. The longer they didn't speak, the clearer her answer was. Cam had to forget it all and just tap into her joy of singing. As she cycled to work, she practiced her scales. If anyone heard her, they'd think she was mad, but she didn't care.

She put her spare clothes and lunch in her locker and reset the combination, then entered the main office of their hut. Carter from MI5 stood over her desk.

He leered at her. "Right, now you're all here, you can all go and wait outside. Don't take anything—not even your coats—and we'll call you back in when it's clear."

They trooped out like naughty children and congregated outside.

"We don't have time for this now. We're so busy," Drew said to no one in particular. He pulled a cigarette case from his pocket then leaned against the wall of the hut.

Jamie stood close to Gloria and Archie, so Cam sidled up to Richard, who stood apart overlooking the lake.

A military policeman watched them all. "Stay where you are."

"What's going on?" Cam asked.

"They say there's a spy in our hut, and they believe they're in our shift."

"Really? I can't see it myself."

"Isn't that the point?"

Cam rubbed her hand down her arms trying to keep warm in the cool air and thought about her shift colleagues. There were no obvious reds, and she couldn't imagine anyone else. "Are you sure they're not trying to pin it on to you or me?"

"I wouldn't put it past them. But they scared the living daylights out of me last time, so there's no way I'd risk crossing them again. And it's wrong to target us."

"You there. Be quiet."

The MP pointed a pistol at Richard, and he shrank back. It was one thing to know they carried arms, it was quite another to have a gun waved around in their direction.

Cam swallowed hard, causing her throat to scrape. The

group was eerily silent. Not even Jamie cracked a joke as he sucked hard on a cigarette. After twenty-three minutes, Carter approached them and poked at Richard's chest. "I'll get you next time." He turned to Cam. "And you need to open your locker unless you want us to break in."

Glad for an opportunity to get out of the cold, Cam followed him in. Her fingers were partially numb, and she fumbled with the combination.

"Hurry up. We don't have all day."

"You shouldn't have kept us out in the cold then." She slid the catch open.

He glowered at her. "Stand back."

"Please be careful with my shirt. I need it for tonight's performance."

His sneer warned her she should have kept her mouth shut. He ruckled through the contents, not bothering to keep the shirt flat. He patted it and shook it to see if it had anything within its folds. Cam gritted her teeth to stop herself making some sarcastic remark. She wouldn't put it past him to ruin it out of spite.

Not finding anything, he tossed it back inside. "I've got my eye on you. If I can prove you're queer, you'll lose your security clearance so fast you won't know what hit you." Then he smiled, all teeth and falsehood.

Cam shifted and tugged at the collar of her shirt that seemed tight all of a sudden. "Are you finished? Can we get on with our important war work?"

"For now." He marched out.

Her hands trembled as she smoothed out the creases as best as she could and reset the numbers. She didn't trust him to come back and put something in there, so she changed the combination again.

When she finally got to her desk, the paper under the desk leg had been removed. What did they think she was going to do, leave decoded messages in plain sight? They must think she was stupid, or they were deliberately trying to rile her. She snatched up another scrap of paper and folded it precisely before wedging it underneath. It wasn't quite as snug as previously, but it would have to do.

The pile of dud messages on the centre table seemed higher than ever, which caused her heart to race a little. The pressure was beginning to tell. Although the messages were prioritised, the urgent pile seemed to increase, and she worried that the one she hadn't got to yet might be a crucial and time-critical message. She huffed out a breath. They were *all* critical. She smoothed down the crease in her trousers and flexed her fingers before picking up her pencil.

None of the usual shortcuts worked, nor checking for the word eins, German for one, which seemed to appear on every message. Nothing. Maybe because she was upset about the change in routine, or because she'd had insufficient sleep, but she couldn't drop into the part of her mind that could tell if something was off. Gloria called it intuition, but Cam always thought it was being able to see and assess patterns, like music. It wasn't coincidental that there was a high proportion of codebreakers who were great musicians, even if they weren't professionals.

Gloria. She looked across at her. She'd been trying to speak to Gloria alone now, for a few days but Jamie was always there. He'd even implemented a system where people couldn't go on a bathroom break at the same time, and Cam suspected it was to keep them apart. And every time she looked up, Jamie was watching or hanging about as if he had nothing better to do. He'd even taken to cycling home with Gloria, as if he didn't trust her.

Dread settled over her. Did he suspect that she had feelings for Gloria? They had always been so careful, not sharing long glances or secret smiles. The hairs on the back of her neck rose. If he knew, then she would be exposed—they both would—but Gloria could laugh it off, claiming a fiancé back home. Cam was clearly queer: the way she dressed, behaved, and refused to pretend to be what she was not.

Carter's threat filled her memory. Losing her security clearance would be the end of everything. She doubted she could go back to Cambridge, and she couldn't stay here or see Gloria every day. She might even have to move, which meant she wouldn't be able to look after her aunt or the chickens. She closed her eyes and made a conscious effort to slow her breaths. No point worrying about what ifs. She needed to concentrate. Even during lunch, Jamie brought sandwiches so he could join Gloria. And they no longer had time to play chess. Dust was settling on their half-finished game still laid out on the top of the filing cabinet.

Jamie rose and collected another message to be decoded. "Another one. I'm in front today."

Cam wasn't going to respond to his baiting. Gloria flashed her an apologetic look behind his back. Of course his tally was higher than Cam's today. Normally she was streets ahead of him, and the rest, but today, she just couldn't focus or settle. She hazarded a glance at Gloria when Jamie turned away from her.

Even from this distance, she could see Gloria's eyes were ringed with shadows as though she hadn't slept for days. She looked shaken when she came in this morning. Cam couldn't wait to speak to her. The only place the men couldn't go was the ladies' cloakroom, so she decided she'd wait and go at the same time as Gloria, whatever Jamie said with his glaring eyes and his stupid rules.

About half an hour later, Gloria excused herself. Before Jamie could call Cam back, she sped out, and they entered the ladies' cloakroom. She did a quick check in the cubicles to ensure no one else was in there. Gloria burst into tears, and Cam opened her arms.

"Jamie knows about us; he guessed. He offered to marry me to save me from marrying Stanley, and I refused him. He knows. I don't know what he'll do. But he's right angry. I'm so sorry, Cam. I didn't want this to happen. And I heard what that ape Carter said to you this morning. It's all such a mess."

Cam didn't have any answers, so she held on to Gloria and let her weep on her shoulder. She kissed the top of Gloria's head.

Now she understood why Gloria hadn't slept, why she looked sad and washed out. Cam's already sore throat seemed to tighten even more. "Do you want to stop seeing me and deny anything is going on? You can still do that. It's not as if we've done much more than kiss, even if it was wonderful." Cam couldn't help a rueful smile at the memory.

"I don't know what to do." Gloria pulled away and took the handkerchief Cam offered. "I know you don't want to be exposed and that you can't afford to lose your security clearance. I can't either, but it's not such a life changer for me. I could always go home and marry Stanley even if I hate the thought of it."

Gloria's trembling reverberated through her own body. She couldn't bear to lose Gloria. "Maybe he won't do anything. It's just for the first time ever, I..." She held Gloria's shoulders. No, she couldn't say it even if she felt it. Not now. This would just add to the mess, and she hated messes. She looked Gloria in the eyes. "I really like you. I think about you all the time."

And as if their bodies took over, their lips met in the warmth of wonder and connection. They could have floated further and deeper when their precariousness pierced Cam's brain. "Stop. Stop. We can't do this here. We have enough willpower not to act on it."

Gloria cupped Cam's jaw, and she seemed to cradle her whole life, her whole soul in her hands.

"Or maybe not." Gloria gave a warm chuckle and swiped a smear of lipstick off Cam's face. "Sorry, I left a mark."

Gloria had left more than just a lipstick mark on Cam's life: she'd turned it upside down. She stared at Gloria's face intently and tried to capture it so she could remember it later. The green flecks in her brown eyes only noticeable this close, the warmth of her breath, the scent of Pears soap, and the surprising comfort of their embrace—she wanted to memorise it all. The words were on the tip of her tongue, and she cleared her throat.

Banging at the ladies' room door caused the whole hut to shake.

"What are you doing in there?" Jamie yelled.

Gloria's eyes went wide, and she trembled.

Cam whispered, "I'll deal with this. See you later." She dropped a kiss on Gloria's nose, then glanced at herself in the mirror to check she had no telltale lipstick on her cheeks and flattened down her hair.

"I'm coming in," Jamie said.

Gloria rushed into a cubicle and slid the lock.

"You can't come in here, Jamie. It's private."

"What are you up to, pervert?"

Cam centred herself despite being tempted to wipe the smugness off his face with a swift uppercut. She focused her rage into a hard glare that cause Jamie to step back. "Women's problems. Things you wouldn't know about. Probably why we have a minimum of two women on a shift, particularly overnight. I'm going back to work, and Gloria will come when she's ready. You should be grateful she's at work at all today."

Cam was unsure where she got her brazenness from. That was probably the most she'd ever said to Jamie in one conversation. He paused and looked at her for a second then whirled around and marched back to his desk. They had too much work to do for all these dramatics.

He glowered at her for the rest of the shift, but she merely smiled, especially when she solved four messages in a row really quickly. When the shift finished, there were three hours to fill before the start of the concert, and Cam planned how she was going to spend that time.

Of course, Jamie had collared Gloria just as they were finishing up in work. "Gloria, I need to speak to you now."

Gloria flashed Cam an apology, and Cam indicated she was going outside. She couldn't stand being in the same room as Jamie any longer.

She unwrapped her sandwiches but, too anxious to eat, she fed them to the ducks on the lake before it got too dark, grateful she had packed extra food. Still no sign of Gloria. When she couldn't leave it any longer, she returned to the hut to change into the white wingtip collar shirt and bow tie and ignored the tingling in her stomach. Singing before a hundred strangers was something she'd never thought she could do. And her throat hadn't eased, despite sipping honey and lemon.

She smiled at the memory of kissing Gloria earlier as she checked herself in the mirror. Gloria, wonderful Gloria, had kissed her and lit up her whole body. Then she thought of Jamie and her shoulders drooped. No, damn him. He couldn't afford to lose his best codebreakers. He would be scuppered without them and surely he wouldn't act out of self-interest. Their shift had the best codebreaking averages, which he was proud to boast about. But that wouldn't stop him making life unpleasant for Cam. She didn't trust him, but she trusted his ego and could envisage his glee at being able to hold the threat over their heads.

The door burst open, and she smiled when she saw Bea, though she looked flustered. Bea was never flustered.

"Cam, I'm so glad I've caught you. The whole concert has been brought forward by fifteen minutes. We're having to change the running order because some of the orchestra have to go to their midnight shift early."

Cam gripped the sink in front of her. "We can't. I've got my schedule calculated to the minute so I'm ready in time."

Bea paused. "Cam, I'm sorry. I know it's very last minute. Can I help in any way? The orchestra pieces are all being played first, including our quartet from *Rigoletto*, and then the Gilbert and Sullivan arias, the piano pieces, Jamie's solo, then you and Gloria will close out the show."

Cam began to shake. "I can't do that."

"Yes, you can. You sing beautifully."

Cam centred herself with difficulty and closed her eyes. *Let whatever happens be okay.* Her breathing steadied.

"Have you seen Gloria?" Bea asked.

Her breathing and heart rate pulsed again. "Jamie took her away for something after the shift ended."

Bea frowned. "Is everything all right?"

Cam caught the flicker of fear in her eyes in the mirror. "No," she whispered. "Jamie knows about us. I don't know what he'll do. At the moment, he's trying to keep us apart, but I'm petrified he's going to shop us to Carter and his mob, and they'll take away our security clearances. Carter threatened as much this morning. I'm tearing myself up here."

"I'm sorry, Cam. I don't know what to say. Jamie is a law unto himself. But we can't afford to lose your skills, especially not with the war in such a critical phase."

Bea opened her arms, and Cam surprised herself by stepping in and accepting the hug. Cam could only cope with a quick hug before she had to pull back. It was all too sharp a reminder of embracing Gloria earlier, and the intense pang of longing threatened to overwhelm her.

"I guess I'd better come along to the hall now then to get myself limbered up and ready."

"That's sensible. In the meantime, I'll try to find Jamie and Gloria."

Cam couldn't help but wince at the coupling. Was he trying to woo her again? She wouldn't blame Gloria for falling for him as he had so much more to offer. Yes, she would. She loved Gloria, and she was sure she had feelings for her too, even if they hadn't managed to express them yet.

Bea squeezed her arm. "I'm sure it'll work itself out. Now let's focus on this evening. You look absolutely stunning, by the way."

"Thank you." Belatedly, Cam noticed what Bea was wearing

a plum-coloured evening gown and high heels, which were probably not sensible for running around trying to find people. "So do you. Would you like me to help you find them?"

Bea's face creased into its usual smile. "Thank you, that would be lovely. Maybe if you could check the dining room and the hall. See you shortly."

Cam locked up her spare clothes and changed the combination again on her locker. It was probably paranoia but better that than the alternative.

Half an hour later, and only ten minutes before the revised start time, Jamie, Archie, and Gloria came in. Gloria looked decidedly annoyed. Cam was frantic by then. She'd even spoken to strangers to ask if they'd seen them on her way back from the hut.

They stood while the orchestra tuned up, and Cam pulled at her too-tight collar. She glanced across at Gloria, who flashed her a puzzled look. Cam then peeped out into the audience. The hall was packed, and the lights were hot. She tried to swallow past the coarse sandpaper in her throat.

Cam coughed, trying to pay no heed to the excited anticipation of the audience. She took out a handkerchief and dabbed at her brow. At some point, she'd been subjected to the torture of having stage make-up applied and didn't want to smudge it, but it felt greasy, as though it was clogging her pores and melting under the heat of the lights.

The orchestra played the opening bars of the quartet at a tempo slightly slower than Archie had been playing on the piano, and it made Cam wince, as it was yet another change demonstrating that this was not just a rehearsal.

Cam would never know if she actually had a sore throat or if it was from the worry about Jamie and the changed concert timing, but her first note was sharp, more squeak than musical. She heard Reggie take a deep intake of breath. She continued, closing her eyes in the hope of not being seen, trying to find a way into the aria but aware that her face burned. Every time before, her rendition had been perfect. Now, when it mattered, when a few hundred eyes and ears were on her, she faltered. She'd let down Bea, Gloria, Reggie, and all of the others who had given their time and effort, and now she was melting in a puddle of sweat and humiliation.

Cam made the mistake of looking across as they came to the closing bars to see Jamie looking smug at the final harmonies. She gave a perfunctory bow, wondering how many of the audience would know she'd failed. Some of the audience had been professional singers before the war for heaven's sake, and she'd shamed herself in front of them. She couldn't go on again. Even though there was over an hour for all the orchestral pieces and the piano solos to perform she needed time not to just to compose herself but also to escape.

She pushed past the Gilbert and Sullivan singers waiting to come on and spilled out of the emergency exit doors at the back. It was still light but heading towards sunset. Maybe a quick pace around the lake would calm her nerves. She strode around in double-quick time, but her throat was still tight and her legs trembled. The wingtip shirt was probably not helping, and if she had any chance of going on again, she needed to be more comfortable. Without a conscious thought, she headed over to their hut. The light coming from the main room and the shuffling and chairs squeaking indicated the next shift were busy working. They were all men she didn't know. It was a relief when she unscrambled the lock on her cupboard to find her other shirt in the same place neatly folded as she had left it. She picked it up and entered the ladies' bathroom. Fortunately, there were no other women in the building, so she removed the tie and constricting collared shirt and splashed her face.

The water was refreshing against her warm skin, and she washed off all traces of the make-up. If she went on again, she refused to look like a clown. She leaned her face against the cool tiles, hoping to chill the burn of humiliation from her cheeks as well as from her memory. The door burst open again, and she snatched at the shirt to cover her modesty then sighed with relief.

"I've been looking for you everywhere," Gloria said. "I came back here first, but you weren't here."

"I walked around the lake."

"It's getting dark. Should we return?"

Cam shrugged. "I can't. I can't go back on."

"Of course you can. We've been practising for weeks, and harmonising beautifully together, everyone says so."

"You sing beautifully. I sounded like a frog."

Gloria laughed. "You absolutely did not."

Cam's shoulders lowered an inch. She croaked like a frog and smiled, despite everything. "I hate to think what everybody is thinking. Reggie sighed heavily."

"Come here. You just need to relax." Gloria took a step towards her.

"I'm not going on again."

"Cam, you've already done the professional thing and continued with the aria. Put it behind you. You're not going to be put off by one wrong note, are you?"

"It was the first note."

"And the rest was spot on. You don't have to be perfect. No one is. You're human." Gloria opened her arms, and Cam walked into them.

The rush of warmth felt so right, so perfect in its imperfection. Cam was just half an inch taller than Gloria in her heels. The taut band around her head released when she could breathe deeply again.

"That's better. God, you look so sexy tonight. I couldn't keep my eyes off you." Gloria stroked Cam's cheek.

Her hand was warm against the cold where Cam had splashed it, and she leaned into Gloria's touch, wishing she could just snuggle against her for the rest of the evening. But she had to go on again and face the humiliation.

"You didn't make a wrong note though. You were perfect."

Gloria curled her fingers around the nape of Cam's neck, brushing her shaved hair at the back and causing all her nerves to tingle.

"What are you doing to me?" Cam smoothed her fingers through Gloria's hair, gently so as not to ruin the style. They inched towards each other, before Cam pulled away and put a finger to Gloria's lips. "My sore throat. I don't want to give you that."

"It won't matter after the concert, and we've been so close, if I was going to pick it up by now, I would have."

She sucked in Cam's finger turning Cam to liquid want. "If you're sure?"

"Yes, I'm sure."

Cam needed no more permission. The weeks of yearning and passion met desire in a flurry of kisses on her nose, her jaw, the column of her throat.

"May I kiss you?"

"With pleasure." Cam met Gloria's lips in a soft explosion of worlds. Gloria's lips parted, inviting her in. The kiss was no longer tentative as their tongues explored in a desperate need to have more, give more, be more, and it melted down all of Cam's doubts and anxiety. With each second, Cam sank into the spell that was Gloria. The hours she'd spent imagining another kiss was nothing compared to the reality. They were devouring each other.

Cam pulled back. Gloria's eyes were wild, her pupils black with desire, her full lips wet and swollen, and her breath came in short gasps, matching Cam's. She gently pushed Gloria against the door of the cleaning cupboard and kissed the long stretch of her neck, inhaling the sweet smell of sweat and soap.

"Oh, I wonder," Gloria said, twisting the doorknob. She grinned as it opened and pulled Cam in. "Keep it dark?" Gloria laughed as she quoted one of the notices up everywhere, reminding them to keep everything secret.

"I want to see you." Cam pulled the light cord, flooding the space and revealing shelves of cleaning equipment, mops, and buckets. She pushed the door to with her foot.

"Come here."

Gloria pulled her closer again in a sensation of hot breath and desire. Gloria pulled at her shirt and unzipped the fly of her trousers.

"Oh, what's this?"

When she put it on earlier, she hadn't expected it to be discovered. "My jockstrap. I wear it for exercise and when I want to feel more, well, me."

"Oh my God. That has to be the sexiest thing." Gloria pulled down Cam's trousers and left them in a crumpled mess at Cam's feet.

When Gloria placed hands on Cam's naked buttocks, Cam groaned and thrust her hips forward.

"Oh my." Gloria trailed her fingers against the leather pouch.

Cam squirmed in delight as glorious fingers traced under the cup to the swollen wetness there. She kissed Gloria again and gently pulled up her dress until she reached the top of Gloria's stockings. As her fingers skated up her thighs, Gloria opened her legs to give Cam better access. The cotton fabric of her knickers was soddened, and Cam grinned. "I'm not the only one who's excited then?"

"Please do something about it. We don't have much time, and I think I'm going to explode."

"Together?" Cam closed her eyes as their fingers explored in tandem, pushing aside the cloth, slipping easily through swollen folds and gently, gently pushing inside. To have the dual stimulation of touching Gloria and Gloria filling her up was almost too much. They moved in synchronisation, faster and faster, and Cam teetered on the edge, barely able to hold it any longer. Gloria flicked Cam's clitoris with her thumb, and she tumbled into an explosion of lights and had to clamp her jaw shut to keep from expressing her release loudly.

Her eyelids fluttered closed, and she stopped thrusting for a moment before she opened her eyes to see Gloria, her expression wild as though she was close to the edge. Cam resumed her thrusting and then stroked Gloria's swollen clitoris. Gloria slammed her head back against a shelf, and her face contorted into bliss.

"That is the most beautiful thing I've ever seen," Cam whispered. "You are the most beautiful person—" She almost said the words but they couldn't quite pass between her lips. "I've never had sex before. Now I understand what all the fuss is about."

It took a few seconds before Gloria responded. "I have, but that was something else. You seemed to know what I needed without a word. Ouch. I need to move. There's something sticking in my back." Gloria shifted a metal bucket so the handle no longer protruded into her back, then she swiped up a packet of cloths and put them onto a dusty shelf. "Not the most glamorous of settings."

Cam stepped back. "I'm sorry."

"No, that's not what I meant. That was wonderful, thank you." Gloria checked her watch. "Oh, my goodness. We need to move. We're on in twelve minutes."

"What?"

"I hope you feel more relaxed now."

"I was until you told me that." Cam grabbed a quick kiss. "Thank you for finding me and thank you for that. It was amazing even if I'm feeling wobbly legged now. I'm not sure my brain can function." She laughed and pulled up her trousers.

Gloria straightened her dress. "It'll have to. I'll just fix my lipstick. You go ahead. Bea and Reggie will probably be frantic by now." She kissed Cam on the nose. "Go."

"All right, I'm gone." Reluctant to let go but conscious of time, Cam stepped back into the cloakroom. She rinsed her hands in cold water and shook them dry. As she walked out of the corridor, she heard a cough from someone in the main room. How strange. Life had changed for her completely, and yet it was the same as normal for all those people on shift.

It was black outside when she exited quickly and quietly. Cam was about to step from behind the blast wall when a shape disappeared around the corner of the narrow alley between the hut and the blast wall. The only people who used the labyrinth of paths between the buildings were the messengers, all young local girls moving from hut to block and back again. But that silhouette was of a big man, not a messenger girl.

Without thinking, Cam followed the man to the end of their hut where he'd turned right at the next hut, which was perpendicular to theirs. At right angles to that was a small path which led around the back of yet another building. She tried to hurry as quietly as she could, but when she turned another corner to face the lake, the man had disappeared into the shadows of the many trees and bushes and total blackout.

Her skin tingled. Who would be slipping between the huts and why? It wasn't exactly a short cut. It was suspicious, or maybe she was just paranoid. Well, she didn't have time to think about that now; she needed to get to the hall ready for her performance. Checking her tie was in place and her hair was slicked down, she jogged around the lake to the hall by the gatehouse and slipped through the back entrance into the green room.

Bea seemed agitated. "Thank goodness you're here. I was worried about you. Where's Gloria?"

"Coming." At the unintentional double entendre Cam had to hide her smile.

Bea's eyes went wide, and she smiled. "What have you been up to?"

"Gloria was just talking me down after my disaster of a

performance."

"It wasn't a disaster at all, but I approve of talking you down. It's all right; we're running a little late anyway. Jamie's only just got back from his cigarette break. He's about to go on for his *Isis and Osiris*, and he cut it fine too. You'll all be the death of me. I'll need a whole packet of cigarettes after this evening's performance, I'm telling you."

Cam squeezed Bea's arm. "I'll happily donate my whole ration to you. You've done a wonderful job of organising the concert, Bea. It's been splendid entertainment."

Bea raised an eyebrow again. "How would you know? You missed most of it. Take a drink of water with you."

Bea hurried off, and Cam stood to listen to Jamie's performance.

A few seconds later, Gloria stepped beside her in the wings, her body warm against hers as they watched Jamie singing in his deep bass voice. They shared a knowing smile. Cam was the happiest she had ever been. She leaned back into Gloria, needing that connection and enjoying the music. Watching him, she had to admit that Jamie had a great singing voice. All too quickly, he was finished. Cam had the sudden urge to visit the ladies' room again, but it was just nerves. She took a swig of water and inhaled deeply, attempting to quell the sensations in her stomach.

They walked onto the stage, and it seemed vast with just the two of them there. They looked down at the orchestra pit, empty now except for Reggie and Archie. Reggie tapped his music stand, and the audience hushed in collective anticipation. Archie played the first notes on the piano that would normally be played by the oboe, and Gloria sang the opening phase, which Cam echoed. "As steals the morn." Like the song, they were back to the land of reason after an evening of dreams and intoxication.

This was her dream, and she was intoxicated with the aftermath of their love-making. Her vision contracted until there was just the two of them intertwining and expressing their feelings to each other. Her lungs expanded, then she expelled the pure sound in harmony with Gloria. They were sharing, and she wanted it to be like this for ever; giving voice to all the emotions of joy she struggled to articulate, unravelling the tangled threads inside her. This was love.

Gloria still looked flushed from their exertions earlier, and Cam tried not to smile, as it would have made it impossible to sing. In her periphery, she was aware of a slight commotion but wouldn't let anything intrude or spoil this moment, which, in a way, was its own climax of their time together. As Archie played the last few notes, Cam wished for it all again. Now she wouldn't have an excuse to see Gloria outside work, but they would make time, surely? They took their bows and exited through the wings.

Carter was waiting for them. "Gloria Edwards, under the emergency powers granted to me I'm arresting you on suspicion of high treason by giving secrets to the enemy. You will accompany me now and the rest of you need to stay behind for questioning."

Two military policemen slipped handcuffs on Gloria and bustled her out of the green room door.

No, no, that's not true. Shock slammed into Cam, and she slumped onto the floor, desperately catching her breath, unable to speak or think.

Chapter Twenty-Eight

"I'VE ALREADY TOLD YOU; I don't know how those messages got into my locker or who put them in there. I didn't." Gloria rubbed her eyes, gritty and stinging after hours of sitting under a bright light being asked variations of the same question. Carter had chain-smoked his way through the whole interview, and the air was thick with smoke and the smell of sweat and fear.

"This is the problem with recruiting northern mill girls: no integrity."

The bastard was clearly trying to bait her, to get her to lose her temper and say something she would regret. "Get your facts correct. I'm not a mill girl, and I do have integrity. I've always done my duty to my family and my country."

Carter sneered. "My mistake. Factory girl. I wonder what your parents will say about you being a traitor."

It would kill her mam if this came out. They were just circling around the same stories. Why wouldn't he believe her? Because he didn't want to. "I'm not a traitor. What happened to being innocent until proven guilty?"

"We have evidence. We have witnesses saying you left the concert, and you were seen entering and leaving the hut where you work. You were in there for approximately forty-five minutes. Everyone else was either at the concert or at work, and the messages were found in *your* locker." He stubbed out his cigarette in the ashtray and put another in his mouth. "In other words, you had lots of time to send on the messages to your commie friends."

"This is all circumstantial evidence. The messages must have been planted there—"

"Come, come, a popular girl like you—even if you are a bit of a firebrand at times—why would anyone want to frame you? It doesn't stack up. I don't think you know how serious your situation is. The sentence for treason is hanging."

The blood left her face, and her whole body drooped. "Hanging? But I didn't do it. I wouldn't do it."

When they'd started this, she'd been confident in the legal process, believing that they'd soon realise she was innocent and release her, but as the questions continued, her confidence slipped like sand through an egg timer. One thing became very clear: Carter was a man with an objective, and he would mould the facts to suit it. Had he interviewed anyone else? What would Cam say? She'd been catatonic when Gloria was taken away, probably locked in with her emotions. Would she say she went back to change her shirt? Or would she say nothing? With a heavy realisation, she was certain Cam would never volunteer any information, not only was she the queen of secrecy, but she would also do whatever she could to keep her security clearance.

Gloria's mouth tasted metallic. She must've bitten her cheek. She blinked back the tears that threatened to overwhelm her, but she wouldn't give him the satisfaction. If he didn't believe her and he, or someone else, had planted the evidence whatever that was she was going to die anyway. Her head began to swim and she thought she might pass out. Yet somewhere deep inside her, through the haze of disbelief a single thought tugged at her. Whatever happened to her she had to save Cam and her job. If Gloria claimed Cam as an alibi Cam would lose her job, lose everything. There was no alibi Gloria could have if Cam was going to continue at Bletchley Park. She would say nothing about her. She inhaled sharply and focused on the odious man again.

Carter leaned back in his chair. "Should we start again? Where were you between the hours of 7:48, when you were seen entering your hut, and 8:37 when you returned to the concert hall?"

"I've already told you; I was in the ladies room."

"The whole time? Pull the other one. In that time, you could have easily slipped in and dropped off the messages, secret messages already typed and translated to go to the admiralty, to give to your commie friends and placed in your locker ready to pick up later and transmit."

"I didn't. How many times do I need to say I don't know how they got there? If I was going to do something like that, I wouldn't be so stupid as to leave them in my own locker."

"Perhaps you were working with someone else then, and you're covering for him."

She shot her head up. This was a surprise.

"A man entered the hut three minutes before you. Who was he? Was he your contact? Or are you protecting him?"

She frowned. "I didn't see a man." She realised Carter meant Cam, who could easily pass as a man day or night. "I would never betray my country. My brother died for England. This would besmirch his memory and sacrifice if I did. I don't know who would want to frame me. Maybe they just placed the messages in any locker, and mine happened to be handy."

"But that isn't what happened, is it? You met the man inside, and he passed you the messages, which you placed in your locker."

"I never met any man."

Carter pulled on his cigarette and checked his watch. "I think you need to cool your heels overnight and consider the implications of your actions."

One of the MPs dragged her from her seat and pushed her out of the door and down a long corridor. "Can I use the facilities, please?"

He gave her a look of contempt and bundled her into a cell with bars on the window in the door. A sink was bolted to the wall. A single tap dripped and a bar of yellow disinfectant soap was attached to the wall.

He pointed to a bucket under the sink. "Use that."

She couldn't see any toilet paper, not even the thin government issue stuff. There was a ledge bed with a grey blanket laid on top, which looked neither comfortable nor warm. There were no windows, just a layer of glass bricks that would normally let in light, but they'd clearly been painted on the outside for the blackout. A single light protected by mesh illuminated the room and cast a lattice of shadows on the stone floor. She shivered and crawled under the blanket. It was thin and coarse against her skin and hardly covered her body. A headache throbbed in her temples. Whether it was from the smoke, constant questions, or the emotional tumult, she didn't know. Who had betrayed her? She felt sick to her stomach, and her mind roiled. She doubted she would get any sleep tonight.

Should she have told Carter about Cam? He already hated Cam. She would be hanged, and Cam would lose her job and have to move away. Then who would look after her Aunty Florrie?

Someone thought they'd seen a man entering, but perhaps a man had entered around the same time, though they'd heard nothing. They had been a bit busy. She allowed herself a wry smile. The evening up to and including the performance had been so perfect, but it had gone so wrong in a second. Who had betrayed her? She hadn't been aware of pissing anyone off. Archie had never been keen on her, but that was because she took away Jamie's attention, and he had been in the concert all evening either playing with the orchestra or accompanying the soloists. Richard was petrified of Carter, and she just couldn't see it. That just left Drew and Jamie. Drew had been at the concert and Jamie said he loved her and even though they had argued, surely he wouldn't do this?

It could have been someone else from the other shift, but Carter had said they hadn't left the room at all, and the C shift had all been rounded up by Bea in one way or another to help with or attend the concert. It didn't make sense. It had to be Richard or Jamie. The sick, icky feeling of betrayal clawed at her. To be framed, particularly by someone she thought as a brother, completely distorted her perspective, not just of Jamie, but also of their friendship and herself. Had she been gullible or blind not to see this coming? Yes, he was angry to be turned down, but she'd still wanted him in her life, and she'd spent ages comforting him when his brother died. Is that how someone behaved towards a friend?

And Cam, would she try and save herself rather than be exposed and lose everything? Gloria was caught in a cleft: if she admitted she was having sex with Cam, they would both lose their security clearance, but if she didn't have an alibi, she would be charged with treason.

The thought of being hanged whirled around her mind. Her food tried to make a reappearance, and she swallowed it down with a cough. The lights glared, and heavy footsteps echoed down the corridors. Gloria turned over to catch some sleep, but it wouldn't come. Maybe she would be better off dead rather than being thrown out of the service. She'd have to go back and work for her da and marry Stanley, if he still wanted her. She certainly didn't want him.

Gloria sat up, wrapped her arms around her knees, and rocked back and forward, humming a nursery rhyme to herself. It would kill her mam to lose both her children, although now she'd re-established a bond with her grandson, maybe she didn't need Gloria anymore. Maybe Cam would be able to continue at the Park if they didn't know about her being in the hut, and they thought she'd been in the concert all night.

Cam. Not to see her again. She had been so passionate during their love making. Gloria had loved it and wanted to share that again. Cam had split open her world with her many little kindnesses, like ensuring Gloria had sugar in her tea even if Cam went without. She opened doors and gave Gloria her jacket. She was everything Gloria had ever wanted in a lover. And now Cam might make a huge sacrifice for Gloria: losing her job and her status, and Gloria would never be able to thank or repay her.

She leaned her head against the wall, no longer able to hold herself up. The emotions, unspoken and unacknowledged until now, hadn't so much arisen as been uncovered one character at a time, until the tiny particles of proof, the skipping of Gloria's heart and the thrill when Cam entered the room, all became clear, and the message was obvious. She loved Cam. And now she would never get to tell Cam how she felt about her. Her tears fell as despair slapped her in the face. She couldn't betray Cam's secret, which meant she had no alibi. Carter wouldn't believe her anyway, so why ruin both their lives? She would stay silent and take that to her grave. Maybe she could do this last thing to give Cam her freedom. It would be her final act of love.

Chapter Twenty-Nine

"YOU LEFT FOR A while during the concert. Where did you go?" one of Carter's men asked Cam. She didn't understand why she hadn't also been dragged away in handcuffs. The sight of Gloria being pulled away was branded on her memory, and she was glad she'd been too anxious to eat earlier, because it would have made a reappearance by now. It didn't stop the churning knot in her stomach though.

She shrugged, trying to affect nonchalance, and looked around the office that had been commandeered into an interview room. "I was upset after my first performance, so I went for a walk around the lake. Then I changed my shirt ready for my second performance." Would they ask her where she'd gone? Her interrogator looked no more than a boy, with dark circles under his eyes indicating he had worked too many hours, and he still had a long night ahead of him. He closed his eyes briefly as if remembering his lines.

"I understand all the performance costumes were held in the green room. Can someone confirm that's where you changed? You were seen going around the lake. I'll need you to account for all the time you were away from the concert hall."

Relief that her paranoia about not wanting to leave her shirt in the green room had given her a pseudo alibi was chased by guilt. He paused and wrote in his notebook. The next question was coming: had she changed in the hut? It was the obvious question to ask. The silence was getting to her. Should she say she was in the hut too? And that she'd seen a man leaving by the alleys between the huts, a man she'd followed but lost? He'd be able to see her pulse throbbing in her neck, but he was checking his notes. She couldn't say what they were doing because that would rip up her heart, her life. But she couldn't let Gloria suffer. She was innocent. She swallowed hard and tried to force the words out of her mouth.

The door swung open with a bang, and an older man entered. He leaned towards her interrogator. "A man was also observed entering the hut. Go check the men on your list." If he thought she couldn't hear he didn't seem to care.

The man-boy nodded, and the older man left. He straightened, flipped his notebook closed and snapped the rubber band around it to keep it closed. Then he looked at her and his lips flashed upwards in what was presumably supposed to be a smile.

"Okay. I need to do an initial conversation with some of the others. Can you send Richard Thomas in please, but I'd like you to hang around. And before you complain, I know it's late, but this is critical."

She stared at him a second before he motioned her with his hand like she was one of her chickens.

"Go on. Go and get your colleague."

Cam bolted upright and fled before he could ask anything else. She found Richard having a cup of tea with Bea. "You're up, Richard."

He looked as wan as Cam felt. Bea gave him an affectionate squeeze, which caused him to smile, but it didn't reach his eyes. Cam took the seat he'd just occupied as he hustled into the office.

She was in a haze and had trouble focusing on her surroundings. Words swirled around her head.

"Cuppa?" Bea poured a rather strong-looking cup of tea from a teapot she must have had brewing for a while. Cam looked around the small kitchenette attached to the hall as if she'd never seen it before. Most of the clearing up had now been done, and Bea sat at a fold-out table.

"What? Oh, Thanks."

Bea pushed across the green institutional cup and saucer. "How did you get on?"

Cam spooned in three spoonfuls of sugar for the shock, unable to look Bea in the eyes. "I couldn't say anything about going into the hut. If it comes out, then that's my security clearance gone, but I can't let Gloria be hanged. She's innocent. I feel so guilty. And scared."

Bea stopped Cam from stirring her tea so vigorously by placing her hand on Cam's. "I can't tell you what to do, but what's it worth to you? Could you live with yourself? Could you watch her being hanged because you can't give up what you've worked for?"

Cam felt as if the whole world was sagging on her shoulders, and she let her head slump into her hands. Hanged. What was she thinking? Of course she couldn't let Gloria hang if there was any chance she could save her. She would never forgive herself if she could have done something. She was nothing but a coward. She simply had to do whatever she could to save Gloria.

"I know. I know. I'll go and speak to him again when he's finished with Richard. But I'm not sure I can drink this. I think I might be sick."

"Cam, look at me. You don't need to say what you were doing, just that she was comforting you after your performance. That's the truth."

Cam expelled a long breath. "Do you think?"

"It's always better to tell the truth. They don't need all the details."

She picked up the teacup and tried to stop it from trembling as she placed it against her lips and took a quick sip. "How long are you staying around for? Are you being interviewed again?"

"No, I'm just waiting for the interviews to finish before I can lock up. There's no point going home now before my midnight shift, so I may as well wait around here. I'll take Gloria's jacket, music sheets, and handbag home..." Bea faltered.

Unless they could save her, Gloria would never come home again and would never need the bag or music.

Cam noticed them for the first time, and her eyes blurred. "Oh God, will she ever sing again? Will we ever see her again? Oh, Bea. I think I love her. I can't let this happen to her. I'll tell them I was there, but will it be enough?"

She didn't mind that Bea stroked her forearm. It was all too much. The whole evening had been like a Big Dipper ride, from her first terrible performance to the bliss of the encounter. She'd never have dreamed that Gloria would want to be with her. And it had been wonderful. Then the second performance which was almost like making love with their clothes on.

"What are you smiling at?"

Cam felt her cheeks burn. She hadn't even realised she was smiling. "I... Until that awful man came around, the evening had improved considerably."

"Your performance was stunning. I couldn't hear a pin drop in the audience."

That was raw comfort now. "Maybe, but where does it leave us? It seems that will be our swan song, whatever happens."

The door to the office swung open, and Richard hurried over to them. "Thank God that's over. Thank you for the tea and a wonderful concert, Bea; I really enjoyed it. You were fabulous, Cam. I hope we'll hear you sing again, and I'm sorry about how the rest of the evening's gone."

With a quick wave, he turned and shot out of the room, clearly keen to put distance between himself and the trauma of the day.

"I'd better go in then."

"Let me go first. I'll just ask if he wants another cup of tea and a biscuit."

"Okay."

"It's the right thing to do." Bea bustled off and returned a minute later. "Mr Davidson will see you now. Good luck."

Cam swung around from the noticeboard that she'd been

pretending to read, strode to the office, and knocked briskly on the door. She was doing this for Gloria. It didn't feel like the right thing to do; it was just the *least wrong* thing to do. "Mr Davidson? I just want to clear something up from what I told you earlier."

The man-boy peered at her and paused in sorting out his papers. "Oh?"

"Yes. Can I sit down?" She took the same chair as previously, before her legs gave way. "I think it might be relevant that I changed my shirt in my hut in the ladies' bathroom. Gloria rushed in and tried to comfort me because I was upset after my first performance. We were there for over forty minutes. As I left the hut, I saw a man disappearing around the back of the hut. I followed him but lost him when I came out by a totally different hut facing the lake. I was worried I'd be late for my performance so I hurried back."

Davidson scribbled down what she was saying then looked up at her. "Really? And you didn't think to tell me this earlier?"

"I was too shocked about it all. I wasn't thinking clearly."

"I see. And you aren't just cooking all this up to try and save your singing partner? What man? There was only one man who went in just before Gloria." He looked her up and down, as though seeing her for the first time. "Unless that was you?"

Cam nodded. "Possibly."

Davison sighed and scribbled in his notebook again. After a couple of minutes of silence, he looked up. "As you've probably gathered by now, we had another inspection when the B shift started and checked all the lockers then. They were empty, and we kept the hut on surveillance until we went in to check them all again. There's only one entrance."

"Not if you go around the backs of the other huts. Did you observe all of those too?"

"Don't tell me how to do my job, Camilla Langley, or I'll charge you with insubordination."

Cam slammed her hand down on the desk. "This is ridiculous.

I'm telling you the truth. The very least you can do is follow it up."

"Maybe *you* put the messages in Gloria's locker." He fixed her with his hard stare.

"I didn't. Ask her. I told you, I was in the bathroom the whole time. I was upset, and she helped to calm me down."

"Frankly, I don't believe you." He raised his hand. "But I will report it to Mr Carter when I see him in the morning. He can decide what he does with this cock and bull story."

Cam wiped her palms on her trousers. Why wasn't he listening? "It's the truth."

"So you say."

She shook her head and returned to where Bea was washing out the last few teacups. Cam picked up a tea towel. "He didn't believe me. I went through all that, and all he said was maybe I planted the messages."

"But he didn't ask what you were doing?"

"No, but he said he was going to tell Carter, and he'll probably ask."

"She was comforting you, that's all. One day at a time. Thank you for this. I can finish off. Go home and say hello to Florrie for me. I hope she won't be worried."

"I said I might be late. Thanks, Bea. It was a great concert, and you worked so hard to make it happen. Good night." She folded the tea towel and aligned it on the rack, then left to get her bike. As she cycled home, her thoughts churned with each down pedal. Cam had just found Gloria, and she'd opened Cam's world, showed her what was possible. She couldn't lose that now, and in the most horrible way. What happened to truth when it wasn't sufficient to sway prejudgement and assumptions? That was the kind of behaviour they expected from the enemy, not here in England when they were trying to fight a war.

She kicked down even harder on the pedals. Her life was already ruined, so she would do what she could to save Gloria, even if she had to take it to Mr Churchill himself.

Chapter Thirty

THE BLANKET SCRATCHED AGAINST Gloria's skin, rubbing her raw and surrounding her in a damp and musty smell, as though it needed airing. She turned, trying to ease the pressure on her hips from the hard bed. If that wasn't enough to stop any chance of sleep, the regular pounding of boots on polished floor, clanging doors, and harsh artificial light would be.

Again, she tossed away from the wall and the unpleasant tang of stale urine from the bucket caught her nostrils. Even putting her finger under her nose couldn't stop her from wanting to gag. The part of her logical brain that was still functioning informed her that this was to humiliate her and break her down. The other part of her brain was slipping into panic. No, not panic: despair. A tiny voice whispered she'd done nothing wrong and nothing to be ashamed of. They had just been in the wrong place at the wrong time. And had been framed. That was the hurt, heavy and sickly. Someone was deliberately trying to harm her. It could only be Jamie, but she never thought he would be that angry with her. Or was it not anger but happenchance? Did he know there was going to be another inspection, and he panicked? He had even less time than they did because he was appearing earlier than them. It was probably a six-minute walk to the hut from the hall and back, and how long would it take to plant some messages? A minute? So in seven minutes, her life had been destroyed.

Whatever happened, it would never be the same again. The inconsequential, the innocence, the fun were all gone. It wasn't a game and had never been a lark, which is how she'd treated it before. It had been her way of escaping the monotony of the cash office, the control of her da, and a means of avoiding the sentence of living with the odious Stanley.

From somewhere down the corridor, a heavy door banged and marching footsteps echoed, accompanied by the clanking of keys. Boots squeaked on linoleum, and the clatter of the lock being sprung rattled her door. Gloria shrank against the wall. Now she was desperate to remain in this stink hole for a few extra minutes of safety. She didn't know where she was going next but knew she really didn't want to go there. Was she going to the gallows already? No, she had to have a trial first. Even during the war, they still needed to work under the judicial system, didn't they?

She wished she'd used the bucket earlier as she now had an urgent need to pee. *Control. It's only fear,* the tiny remaining rational part of her brain said.

"Get up, you need to come now."

The guard was young and carried himself with the slight jitteriness of someone not entirely sure of his role. Gloria tried to smile as wide as possible, although she must look a sight with her creased evening gown. She tried to smooth her hair to look more acceptable. "Where are we going?"

"I'm not to talk to you." He advanced towards her.

"But what harm can it do?" She scrambled off the ledge bed to avoid him touching her. Her wrists were still raw from yesterday's manhandling and with any luck, she would avoid handcuffs. Pride made her want to show some defiance. She rubbed at the red patch where the skin had peeled.

The young guard pulled her by the shoulder so hard that she stumbled out of the cell, then he pushed her in front of him down a corridor. No handcuffs must mean it wasn't the courthouse. Another interview room maybe? She didn't know if she could answer the same questions as yesterday over and over. Would they wear her down until she broke down and confessed to something she didn't commit?

The guard opened the same door as yesterday. Was it yesterday? She'd lost all sense of time.

"In," he said with more formality, presumably to impress his superior in the room.

There were two people in the room already. A man sat by the wall with a notebook, presumably to record the conversation. The guard positioned himself by the door. Carter sat where he had yesterday, looking freshly bathed and sporting a look so smug, she wanted to slap him. The spark of anger fizzled like a match in water. She was innocent, of spying anyway, yet they were determined to frame her.

"So," Carter tapped his cigarette on the table prior to lighting it, "Camilla Langley says she was in the hut at the same time as you...in the ladies' cloakroom."

The tiny thread of hope she'd had that she could keep Cam out of this unravelled. He must have seen her shoulders sag because he smirked. God, she detested this man.

"Would you like to explain what you were doing there? Does it really take thirty-nine minutes or so to powder your nose? I don't think so. Shall I tell you what I think happened? No? Well, I'm going to tell you anyway, Mill Girl. Oh, sorry, Factory Girl, as if that makes any difference: full of commies, all of them."

She couldn't stand this, listening to his unfounded prejudice even though she knew he was trying to goad her. "My father owns the factory. He's hardly likely to be a communist, is he?"

Carter inhaled deeply and sat back in his chair then blew out a perfect smoke ring. "Well, that's the interesting thing. We've been doing a little digging about you and the *factory*. It appears you made a big fuss about some lad not getting fair wages and complained to the boss about it. You could have started a riot or stirred up a strike. Just the kind of anti-war effort your commie heart would like. It appears you're like a lot of young people and have no respect for your father, going against his wishes."

He paused to take another drag on his cigarette and watched

her, as she scrambled to catch up. Who had he spoken to? Da? Nancy? Oh, God, if her da knew, he would have told her mam. She let out a groan of anguish before she could stop herself.

Of course this is what Carter wanted, to see her squirm and sweat, to let her know he knew everything. And he knew about Cam. She'd tried so hard yesterday not to reveal anything that could link to Cam, and now it was for nothing. If Cam had confessed, or they'd guessed, they must have all been interviewed by now. She swallowed hard and had to blink to keep the tears back. She couldn't save Cam. She couldn't protect her or their secret. They were finished. Even if they let her off the charges, although she was sure Carter would find something to pin on her, neither of them would work at the Park again.

Carter puffed smoke in her direction, making her cough and dragging her attention back to him. He leaned across the table. "As I was saying, Factory Girl, you came out to hide the messages or pick up the messages before you passed them on to your contact. Did you hide them in your knickers to get them through gate security? It will be interesting to see what we find under the floorboards in your lodgings."

"You won't find anything there unless you planted it yourself."

He raised his eyebrow. "Then you went into the ladies' cloakroom and found Camilla Langley changing her shirt and crying over her performance."

"She wasn't crying." Even as she spoke Gloria knew she'd been broken, betrayed Cam and herself. She had to stop herself from heaving up the gloop of porridge that passed as breakfast.

"No? But she was upset and you comforted her, put your arm around her. I bet she enjoyed that, invert that she is. And you probably thought you had the perfect alibi, but it doesn't take that long to hide secrets, does it? So you had to have an excuse to hide away. Perhaps she was in on the whole scheme? Was she your contact? Can't trust queers. Were you supposed to meet her?"

"Why would I do that when we work together? That doesn't make sense."

"You were spying together. A queer and a commie; that ticks all the boxes. Meanwhile, we know the secrets have been getting to the Russians. Yes, you can say they're our allies, or rather they're our enemy's enemy, but they've told us they've received information from here, from your hut, and we've narrowed it down to your shift. We've been watching and waiting, and lo and behold, two people disappeared from the concert at the crucial time between full inspections. Meantime, you were working out your next plot to sell the secrets, or did you do it for the glory of it all? And Cam was sobbing into your pretty dress. Shame it's a bit more creased now, but don't worry, we'll soon exchange it for a very unattractive prison uniform which will be the last set of clothing you will ever wear before you're hanged."

He leaned back on his chair, his fingers entwined behind his head, a picture of relaxation. There was something important in what he said, and she struggled to bring her thoughts into focus. He hadn't mentioned what she and Cam had been doing, and he would have done if they had evidence. So maybe they didn't know everything. She would hold onto that. She stared at the bare bricks behind his head not wanting to incriminate herself by talking.

He rocked forward again, frowning. Maybe she hadn't given him the reaction he hoped for.

"Do you know it's a particularly unpleasant death? If you're lucky, the hangman will place the knot to break your neck, but they usually need an incentive to do that, or if they've been requested to make it as easy as possible. Occasionally, we make a request when someone tells the truth, but you haven't been telling the truth, have you? Not the *whole* truth. You didn't mention Camilla Langley yesterday. Were you trying to protect your girlfriend? Or did she fuck you and you thought you'd given yourself an alibi?"

Gloria took in a sharp intake of breath. He knew? Had Cam spilled everything? It would destroy her, destroy them both. Gloria retched but swallowed back the bile. The catch of vomit sticking in her throat caused her to cough. Her nostrils flared and stung.

"An interesting response. You did think it would give you an alibi. There was still time to do both, and you did."

"It wasn't like that," Gloria whispered, then cursed herself for letting even that slip.

"Did she take you by the basins? Classy. Probably the kind of thing you think is acceptable in the North. Or was it on the floor?"

"She was upset, and I comforted her, that's all." Was she already caught in a lie?

"No. It was the cleaner's cupboard. We discovered it had been disturbed in there. We could tell by the dust. Pretty disgusting the state the cleaners keep the cupboard in. We'll be taking fingerprints later."

Gloria shook her head but felt her cheeks burn.

He laughed, a bark not unlike a hyena. "So, you fucked in the cleaner's cupboard. Thank you for confirming my suspicions."

"I was comforting her, that's all."

He stubbed out his cigarette and looked her up and down. "I don't believe you. This is just obfuscation to cover your tracks. Pity it's not going to save you. Did you get all that?"

The man who'd been taking notes nodded.

"Well, I need to have another conversation with Camilla Langley. You'll be taken back to the holding cell."

Gloria emptied the contents of her stomach all over the floor.

A drop splattered on his shiny shoes, and he shook it to dispel the globule. "Ugh. Disgusting. Guard, get someone to clean up this mess, and take her back to the cell."

He sidestepped the vomit and strode out of the room.

Gloria put her head in her hands. She'd betrayed Cam. They were both finished.

Chapter Thirty-One

CAM LEANED HER HEAD back against the wall of the hen house, even though it was not the most comfortable or clean environment to contemplate her situation. The chickens fluttered around in a flurry of feathers, clucking their indignation about her presence since she wasn't feeding them. She held Three in her lap and stroked her feathers, unsure if she was soothing the chicken or herself.

She heard shuffling outside followed by a gentle tap on the door, which cause a further cacophony of squawks and flapping feathers.

"Cam, are you all right, sweetheart? You've been in there a long time. I thought you might be doing your boxing, but you weren't there."

Cam sighed. "Hang on, Aunty. I'll come out." She gave Three another stroke then put her back in her nesting box and rose, brushing the shreds of newspaper bedding off her overalls. She brought out the five eggs she'd collected and checked the wooden catch was secure before she joined her aunt on the path.

Aunty Florrie peeped into her bucket. "Ooh, lovely. I'll make a cake for the Women's Voluntary Service." She tucked her hand in the crook of Cam's arm and leaned on her heavily as they made their way back to the house. She pointed at the tilled ground. "Will you be able to plant the potatoes this week, Cam?"

Cam surveyed the plant beds, unsure how to tell her aunt about the trauma of the night before. But she recognised her aunt's attempt to keep the lines of communication open, so she fought the urge to shut down. "Yes, depending on my shifts." How could she admit she might not be at the Park much longer?

"I'll make the tea if you want to freshen up. You're on the four p.m. shift this afternoon, aren't you?"

"I don't know. I guess. I might need to go in earlier."

Her aunt stopped and turned to face her, but Cam couldn't meet her eyes.

"Are you going to talk about whatever's troubling you? Did the concert not go well? Sorry I didn't wait up for you; I was tired."

Cam shook her head. "I didn't expect you to wait up. I'll just use the bathroom and join you." She would have to talk soon, but where to start?

Even after she sat down a few minutes later with her cup of tea, she still couldn't talk about the previous night. But her aunt was watching and waiting. "I don't know where to begin."

"Did it not go very well?"

"It's much more than that." To her utter mortification, tears welled over her eyelids and poured down her cheeks. Aunty Florrie came to her side and hugged her close. Cam clung to her and wept into her apron, holding on like she did when she was a little child. "Gloria's been arrested for treason, and it's all my fault."

"What? That doesn't make sense."

"I know." Without withdrawing from the embrace, Cam gave a brief and censored version of events; she didn't need to scare off her aunt with details of sex, and she couldn't risk divulging any secrets.

"Seems obvious to me that he's the one responsible for the troubles. But how did you know it was a man?"

"He was big and bulky, whereas the messengers are all young girls just out of school. And there was the smell of cigarettes in the air. As far as I know the girls don't smoke." She cast her mind back to the vision of the man's silhouette disappearing and the smell of– "Wait, they weren't British cigarettes; they were exotic, like the French ones Jamie smokes. He boasted he got them from a friend in London."

Bile rose in her throat. *Bastard.* She knew there was something off about him. That he'd betray Gloria though, was something she couldn't stomach—or forgive.

"It sounds like you need to tell the authorities that detail."

Cam pulled back and looked into the concerned face of her aunt. "I do. Not that it will help me save my job, but it's the right thing to do."

"It is. And even if you have to leave that hush-hush place you aren't allowed to talk about, I'm sure you could get another job. Maybe you could go back to Cambridge? It won't be the end of the world."

"It might be for Gloria if I can't convince them to look into Jamie." Cam shuddered. She couldn't bear the thought that she wouldn't be able to save Gloria. "Aunty, I need to go. I'll do what I can to make it right, to clear her name." Life would not be worth living if she failed. Love meant having to sacrifice and compromise, and if she had to sacrifice her job for Gloria to go free, she would do it with a brave and willing heart.

Chapter Thirty-Two

"Ah, Camilla Langley; I was looking for you." Carter hardly bothered to open his lips as he spoke.

The ashtray full of cigarette butts and the deep circles around his eyes were testament to his not getting much sleep, not that Cam had any sympathy for him.

The interview room was in one of the newly built, blast-proof concrete blocks. It was just one anonymous office in a long corridor of similar bright green doors. The guard stood just inside, and a stenographer sat at a small table beside the wall with a black machine like a small typewriter. Carter sat in a miasma of smoke as if he'd been there some time.

"So good of you to give yourself up."

Cam halted mid-step on her way to the interview chair. "What? No. I've come to tell you who I'm sure has done it—who you need to interview."

He shook his match vigorously to extinguish it and added it to the mountain of matches and cigarette stubs in his ashtray. "Is this some excuse to shift the blame from the woman you fancy? Ha. That's shocked you, hasn't it? Yes, she told me all about your sordid little pity party in the cleaner's closet. Now we've got the fingerprints too."

There was nothing sordid about it, Cam wanted to scream. She closed her eyes for a second, attempting to block out his contempt buffeting against her senses. He was just goading her. She gripped the top of the chair and didn't sit. This was a waste of time; his mind was closed. "I told your man I saw a tall man dashing around the side of the hut when I exited. What I didn't recall until this morning was the smell of cigarettes—"

"Everyone smokes." As if to emphasise his point, he belched out a puff of smoke. "This is ridiculous."

"Not French cigarettes. They have a particular smell about them, like burning tyres; it's disgusting. Even the expensive ones, the Gitanes reek. The ones that Jamie Gordon smokes—"

"That's enough. You can't go around casting aspersions to deflect from your activities. If I had my way, you'd lose your security clearance today, but sadly, it's not up to me. Jamie Gordon could sue you for slander."

"Not if it's true. And what about the wrongful arrest of Gloria Edwards? She's innocent, yet you persist on thinking you've got your woman. She was framed, almost certainly by Jamie Gordon because she turned him down, but you can't accept that because he's a golfing chum of yours. Being popular doesn't make him innocent. Instead, he can charm his way out of trouble. Go and interview him and extract the truth from him."

Carter leaned his chair onto the back two legs. Cam was so tempted to tip him over.

"We have. He was in the concert the whole time—"

"He went for a cigarette break and only returned a minute or so before I did. Ask Beatrice Williams; she was frantic that he was going to be late for his performance."

"A cigarette break isn't time enough to go from your hut to the concert hall."

"It is if you go through the rat runs between the huts and pass in front of the house. It takes two minutes forty-five seconds at speed, and how long does it take to hide a message? Two minutes? That's easily within the time Jamie normally takes for a cigarette break, which is twenty-one minutes."

"And how would you know that?"

"Because most days he goes for one, even though he smokes in the hut, and we aren't supposed to take a break during the day, but we don't say anything because he's the shift supervisor.

Why does he need a break anyway? He could be up to all sorts of mischief. His breaks seem to be getting longer. Initially, they were just sixteen minutes."

Carter slammed forward on his chair and looked slightly rattled now.

That was her cue to leave before he asked her more questions about what she'd been doing with Gloria. "I'm wasting my time here. Save yourself the embarrassment and interview Jamie properly." She turned and strode out to the main house. What she would give for a punching bag now. Rage kept her walking when normally she may have paused to reconsider what she was about to do, but she had nothing to lose. Gloria's life depended on it.

Cam didn't often go into the Victorian gothic building that housed the administration and command offices. There was no need. Each hut and building was self-contained, although they all took an educated guess on the activities within each hut. She walked through the ornate wooden doors into another world. The large front drawing room had been converted into an office for the commander of the Park, but she was going a bit lower in the hierarchy to Jamie's boss, Mr Needleman who worked on the first floor.

His secretary looked at Cam over her glasses. "Mr Needleman's not available," she said without even checking with him.

Cam glowered at her and didn't move from her place by the desk. "This is a matter of utmost security—"

"Everything we do is of utmost security. If you have a concern, bring it to your supervisor."

"What if my supervisor is involved? Would you recommend I go right to the top? Maybe Mr Churchill would want to hear about this?" She was bluffing, but the secretary didn't know that.

The poor woman blanched. "I'll go and see if he's free now. What's your name?"

"You do that." Cam gave her name and hut number, then paced while the woman slipped into the room behind her desk.

A few minutes later, she came out and held open the door. "You can go in now."

"Thank you." Cam entered the oak-panelled room. The ornate carvings and patterned ceilings may not have been intended to intimidate, but it was a different world here, and she was grateful she didn't work in somewhere so pretentious.

An older man with a lanky body and even thinner hair peered at her over his half-moon glasses. "Miss Brown tells me you have important security information. Don't you think it's something Mr Carter of MI5 should be involved in?"

"He is, but his judgement is clouded because he's friends with the individual concerned."

"Sit down and tell me what's on your mind."

She briefed Mr Needleman with the facts.

He shook his head and flicked at the corner of one of his papers as she spoke. When she'd finished, he stared at her through half lidded eyes. "Jamie Gordon is a star codebreaker and a good fellow. He's got a single figure handicap in golf and is very popular up at the club."

Of course Jamie would be part of the establishment. Would she have to go even higher to be listened to? What happened to the truth? This was starting to feel like being thrown into the *Brave New World* and similar novels that Auntie Florrie liked to read.

"You can't just go around accusing people without proof."

She rose, determined to escalate the issue if it meant Gloria lived. Perhaps there was something in her look of resolve, because he leaned forward.

"I tell you what, let's come up with a plan."

She sat down again, and ten minutes later, she returned to work, having to pretend it was just another ordinary shift.

An hour later, Jamie stood in the centre of the room and threw a piece of paper at Drew.

Drew caught it one handed. "Howzat?" He raised his arms as if doing a victory dance.

Cam unclenched her jaw. "Do you have to behave like school children?"

Jamie turned away. "One for you, Drew, and if you solve it before Miss Grumpy solves hers, I'll buy you a scotch."

Drew unfurled the paper and smoothed out the crinkles. "That's incentive enough. Oxford for the win."

They settled down, and Cam continued to watch Jamie surreptitiously as she affected concentration. She chewed on her pencil, waiting for her moment. Her heart hammered in her chest. She couldn't be a spy or do clandestine work; she liked openness and honesty, not dissembling or lies. The people who did spy were so brave.

Jamie wasn't being himself either. He hadn't been out for his cigarette yet, which was when she had to make her move. She tried not to focus on everything that could scupper them. The location was critical and now it was starting to cloud over. If it rained, would they be able to hear?

Just when she thought she would explode with the anticipation, Jamie rose.

"Fag break, Archie?"

No, no, she needed Jamie to go on his own. She couldn't accost two of them simultaneously. The plan was slipping through her fingers. She would need to adapt, and she wasn't great at thinking on her feet.

"Give me a few minutes."

Archie nodded his head without looking up, clearly at that moment just before a code became clear. Thank God for once his duty came before his need to pander to Jamie's every whim.

"I'm going now," Jamie said and made for the door.

Cam waited thirty seconds then stood. "Bathroom," she announced to the entire shift and followed him out, ignoring

Richard's raised eyebrow.

The corridor was empty. *Damn, I've waited too long.* She walked down the corridor, trying not to make too much noise and praying that the contingencies she thought of would be enough, and that everything was in place as they'd arranged. She didn't fancy challenging him in a fight. He was much bigger than her.

She exited the hut and caught sight of him disappearing around the end in the alleyway, almost in a replica of the night of the concert. Anxious to catch him before he went too far, she hurried after him. "Jamie. Wait a moment."

He turned at the mid-point along the hut. Good. She had to force herself not to glance and see if the window was opened a crack.

"What?"

His snarl made her regret her choice of plan. He extracted a packet of cigarettes from his breast pocket and flicked a lighter until it caught. The distinctive tar-like burning smell of the French cigarettes drifted into her nostrils.

She took a couple of steps towards him so she was in touching distance. "It's you, isn't it? You're the spy. I thought it was Archie, but he had an alibi all evening because he was in the concert. You slipped out, and I caught sight of you as you rounded the corner of the hut. And I smelled the same French cigarettes you smoke—"

"What the fuck are you talking about? Have you completely lost your mind, Langley? You can't go around making false accusations."

"But they're not false, are they? You planted the message in Gloria's locker so they wouldn't find it in yours—"

"You've got a vivid imagination—"

"And escaped down these rat runs between the huts, then back to the concert just in time for your solo."

He laughed, but it wasn't his usual full-bellied laugh. It was too thin and false. "You'll have to try better than that."

The tightening of his fingers scrunching his cigarette packet belied his nonchalance.

"I saw you when I came out of the hut."

"It was dark. It could have been anyone."

He walked towards the window, and she thought he might see Carter listening in there. *If* they were there. She needed to distract him. "Except it *was* you. There was an overwhelming stench of those disgusting French cigarettes you smoke. Exactly like now."

He exhaled smoke through the side of his mouth, seemingly unperturbed, but his back stiffened. "That proves nothing. There are thousands of people on site. I'm sure I'm not the only one who appreciates Gitanes."

"But you're one of the few who can secure them when you visit the Savoy each month. And how many people have access to our huts? You know the protocols. All inter-hut communication is via telephone or memo. No personal visits. The only people who get to traverse the site are the messenger girls, and they're not large men who smoke Gitanes. Everyone else from the hut has been accounted for. You lied and didn't say you disappeared for your cigarette break."

His face reddened, and he got in her face. "You mean like you lied? Fucking Bradford in the cloakroom. I heard you from the corridor. What did you do to twist her mind and convert her to your devious ways, you fucking queer?"

Cam closed her eyes briefly to wash away the hateful words. The only way she'd get through this would be to ignore his insults. "The only person unaccounted for is you on your twenty-three-minute cigarette break. You only just made it back to the hall for the concert. Bea said you looked harried and stressed."

"Beatrice Williams is a busybody, poking her nose in where it doesn't belong."

"That's not true. But why did you frame Gloria? I don't understand. She really liked you. Were you really that angry with her? Why hide the messages in her locker? What prompted you to make a dash to the hut?"

He threw down his cigarette and stubbed it out with his toe. She needed to provoke him into talking. "All the time you've been visiting the Savoy... Is that where you meet your contact? Ah, that's what Archie's been to you: an alibi. And later on, it was Gloria."

"That's all conjecture."

"You haven't denied it."

"Archie has nothing to do with anything."

"Yet he follows you around like a lamb. What's your relationship to him? He clearly loves you—"

Jamie stepped forward his hand raised as if he was going to strike her. "I'm not some fucking homo. I saved his life in Spain that's all, and he's grateful. I've had enough of these lies."

"Interesting you seem more concerned with protecting your reputation as a full-blooded male than your so-called innocence. Did you first meet your contact in Spain? Is that where you discovered your love of foreign cigarettes? You fought for the reds, and you came scurrying home when they lost. But you'd already made your bed then and had to lie in it—"

He turned and stalked away. "I don't need to listen to this—"

She'd failed. She had to act now or her chance to save Gloria was gone. "Why Gloria? I thought you wanted to marry her. Or was that just a ruse?"

He ran back and towered above her. "You think you're so clever, don't you? You may have the smarts, but you're a charmless pervert." He slammed his hand against the wood, and it flexed and creaked. His expression was pained. "Why would she choose you? I heard you rutting like rabbits in the cloakroom. The walls are so thin, I heard every grunt and moan. It was disgusting. I would have put it in your locker, but you're always changing the combination, paranoid fucker that you are. I was so angry—"

"You're so angry? You framed someone you said you loved out of spite and jealousy."

"Who cares? I'd originally planned to pin it on Richard, but you disgust me, all of you. I'm not sorry. You deserve what you've got coming to you. It won't make a difference; I've already poisoned your credibility and told Carter you're an invert. He's going to get you thrown out anyway. It doesn't matter how great your codebreaking skills are."

She held onto her neutral expression so he couldn't see how his words affected her. "Why would you betray your country?"

"Does it matter? This fucking country, with its class system and old boys' network... It's finished."

"You're part of that."

"No, I'm not."

Where were the others? Weren't they coming? Had they heard any of this or had it all been a waste? Without a confession made within earshot of others, she had not an iota of proof. He was so smug, thinking he'd got away with it, and Gloria would hang for this piece of shit.

The rage that had simmered for days boiled over, and she lunged at him, but he was surprisingly quick for his bulk, and he darted to the side, then took a pace towards her. She looked up to face the barrel of a gun. Her blood turned to ice. So much for her heroics. She couldn't escape now. This plan had backfired, and she wasn't going anywhere.

"It's time to shut you up. I'll make it look like you committed suicide because you couldn't cope with knowing you'd got your lover killed because of your unnatural lust."

She tried to straighten up, but her knees crumpled. "Put the gun down, Jamie."

He laughed. "What you've forgotten is that you don't have the power. I do. You have everything to lose, and I have everything to gain."

There was a shuffling behind him. "Drop your weapon,

Gordon. You're under arrest for high treason."

Carter. Thank God! Not a moment too soon.

Jamie grabbed at Cam and pulled her in front of him, so close she could smell his sweat. The barrel was cold against her temple. She tried to recall. Had he switched off the safety?

"I don't think so. We'll be going on a little trip, me and this little pervert here." He dragged her backwards towards the other entrance of the alleyway. "You've got nothing on me."

"Put the gun down, Gordon," Carter said. "We just heard your confession. As you said, the walls are thin. That's the trouble with wood. And we heard you clearly through the open windows."

"So what? Your precious secret about the existence of the Park is blown wide open. The Russians know you've broken Enigma."

Carter smiled, the first time Cam had seen his crooked and stained teeth. It gave her the shivers.

"Not quite. Don't you think we've been intercepting your outgoing messages, letting out a few less important facts and feeding them a lie? You disappoint me, Gordon. I hoped you'd be club secretary."

Club secretary? They were talking about golf when he had a gun to her head. Cam had always thought she would fight back if something like this happened to her, but she couldn't move, and he could probably feel how fast her heart was beating.

"Drop the gun, Gordon." Carter took a step towards him.

Jamie dragged Cam backwards away from Carter. "Don't come any closer. I'd take great delight in putting a bullet through Langley's brain. All that intellect splattered against the path. Serve her right for stealing my girl."

A military policeman appeared at the other end of the alleyway, so Jamie was effectively cornered. She remembered her aunt saying a trapped rat is the most dangerous. Would Jamie shoot her?

The MP approached.

"Tell your man to stand down, Carter. I need a car out of here." He waved the gun towards Carter.

Cam slammed Jamie's arm upwards with one hand and elbowed him in the gut, then she spun around and threw an upper cut that sent him sprawling backward. Her blood throbbed in her brain, and she was about to follow up with a hook when her hands were pulled back.

"Stop, Miss Langley. We need him conscious." Carter again.

The MPs bustled Jamie away, and Carter followed them.

Cam bent over double, trying to catch her breath and control her trembling body. She heaved but managed to keep down the nausea.

"That was very impressive, Miss Langley. I would never have believed it if I hadn't seen it with my own eyes."

Mr Needleman. When had he arrived? After the dirty business, no doubt. She staggered and slumped against the hut wall.

"Would you like a cup of tea?"

She rubbed her bruised knuckles. "No. Please, just release Gloria Edwards as soon as possible. She shouldn't be held one minute longer."

"I'm sure that will be arranged."

Her rage sparked again. She hadn't endured all of that for everything to be caught up in some bureaucratic nightmare. If her job was gone anyway, she had nothing to lose by arguing with her boss's supervisor. "No. You arrange it now. You have the authority, don't you? Or do I have to go higher up?"

"You're certainly not to be messed with, are you?" He turned to one of the remaining MPs. "Go to Holding Block A and start the paperwork for Gloria Edwards' release."

"I'd like to go too and take her home."

Mr Needleman looked as if he was about to object but seemed to reconsider. "That's sensible. You probably need the rest of the day off too after your ordeal."

Now he was being conciliatory. It really didn't matter if she could just get Gloria out of her nightmare and back home safe and sound. They would deal with the consequences tomorrow, when she would discover whether she still had a job or not.

Chapter Thirty-Three

GLORIA BLINKED AS SHE was finally released out of the anonymous block she'd been held in since the concert. The light was clear, and the low sun indicated it was heading towards evening. She inhaled deeply, revelling in the sweet smell of spring instead of the rank musty air of the cell. She almost couldn't believe it. Where to now? Home or work?

They hadn't told her any details of why she'd been released, but that she would be contacted about the "other matter" in due course. A little sick feeling in her stomach told her they weren't about to let her and Cam get off lightly. But she would deal with that another day. Now she wanted to slough off the taint of the place.

Her indecision was disconcerting. Perhaps the incarceration had affected her emotionally as well as physically. Of course it had. The clanging of doors and heavy boots had been the backdrop of the last few days, but now there was the bliss of silence. No, she listened more acutely. Not silence: the sound of a motor car disappeared in the distance, birdsong and the squeak of a bicycle swirled around. And it wasn't just the cheeps and twitters of the little brown birds she could never identify but also a solitary blackbird perched on the apex of the roof opposite. The simple melody of notes and whistles and cheep-cheep at the end like a full stop reinvigorated her soul. The trill staccato phrases of pure joy cleansed the drudgery of the past few days. That blackbird was her kindred spirit, alone and calling to the evening air, celebrating the moment.

Then she looked down at her clothes, disgusted by the smell

of stale sweat and dirt clinging to her. A bath had to be her priority. Decision made, she edged down the steps to the road. The wind was cool on her cheeks and bare arms—she still had on her evening gown from the night of the concert—and there was a touch of ice on her nostril hairs. *Who cares? It's fresh and clean.*

She threw her arms to the lowering sun and twirled around. The sound of laughter stopped her short, and she looked around to see Cam walking towards her, wheeling their bicycles.

"You came, you came!" Gloria rushed towards her, unable to stop the laughter bubbling up and not caring if anyone had witnessed her. But then she halted a couple of steps away to check it was okay to hug Cam in a public street.

Cam had shadows under her eyes, but her deep brown eyes glittered, and her smile was so broad it formed dimples in her cheeks.

"To hell with it!" Gloria flung her arms around Cam's neck.

"Wait. Let me put the bikes down."

Gloria wrenched her bike from Cam's hand and tossed it down at the side of the road. Cam placed hers carefully against a lamppost.

"It's wonderful to see you," Gloria said as she and Cam finally came together in a hug, and she was enveloped in the warm spicy scent of Cam. It suited her well and Gloria snuggled closer to immerse herself in it.

Her nipples hardened at the brushing of her breasts against Cam's chest, and she shivered as Cam feathered a kiss to Gloria's cheek, then held her in her arms, giving her the illusion of safety and freedom.

"Thank you for coming to meet me. I wasn't sure how I was going to get back home - or to work." She pulled back to look Cam in the eye. "Wait. Shouldn't you be on shift? It must be after four o'clock now, but my watch has stopped. I'm babbling, aren't I?"

"It's adorable." Cam squeezed her hands. "You must be

frozen. Here, take my jacket."

Before Gloria could protest, Cam wriggled out of her jacket and held it open. Gloria turned and slipped into it, nestling in the warmth and smell of Cam.

"Thank you. I can't tell you how chuffed I am to be free." Needing both comfort and the reassurance of touch, Gloria held onto Cam's arm.

"Bea took your jacket and bag back to your lodgings but left your bike at the Park, so I thought I'd bring it down for you."

"Thank you." Dread slid over Gloria like a snail's slimy trail. "Have you been suspended from work because of us?"

Cam shook her head. "No. Bea swapped her shift with mine when I said they were letting you out. They're short of people now on our shift with Jamie being gone and you being—"

"Jamie? It was Jamie?" Gloria sagged a little. Confirmation of his betrayal smacked her so sharply, it was like a physical pain in her chest. She'd hoped it hadn't been him.

"Evidently he heard us...in the bathroom. But I'll tell you all about it while we cycle home. Will you be all right on your bike or shall we walk?"

"I'd rather cycle, but I'm not sure I can in this dress."

Cam got to her knees at Gloria's feet; she pulled and pleated the folds of Gloria's dress to make pseudo pantaloons and used her own bicycle clips to secure it all. Gloria couldn't resist trailing her fingers through Cam's hair. That Cam would sacrifice her trousers to being caught in the bicycle chain touched Gloria in a way she didn't believe possible. Cam was so proud of her appearance, she couldn't imagine wanting to keep a marred pair of work trousers, even with clothes rationing. It was an expression of devotion that needed no words.

"Okay?" Cam rose and brushed dirt off her trousers.

"I feel like I've got whiplash from being inside with the threat of hanging one minute and being released with no charge the next. I'm so glad you're here. I feel right wobbly, although I'll be grand when we get going. I want to get out of here as soon as I can."

"Let's take it steady. I'll cycle behind you so I can check on you, and I'll tuck my trousers in my socks, so you won't see that travesty." Cam grinned.

It was the first time Gloria was aware of Cam making a joke about herself, and it warmed her to her soul. She was obviously feeling more relaxed around her. "I'm not entirely sure which way to go," Gloria said.

"I am. We go down here, and it takes us up to the normal road you cycle home from the Park."

"Thanks." With that, Gloria pushed down on her pedals and wobbling just a little, set off towards home and away from the trauma of the last few days. As she cycled, a twinge of guilt kept popping up, as if she'd absorbed the narrative of Carter and his chums. When they dropped down onto the old Roman road, she pushed her head down and sped along as fast as she could. People dressed in their finest clothes were hurrying towards the church in their droves.

She pulled to a stop, and Cam nearly careened into the back of her, avoiding her by scuffing her feet in the gravel.

"Oh, it's Sunday. I'd forgotten that because they don't ring the bells. It doesn't seem the same." An overwhelming urge to attend and sing and give thanks overtook her. Despite everything, she'd never lost her faith. It had kept her going in the bleakest of hours, when despair had gripped her soul that her last home would be an eight-foot cell with bars on the windows, before being dragged to hang from the gallows like a criminal. The faintest pin-light of faith had comforted her; that truth would prevail, that she was being looked after.

"Do you mind if we go into evensong? I need to pray for deliverance from that awful place."

Cam looked up at the bluff building. They hadn't really discussed religion, but Gloria knew Cam didn't attend church regularly. She hoped she would join her, but if she decided to cycle home, Gloria could understand that.

"Of course. As long as you're sure you don't want to go and change first?"

"No time. Come on. Let's leave our bikes in the rack over there."

They entered just as the verger was about to close the door. They smiled and threaded their way to the back. The rector welcomed all to the service and a series of call and responses followed before the choir sang the canticles and psalms. When the choir sang Psalm 23, Gloria couldn't help but let the tears flow. Finally, the fear that had clamped around her heart unshackled and broke away, leaving her shaking. She was relieved to be here, furious at Jamie and at herself for being taken in by him, and thankful to her saviours who had insisted on the truth. She stood in dirty clothes and messy hair, ashamed and overwhelmed but renewed. Cam squeezed her hand, and she took comfort and support from the contact. When the congregation was asked to sing a hymn, they both joined in, their voices blending as normal, and they got a few amazed looks from other members of the congregation. This was joy.

The service finished before it went dark so there was no problem with the blackout. Gloria was grateful the country was on double summertime because the route seemed different, and she needed the visual clues.

When they returned to her lodgings, Gloria looked around with new eyes. They were familiar but it was as if they belonged to the distant past.

"Sit down, you must be exhausted. I'll make the tea." Cam was already filling the kettle at the tap.

She did feel bone-weary as the last of her energy seeped away now she was finally home and the horrible ordeal was behind her.

Cam opened the cupboard above the kettle. "Where's the tea?"

Gloria pointed to a cupboard two along.

"Really? That's illogical." Cam shook her head and retrieved the battered Lyons tea tin and placed it on the counter. Then she opened the other cupboard doors. "Don't tell me: the crockery is in the cupboard under the stairs."

Gloria laughed. "Honestly, it might be easier to make the tea myself."

"No. I said I'd make it. Ah, here we are. The last place I looked." She selected two cups and saucers, having rejected one cup with a chip in it.

"Technically, anything you find is in the last place you look."

Cam raised an eyebrow and her eyes twinkled. "Now, you're just being a smarty pants."

She placed the sugar bowl in front of Gloria. The end of the spitfire-shaped spoon dug into it and reminded her of a cross.

Now wasn't the time to think of Ben.

Gloria picked up the spoon and dragged it through the congealed sugar, unclogging it. Cam was probably cringing that the spoon had obviously been transferred from stirring the tea back into the sugar, but she didn't show any signs of discomfort. "Tell me why they dropped the charges. They didn't say why or what happened."

While Cam bustled around the kitchen preparing the tea and rewashing the crockery, she filled Gloria in with the details she'd missed. It was clear that Cam had been instrumental in securing her release although she didn't boast about it. Gloria's heart was too full to express the love and thanks she had for Cam. Instead, she played with the sugar, pouring it from the spoon into the bowl, and scooping it up again. "Thank you for everything you've done. What I can't get over is Jamie's betrayal. I know you and he never got along, but I always saw him as another brother. I couldn't have been more wrong."

She knew it was true but didn't want to believe it or accept it. Jamie had said he loved her, he'd said he wanted to marry her, yet he'd been betraying his country and her all along. Cam had warned her, had seen through his charm for what it was: brittle bluster.

"He'd originally planned to target Richard, then heard us and in his rage placed it in your locker because he couldn't access mine. So it was anger rather than premeditated if that makes sense?"

"I suppose that makes me feel a little better. Except you said the authorities now know about us, and they're not going to let us be." Her stomach roiled in dread about what would happen.

Cam busied herself with the cups and saucers, clattering them as she straightened them, but her shoulders trembled.

Oh Lord. Cam had given up everything to save her. Bletchley Park was her whole life, that and looking after Aunty Florrie. Almost without thought, Gloria got up and wrapped her arms around her from behind. As expected, Cam was stiff in her arms initially, then softened her stance and relaxed into Gloria. "I'm so sorry and thank you. I know it's nowt like adequate enough to express what I feel about your sacrifice: gratitude, guilt, amazement that you would do that for me. For you to give up everything to save my life. I'll never be able to repay the debt I owe to you."

Cam mumbled something then cleared her throat. "You don't have a debt; I did it willingly. I wish it hadn't come out because they can't ignore it, so I've been wondering about what I can do. I could write to my old Cambridge professor and see if I can go back to my old job. It's unbearable that I wouldn't see you again. I've just found you, just connected on a real level for the first time in my life. You accept me with all my foibles, and I want nothing more than to explore what we have together. But at least now I know you're safe. And if all we have is that one short period of time—"

Gloria nuzzled under Cam's ear. "No. It won't be like that. I'd like you to stay the night if you can, as long as your aunt will be okay?"

"I have to do Bea's midnight shift then get some sleep before our evening shift tomorrow night, assuming we're still required."

"Mrs Jones will be home from church any minute but is working at the factory from eight this evening, so she won't be back until morning. That gives us a couple of hours. Please stay the evening at least."

Cam inhaled deeply. "Okay, thank you."

The kettle whistled on the hob.

"Excuse me." Cam prepared the tea.

Gloria admired the precision of Cam's movement and her watch checking, doubtless to store the data for the next time—if there was a next time. This could all disappear. Their precious time together, where they'd done what they loved, had the independence to be who they were, and made a difference, was hanging by a precarious thread.

She feathered kisses up Cam's neck as Cam cleaned down the surfaces. "Thank you for everything you did, for being you."

The outside latch rattled, and Gloria stepped away just before Mrs Jones entered, her nose tinted pink from the cold. She seemed surprised, but not particularly pleased.

"Oh, you're back. I'm glad you found time to go to church. Who's this?"

Cam swung around to face her and turned on the charm. "Cam Langley. I'm a friend of Gloria's. I've just made her a cup of tea because Gloria is exhausted. Would you like one?"

Mrs Jones looked Cam up and down, and her mouth's grim line signalled her disapproval. A protective flare of anger flashed in Gloria's gut, but before she could say anything, Mrs Jones had whirled around and marched towards the door.

"I don't mind if I do. Now I need to get changed for work."

"May I take a bath, Mrs Jones?"

She swung around to face Gloria and stared as if she was asking for the moon. "Bath nights are on Tuesday."

"I realise that, but I hoped—"

Cam put down the cloth. "I presume you know where Gloria's been for the last couple of days because some man framed her to avoid being caught himself?"

"Difficult to miss given the policemen swarming all around here with their dirty boots trampling on my carpets and turning the place upside down, lifting floorboards, and checking behind pictures with not so much as a please or thank you. It took me two hours to clean up after them. Two hours I don't have, mind you."

"Very disturbing, I'm sure. Can you imagine how much more disturbing and upsetting it was for Gloria to be wrongfully imprisoned without the proper facilities? She needs a bath to wash away all the grime—"

"All right. You've made your point. I'll put the copper on when I go upstairs, but mind you switch it off later, young lady."

Gloria nodded, and Mrs Jones disappeared with much huffing, and puffing, and clomping up the stairs.

This take-charge Cam was thrilling. Gloria joined her at the counter and touched Cam's cheek.

"What?"

"Thank you for being strong when I feel weak, for standing up when all I want to do is sit. For being you."

Cam grinned. "It's a little difficult to be anyone but me. Most people would see that as a disadvantage given how odd I am."

"You're not odd. You're unique, and I love...that about you." She almost said what came to her mind, but was it too soon or too much? She didn't know how Cam felt about her, except maybe she'd demonstrated it through her actions.

"Now, stop it. We need to have this tea poured before Mrs Jones returns. She likes hers white with two sugars. Leave mine to brew; I want tea I can taste. Thank you." Gloria stepped away feeling more charged than she thought. Was it just the impact of having been released, of literally having a new lease of life?

Or were her feelings deeper than that? She'd never said the words before. How did you know if it meant anything? What if Cam didn't or couldn't love her back? How would she feel then? There was too much going on in her head to concentrate. Cam had given up so much to save her. Would she eventually come to resent it? Would Gloria have to return home, or would Cam go back to Cambridge? How would they see each other? Was this all doomed to fail before it started?

"You started it." Cam placed the teapot and strainer in front of Gloria. "I won't get in the way of you and your proper northern cuppa."

"Are you teasing me?"

Cam grinned again. "Possibly. It's just so wonderful to see you here, free and exonerated. I just want to laugh and sing."

Finally, Mrs Jones left for work with a bang of the door and hurried footsteps disappearing down the pavement.

Gloria grabbed Cam's hand. "Come and have a bath with me."

Cam accepted the offer and was tugged up the stairs and into the bathroom before she had time to think. The bathroom was all sparkling tiles and shiny taps, much more modern than Aunty Florrie's, but without the personal touches of a hand painted picture of a sailing boat and lighthouse. Cam shivered. She would miss it if she had to leave where she was.

Gloria inserted the plug and turned on the taps with a gush of water.

Cam pointed at the line painted around the tub at the regulation five inches. "Using Archimedes' principle, with two of us in the tub, we'll displace a greater volume of water, which will give us a deeper bath."

Gloria laughed. "That's such a you thing to say. Are you

suggesting I invite more people to join us in the bath? Mrs Jones, perhaps? Or Bea?"

Cam flicked some water at Gloria, and she squealed.

"No. Just me, more often, until we're told what happens to us."

Gloria's smile faltered, and Cam could have kicked herself for bringing down the mood. Why couldn't she just enjoy the moment instead of worrying about the future?

"Let's not think of that now. We've still got a few hours until you need to leave for the midnight shift." She held up her hand as Cam moved towards her. "Before you kiss me, I must clean my teeth. My whole mouth feels furry and sour-tasting. Choose a towel from the airing cupboard in the landing."

Cam smiled as she obeyed. A thrill went through her at the invitation to kiss, as if there was any other suggestion. Gloria hadn't been put off then. Maybe the lovemaking hadn't been a one-off either, but she couldn't make any assumptions. She would do what she never did and just let flow whatever was to happen. With each minute, Gloria seemed to be rediscovering her normal confident feisty self. The shrunken withdrawn woman she'd met at the steps of the police station was fading, as though her real self were expanding inside her, filling her with her normal energy.

Cam returned to the bathroom, and Gloria grabbed her hand as she cleaned her teeth, as if she couldn't bear for them to be parted.

"Can I use some of your tooth-powder, then at least I'll taste the same."

After Cam patted her mouth dry, Gloria pulled Cam towards her, kissing her as if it might be their last, and Cam relaxed into it, losing herself in the pure physicality of it. It was a kiss to burn away the trauma of the last few days, a kiss to comfort and to heal and Cam leaned into it, wishing it could last forever.

Gloria pulled away suddenly. "Oh, the bath. One moment." She turned off the taps. "It's just over the line. I'm sure you won't tell on me to the line police?"

"If there's two of us in the bath, could we have more?"

"Ready?"

Her seductive eyebrow tweak had a direct impact on Cam's core. Gloria pulled up the fabric of her dress to reveal her long legs as she unclipped her stockings. Slowly, she uncurled the stocking down her thigh over her knee and shin. Cam swallowed hard and sat down on the chair beside the sink. Without taking her gaze away from Gloria, she reached underneath her to remove the towel on the seat.

"Oh, you like that?"

Unsure whether the question was rhetorical or not, Cam nodded. Gloria removed the stocking and let it drop to the floor. Then she placed her other foot on the side of the bath, displaying the enticing flesh at the top of her thighs. She proceeded to unravel the second stocking, simultaneously uncoiling Cam's arousal. The second was despatched with equal disregard for where it landed. Given how difficult it was to obtain stockings, Cam paid a passing thought to carefully picking them up and washing them in the sink by hand, but Gloria had already moved closer and turned around, presenting her back to Cam. She peered over her shoulder and flashed a smile. "Unzip me."

It was a command not a question, and Cam's heart pounded. "Of course." The dress was silky, obviously expensive, and the volume of material indicated it must have been purchased before the war and clothes rationing. It was sacrilege that Gloria had been forced to keep it on since she'd been arrested at the concert.

Gloria shivered as Cam touched her skin.

"Cold?"

"A little."

"Let's get you in the bath." Cam gently tugged at the zip until cloth spilled around Gloria. Cam dropped to her knees and helped Gloria step out of it, then began to fold it.

Gloria leaned on her shoulder. "Leave it. Come up here."

Cam's arousal spiked at the sight of Gloria in lacy underwear.

"I'd hoped you'd be able to see this all properly after the concert."

"You dressed like this for me?"

Now Gloria seemed slightly shy as she nodded.

"You're beautiful," Cam said in a breathy whisper. "And thank you. I can't tell you what it means to me that you did this for me. You're doing things to me that I can't describe."

"Mm."

Gloria brushed her mouth against Cam's, then licked and pulled at Cam's bottom lip, demanding entrance, not that Cam would say no. Eagerly, she met Gloria's tongue with her own and had to inhale sharply as the stirring between her thighs became more insistent. She lost herself in the kiss, surrendering herself to the wonder that was Gloria.

"The water will be getting cold," Gloria said. "And you're overdressed." She pushed Cam's jacket off her shoulders and hung it over the back of the chair. "Hmm, that's better. Let's remove this."

She slipped her fingers into the knot of the tie and unthreaded it, before tossing it over the jacket and returning to unbutton her shirt. She paused by Cam's breasts, tracing the back of her hand over her nipples. Cam arched towards her, breathing hard.

"Nice."

And just when Cam thought Gloria would do something about the ache in her hardening nipples, she returned to the unbuttoning of the shirt. She folded it quickly and placed it on the seat of the chair.

"You're a tease."

"Aye, but I don't see you protesting too much. You need to have your shirt neatly folded if you're going to wear it for the overnight shift."

Cam groaned. "Don't remind me."

"Okay. Pretend I didn't say it then." Gloria's fingers drifted over Cam's belly, causing goosebumps to break out. "You can tell you train hard. Your stomach is so hard and well-defined."

Gradually, she traced her hand lower to the top button of Cam's trousers and unzipped the fly so slowly and provocatively Cam wanted to shout at her to hurry up and take them off, but she held her tongue and stepped out of them. Gloria withdrew and folded the trousers and placed them on top of the shirt.

She studied Cam. "I remember this." Gloria released a little groan as she ran her palm over the jock strap leather pouch, then slid both of her hands down to grasp her buttocks firmly. "This is so sexy. It does something to me. Makes me shiver. I think I'm going to leave it on for a moment."

"You make me shiver, and I'm so wet."

"Mm, I look forward to exploring that."

She ran her hands over Cam's thighs, causing Cam's hips to buck. Again, Gloria didn't dally and stroked down her thighs and calves before she knelt to remove her socks and shoes. When Cam looked down at Gloria at her feet, her knees weakened, and she thought she might not be able to stand. She ran her fingers through Gloria's dark hair and realised that Gloria on her knees in front of her had been a fantasy—a fantasy she'd thought could never be a reality.

Cam glowed, knowing she was having this effect on Gloria, and that it was mutual. It was easy, and relaxed, and nothing like as angsty as she had imagined. Gloria made it easy by her confidence, which seemed to grow with every minute.

"You are stunning," she said and helped Gloria to stand. She pulled her into an embrace, and they swayed together. Cam wanted to savour this memory for ever, kissing as if they'd never stop. She couldn't believe she was welcoming the bodily contact, and that she didn't feel overwhelmed or overstimulated. This was unprecedented on so many levels and a complete revelation. This was freedom.

They parted for breath, and Cam realised Gloria must have undone her bra while she was occupied, as the cotton garment fluttered around her torso. She let it fall, not caring where it landed. She was about to apologise that it was only a simple cotton bra and not like the expensive lace Gloria was wearing, but then she saw the look in Gloria's eyes. Her pupils were wide and shining, full of want. Cam had never been the recipient of such a look before; it had been too dim in the cleaner's cupboard to see. The gift was a delight, warming her heart and heating her own desire, and her clitoris tingled.

Gloria trailed her fingers down Cam's chest and traced the outline of her breast and across the peak of her hardening nipples. Cam arched into Gloria's hands needing her to explore there. "Touch me," she whispered, almost begging.

"With pleasure."

Gloria tweaked and pulled, and Cam responded as though she had a direct connection between her nipples and her clitoris, which had hardened in harmony. Cam let out a breathy moan. "We need to have that bath now, or we won't get there."

Gloria smirked. She was so self-assured it was hard to believe she was the same woman who had been so broken a couple of hours before. Her wrists were raw, and she had a bruise on her side. Cam traced it with her fingers, her arousal subsiding with an increase in her concern and protectiveness.

"They weren't too careful how they treated me. They assumed I was a traitor and deserved everything I got. But I don't want to think of that. You're right, we do need to bathe now, although I do love this on you." Gloria snapped the belt of the jock strap. "But maybe it should come off now."

Cam obliged and wriggled out of it.

Gloria groaned. "Oh, yes. Lucky me," she said quietly.

Cam felt the same, simultaneously wanting to step into the bath and take it slowly so she could spend an age admiring Gloria's body, naked and exposed just for her. "Let's have that bath." Cam ran her fingers up and down Gloria's side, avoiding the bruising and revelling in the goosebumps that followed the path of her exploration. She eased down the straps of Gloria's bra, keeping her eyes fixed on Gloria's darkening pupils. Gloria assisted by undoing the clasp and dropping it to the floor. Now it was Cam's turn to groan in delight at the sensuousness of skin on skin as she cupped the full breasts in her palms. The warmth of Gloria's breath contrasting with the cool air made her shiver. "Let's take these off and warm up in the bath, otherwise we'll need to add extra water and the line police will be after us." She slipped down the lacy underwear, uncovering a dark triangle of hair inviting her in.

"Later," Gloria said and tugged Cam towards the tub. She stirred the water. "Good, it's still warm."

"I'll take the tap end," Cam said and joined her. The water rose, and they sank into it.

"The best example I've seen of Archimedes' principle," Gloria said as she picked up the soap and lathered it round and round before handing it to Cam.

Cam took a smaller amount and replaced the soap on the ledge of the bath. Gloria smothered the lather all over her body, paying particular attention to her nipples and between her thighs. She raised her foot elegantly and lathered between her toes, before repeating it for the other. Cam wanted to kiss all the way down those silky legs.

"I need to wash my hair too. I can't bear to have the taint of that horrible place anywhere on me. I've run out of my shampoo ration so it will have to be soap."

With that she submerged herself in the depths. The water surged and shimmered in a wonderful, distorted image.

That Gloria had invited her into her bath and promise of more to come was more than Cam had ever dared to dream. But this was much more vivid than a dream; the feel of the warm water lapping at her hips, the sight of Gloria's naked body displayed with joy, not shame, the steamed-up mirror, and the mild spicy scent of Pears soap were all too visceral to be dream-like. Gloria hauled herself from the water and shook her head like a dog, laughing when she splashed Cam, then repeated the process. Cam watched, mesmerised by the intimacy and the confidence returning to Gloria with every drop she shook from her hair.

Cam finished off her own ablutions and rose, the cold air causing goosebumps all over.

"Be a darling and hand me my towels."

"Of course." Cam stepped onto the bathmat. She held out the larger towel so Gloria could wrap herself in it, then rubbed Gloria's back to warm her. She handed over the smaller towel then cleaned the bath, removing all traces of soap suds so there was no evidence they had shared the sensuality of a bath.

Gloria expertly twisted the smaller towel and piled it on her head like a turban. "Thanks for doing that. Come into my bedroom. I want to take this further; you've been turning me on all evening. If you want to, of course." She gave a knowing smile.

Cam would never say no to that. "I want to." What had happened to her brain? She'd become completely inarticulate due to the chemicals coursing through her body, drugging her with desire.

She padded behind Gloria, leaving damp footprints on the linoleum and followed Gloria upstairs into the attic bedroom. Gloria turned and dropped the large towel, exposing herself in all her glory. "Shut the door, Cam, and come into my boudoir."

The walls were steep sided to the apex of the roof, so Cam had to duck to traverse the room to the small bed. Gloria reclined on it and spread her legs wide, inviting Cam closer.

In the cleaner's cupboard, it had all been so quick that Cam hadn't had time to relish being with Gloria, and then everything had gone arse over elbow after that. Nothing compared to seeing her now, stretched out on her bed, arms above her head and naked except for the towel still wrapped around her hair. The pose, which could have been from an ancient painting, caused her blood to race, and the display was all for Cam. "How did I get so fortunate?" The words tumbled out before she could stop herself.

Gloria peered up at her. "Are you serious? You're gorgeous, smart, funny, and kind. I'm the lucky one." She pulled Cam toward her and kissed her palm. Gloria patted the mattress, and Cam shuffled closer.

"How come you don't seem nervous? You said you'd never been with a woman before."

"I haven't, but I know my body, and I know what I like. I'm attracted to the person first. And I like you."

Cam's heart lifted with the dazzling smile Gloria sent her way when she spoke. She caught the unmistakeable widening of Gloria's pupils and the glistening evidence of her desire at the apex of her thighs. This was proof that Gloria was serious that she wanted to be with her, and Cam was beginning to believe it. She knelt on the bed and hovered above Gloria. "As you're so much more experienced, what do you like?"

"How about I show you?"

Taking courage, Cam straddled Gloria and sighed when the heat of Gloria's skin matched her own centre as she pressed down. She almost hummed at the sight of Gloria's full breasts and pert pink nipples. "You're beautiful," Cam said, her breath catching on her words.

Gloria reached up and stroked Cam's cheek. "So are you—handsome, I mean. I love your blend of masculine and feminine."

"Thank you. It means so much that you see me." She lowered her head and placed a kiss on Gloria's lips, then made her way down her throat. Gloria raised her head to give Cam better access to the slender column of her neck. She returned to kiss Gloria's mouth, but the gentle languor was gone. Their fevered kiss crushed their lips together and their tongues met. Arousal stirred in Cam's brain and core, and her whole body trembled.

She trailed her fingers down Gloria's face and stroked her lower lip. Gloria sucked in her finger, causing Cam to clench her thighs together. She should not get this aroused so quickly; this was about pleasuring Gloria. Cam trailed her wet fingertip over Gloria's chin and down to her chest, following the path with her mouth until she took Gloria's breast into her mouth, causing Gloria to moan and arch up towards her, demanding more without words. This was communication Cam could easily read. Not needing clues or instruction, she could feel Gloria's response on her skin, by her shudders, by the goosebumps.

Cam ran her hand along Gloria's hips. She glanced up to check Gloria was still okay; her wild dark pupils spurred Cam on.

"I need this. I need you."

That was all the permission Cam required, and she brushed Gloria's thighs, her skin warm and glistening with desire. Gloria spread her legs and pulled Cam's hand to her centre, so swollen and hot.

"Inside me now, please."

Gloria guided Cam's finger into the warm softness within, so welcome, so perfect. Cam thrust in harmony with Gloria's undulations, Cam following Gloria's lead like they did when they sang. It seemed only a few minutes before Gloria's breath came sharp and fast, and she pulled Cam closer like she was trying to consume her. The hot scent of arousal tickled Cam's nostrils and urged her on, which sparked Gloria into bucking her hips frantically. Cam slid her thumb over Gloria's clitoris, and Gloria moaned so deep, Cam thought she might climax herself.

"Faster." Gloria thrashed about, until her half-lidded eyes closed altogether and with a stifled cry, she shuddered and the tension left her body.

It took a few seconds for her to come back around. She stretched and almost seemed to purr, much to Cam's delight.

"That was grand. I can't believe that was your first proper time being intimate."

"I was given instruction and not all of it verbal. Have you ever been told you're bossy?"

"Yes, but never in bed. I loved that you asked and responded to what I wanted and didn't just assume you knew what I liked."

Her previous lovers must have been arrogant, but Cam just preened under the praise.

"Now it's your turn."

Before Cam could let her anxiety take over, Gloria had quickly shifted on top of her. She stared down at Cam, a coquettish smile causing her eyes to gleam.

"Are you ready?" Gloria swept her hand between Cam's thighs. "My, my, you're wet. Delicious."

How could she be so confident with something she'd never done before?

"May I?" Gloria asked.

Cam nodded, the stimulation to her core was sending sensations throughout her body.

"Good."

Gloria slipped between the slickness and gently pushed inside. Their gazes met with an intensity that made her shiver. Her muscles contracted and released around Gloria's finger, welcoming her in, and Gloria set up a rhythm, more allegro than allegretto. She might have said something to that effect but was rendered speechless as Gloria flicked her clitoris, then stroked it with her thumb. Cam whimpered and begged for more as the tension built, suspended like an unresolved chord-progression, leading her higher until it was almost too much. Then, with an intoxicating rush, her brain became a kaleidoscopic mind storm as her climax swept over her, resolving into one tonic chord spanning many octaves, vibrating her whole body and curling her toes.

All the energy seeped out of her body, leaving her buzzing and out of breath. When she finally found her voice again, she turned her face to Gloria. "I can't believe how skilled you are, and how different it is with someone else." Cam opened her eyes to catch Gloria's frown. "I mean, as opposed to pleasuring myself."

"I'm glad you do that, rather than believe all the nonsense they spout about such things being unholy."

"If I didn't, I'd have been celibate my whole life. But this is so different. I've never felt so alive, and I wasn't overstimulated. You were perfect."

"We definitely need a repeat performance, and soon."

"I agree."

Gloria cupped Cam's cheek. "We'll need to make it soon and often, until we know what's happening."

And just like that, the afterglow vanished, and reality came screaming in. This was just a hiatus before their real lives demanded their attention. But if it all collapsed tomorrow and this was all they had, it would have been worth it.

Chapter Thirty-Four

IT FELT LIKE A strange new world when Gloria stepped into the hut, unsure of her reception. She had always enjoyed flouncing in after she'd fixed her make-up, making a bit of an entrance, seeing the delight on Cam's face, passing a jokey interaction with Jamie, and countering Archie's scowls with a smile. Now the dynamic had changed because of a betrayal from within, and she wasn't sure how she'd be received. *Here goes.* She plastered on a smile and opened the door to be smacked by the fug of fumes and smoke. "Good afternoon, all."

Cam sat at her squeaky trestle table by the door, smiling at her with unabashed joy. The temptation to kiss her was overwhelming. It must be so obvious to everyone what they were thinking, what they were feeling, what they'd shared.

Richard puffed on his pipe and looked up. "Good to see you back, Gloria."

"Thanks." Did he know he was Jamie's first target? There was no need to say anything. Sometimes it was kinder to keep a secret where nothing can be gained by divulging it. It would hurt Richard unnecessarily.

Their game of chess lay half finished, gathering dust on the cabinet. It seemed like a lifetime away when she and Cam had played it last. She felt like she was emerging from some long and terrifying nightmare, full of evil spirits and malevolence, and on waking, she'd lost her naivety and optimism. She'd startled awake the previous night, her chest tight and gasping for breath, and had to talk herself down. There's nothing like facing the hangman's noose to make a person reevaluate what's important.

She walked towards Cam. "Chess at supper?"

Cam looked up from her dud message as if she'd forgotten there were other people outside the patterns and complexities of maths that swirled in her oversized brain. Cam blinked then gave Gloria the full and genuine soft smile that she reserved just for her, the one that made her tingle inside.

"Of course. Trying a different opening gambit?"

Gloria laughed and went to her own desk. "You wish."

Archie glowered at her. Did he blame her for Jamie? She had no doubt he would have preferred if she'd been guilty. He seemed like the shadow when the sun disappears: unseen. He must be feeling bereft at losing his hero.

"Welcome back," Archie said. "We missed your input."

She stared at him. "Thanks, Archie, that means a lot."

He shrugged and pointed to the burgeoning duds pile in the centre table. "That's not getting any smaller; we need all the help we can get."

So it wasn't her so much as her brain. At least it was a compliment of sorts. She tried not to stare at the empty desk beside her. Jamie's betrayal sat thick and sticky in her heart. That he'd been willing to blame her after he had been so charming and friendly weighed heavily with her, breaking her trust in her judgement. But he had fooled a lot of people and she needed to put all of that aside, but it was hard. He'd been funny and welcoming and he'd included her. And yet he'd turned out to be a clandestine communist. Given he was born into a wealthy family with all the privilege that entailed, it was a strange choice. To betray his country seemed inconceivable. Ben would never have done that; he'd always been so proud to serve and had willingly sacrificed his own life for the safety of them all. Jamie was nothing like her brother, and now she couldn't imagine how she'd ever thought that.

Drew stopped by her desk as he went to pick up another coded message. "I've arranged for another raseball game with the Yanks. Will you play?"

The churning in her stomach reminded her that nothing was certain, that they were waiting for the hammer to fall on her and Cam, but she managed to smile. "If I'm free, sure."

She exhaled loudly. Maybe it would all settle down now. She couldn't bear to think that she would be stopped from doing this with this group of people, her friends, trying to win the war. After a bit of shuffling, puffing, and tapping of pencils, a stillness fell on the room as they each dropped into the mental space they needed to explore the logic of patterns or codes.

Cam stood and put her completed message into the recently installed pneumatic message carrier, like they had in expensive department stores. Gloria caught her eye, and Cam winked as she drew another code to be solved. That wink told of promises to come. Gloria stared at Cam's bum and wondered if she had her jockstrap on and her buttocks were bare. She licked her lips, and her heart thudded hard. She should definitely not be thinking of that at work when she needed her whole higher brain to function.

Cam swung around to sit. There was no way she would have missed where Gloria's gaze had been. Cam smirked and wriggled a little as she sat and wobbled her desk. How could she be so calm? It was purgatory sitting here, wanting to undress her, to make love to her again. Cam shook her head slightly and drew her brows together as if telling her to keep working. And she was right, of course, so Gloria dutifully bowed her head. They needed to work as much as they could now in case it was snatched away from them.

As if she had willed the evil spirit to reappear, the door burst open and Carter entered. Gloria groaned, and Archie flashed a glance at her.

"Camilla Langley and Gloria Edwards, we need you in Mr Needleman's office."

Cam's eyes widened and signalled the same terror Gloria

felt as their gazes locked. Were they not even going to get a day to redeem themselves? Was this the end? She replaced the message she'd been working with onto the centre table and popped her personal items into her bag. She flashed a hollow smile at Richard as she followed Cam and Carter out. Why hadn't they just telephoned to ask them over? Was it so they couldn't confer about their stories. Perhaps they should have talked about it, but they'd been too busy. Despite everything, she couldn't hide her smile at the thought of being with Cam.

"What are you smirking at?"

If she had it in her to kill someone, now would be the time and Carter would be the person. "Nothing. I trust this is important as we're trying to do critical war work without being disturbed by your malicious mischief-making."

Cam shot her a worried look, but she'd had enough with this farce.

A few minutes later, they were let into the office in the upper floor of the main mansion. Mr Needleman looked over his glasses at them as they sat on the two chairs at the other side of the desk. Carter sat on Mr Needleman's right, and another man sat on his left. The leer in the new man's eyes and the barely disguised smirk suggested he was getting some titillating pleasure from this. *Creep.*

Miss Brown sat at a side table, her pencil and pad at the ready to take notes.

"Miss Langley and Miss Edwards, thank you for coming. Don't look so petrified, Miss Edwards. This is just an internal welfare matter, not a criminal charge." He gestured to the man sitting to his left. "This is Mr Taylor; he's head of welfare." Mr Needleman glanced over at Carter. "Mr Carter has made an allegation about you both that came about as a result of the inquiry into the Jamie Gordon case. His contention is that your... relationship ... leaves you open to blackmail and that you are therefore a security risk and should lose your clearance to work as codebreakers. Sorry, but I have to ask if it's true what he suggested you were doing in the cleaner's cupboard?"

Gloria's heart raced at being back in the nightmare of being questioned and her life hanging in the balance. She couldn't breathe and sweat formed on her forehead. A hand on her forearm steadied her. She inhaled sharply as she tried to take a full breath into her lungs but they felt crushed by a tight band.

"I was upset," Cam said. "Gloria was comforting me. It was me who initiated more...intimacy. Please leave her out of this; she's been through so much already with the wrongful arrest and the threats."

Even now Cam was trying to protect her and take the fall for both of them, although she had so much more to lose. Gloria tried to speak, but it was all she could do to breathe.

"Threats?" Mr Needleman frowned.

"Mr Carter was determined to fit the facts to the story he concocted in his head and was happy to see Gloria hang for it. He threatened her life and seems to believe that unless you were born in the south of the country to a well-to-do family, you can't possibly be trustworthy. Yet the traitor was a friend of his from his golf club. It makes me wonder if he was trying to cover for his friend—"

"That's ridiculous," Carter said.

"You can't make that accusation," Mr Needleman said. "Strike it from the record, please." He looked down at the manila file on his desk. "Thank you for your perspective—"

"What we did was not illegal in this country, and therefore would not make us at risk of blackmail. Some people may not approve, but Gloria sings in the church choir every Sunday and her brother was killed in the Battle of Britain, sacrificing himself for this country."

Cam was on a roll now. Gloria had never seen her so fuelled by anger, judging by the tight grip on her arm. Her eloquent protectiveness was enthralling.

"I'm sorry about your brother," Mr Needleman said.

She nodded, but her throat was still constricted so she couldn't speak.

"We're fighting against a prejudice and ideology that underpins a monstrous regime, yet these suggestions are targeting the exact same prejudices against women, against anyone who is other—"

Mr Needleman held up his hand. "Miss Langley, you are a remarkable...person: bright, brave, and loyal. I will never forget the sight of you knocking out a man twice your size. You argue the case so passionately, and you impress me immensely, but those are not deciding factors. I understand that when you worked for Dilly, God rest his soul, you were instrumental in the breakthrough on the Italian navy, and that level of intellect is desperately needed at this crucial time in the war. Your work is vital, and we need your skill and expertise." He glanced towards Gloria. "And you have more than proven your worth in the short time you've been here. We need you both. Case dismissed. *But* please keep your extracurricular activities off-site. I can't deal with another complaint from the housekeepers. Please return to your work. Mr Carter, a moment, please."

Carter looked like he'd just swallowed a bucket of lemons. Gloria hoped he wouldn't take it out on them in future inspections. She couldn't believe there were going to be no further implications. "We're free to go?" The relief had finally loosened her vocal cords, enabling her to breathe again.

"Yes. Thank you for your work and discretion. Needless to say, anything said in this room is confidential. I don't need to remind you that you've signed the Official Secrets Act. Good evening."

Cam tugged at Gloria's sleeve as if she couldn't escape fast enough. Gloria followed her out, surprised that Cam skipped out of the main front doors into the pitch black.

"What did he mean about knocking a man out?" Gloria asked in the darkness, feeling in the dark for Cam's hand. She gripped it tight, and Cam's fingers folded over hers.

"When Jamie didn't appreciate being called out he took me at gunpoint, and they were too scared to do anything about it, so when he was distracted I landed an upper cut on him to stop him."

Her voice was so nonchalant, but Gloria felt sick. "He held you at gunpoint?"

Cam grunted. "Sorry if your hero let you down."

"He was never my hero. He was a so-called friend who reminded me of my brother. But I realise now he was nothing like my brother either. The real hero is you." That was blindingly obvious and had been for a while. "You would have given up everything you hold dear to help me, even risking your life to save me. *You're* my hero. Thank you."

"You're welcome."

"I can't tell you how relieved I am this is all over."

"Now will you start locking your cupboard?"

"Yes. I'll buy myself a padlock on our next day off. Would you like to come with me to choose it?"

"I'd love to."

It was funny how that option sounded like a date. Gloria's heart sped up.

"When I was locked up in that horrible cell, I promised myself if I got out alive, I'd be grateful and would take the consequences of losing my job and being separated from you, hoping that at some point, we could reconnect. Now all my wishes are granted: my freedom, my job, and the possibility of being with the brave, handsome woman beside me." She squeezed Cam's hand in the darkness, taking courage from Cam's even breathing and the warmth of her palm in hers. "This is the best day of my life."

Chapter Thirty-Five

THAT EVENING, GLORIA'S LANDLADY came into the lounge where Gloria was reading. "Gloria, it's for you. It's your father. And don't let that cat scratch my furniture."

"No, Mrs Jones." Gloria placed Bea's stray on the rug and stood to take the phone call. What did her da want with her? She had nothing else to say to him. If he was going to try and get her to come back, he would be unsuccessful. "Hello, Da."

"What's this about you being incarcerated? No daughter of mine will be found guilty of treason."

"I was framed, unfortunately, but it's all sorted now."

"I've never been so ashamed. It caused your mam to flip. She's gone down to live with our Ben's Ailish, leaving me all alone to fend for myself. It's not right."

Ah, so it was his self-interest that had stirred this phone call. "Isn't Mrs Henderson still there? And maybe Nancy Ramsbottom would come along and help look after you. How many women do you need running around after you?" She heard a sharp intake of breath down the phone. He clearly hadn't expected her to be so feisty. Well, tough. She'd had enough of pandering to him and his control. "If Mam has gone to help Ailish with the bairn, that's great news. She seemed really close to him, and it will be best all around. You'll all be happier."

"But what about you marrying Stanley Arkwright?"

"This again? I've already told you that I'll never marry him. I'm twenty-one now so I'm an adult, earning my own money and doing important war work. Offer him the job to take over when you retire. Or don't. Do what you like, but it's nowt to do with me."

She smiled as she recognised her own strength. He no longer had the power over her, or her mam. Gloria would write to her, congratulating her on her escape.

"You're not coming back?"

She almost felt sorry for him. *Almost.* "No, Da. When the war's over, I may come to visit, but that's no longer my home."

"What about the young man you were seeing?"

"It appears he bamboozled everyone; he was the one who tried to frame me."

"He what? No man will ever do that to my daughter."

Gloria twisted the cord around her fingers tighter and tighter until she thought she'd stop all the circulation. "Da, I don't need you to do the protective bit. I'm fine." *I have my own protector. A rather gorgeous, fascinating protector.* The thought made her smile. Not that she'd ever tell her da about Cam. But she didn't care what he thought. The realisation was liberating. She was free of him and his expectations; she was free to create her own life. And she would.

"So you're settled there then?"

"Yes. I am. I'm happy here, I work hard, and I sing in the church choir."

"So you won't be coming back?"

"No, Da. My life's here now. Goodbye."

"Aye, well. All the best then."

And that was that, she thought as she replaced the receiver. Surprisingly, she felt no regrets, just sadness and a sense of relief that she hadn't had another argument with him. She was about to return to the sitting room when Mrs Jones appeared at the kitchen doorway.

"I'm sorry, but I can't have you in my house anymore."

Gloria's heart sank. "What? Why?"

"It's too much trouble what with the police coming in turning the house upside down. Besides, I've let out your room. Talk to welfare at that place of yours and see if you can arrange alternative accommodation. I'll give you a week to find something more suitable. Goodnight, and don't forget to put the guard in front of the fire when you go up."

As if she could read now. She stared at the fire as it crackled and hissed with the brownish coal they could get on ration. Lovelace jumped back onto her lap and proceeded to twirl around until she made herself comfortable. Gloria stroked her, eliciting a purring of contentment, and she sorted through the tumble of her emotions.

Sometime later the door squeaked open, and Bea popped her head around. "Hello, I thought it might be you in here. Lovie's made herself at home on you, I see." Bea frowned. "Are you all right?"

"It appears I'm being thrown out of my lodgings."

Bea plopped down on the armchair on the other side of the fire. "What?"

"Mrs Jones doesn't want the trouble I caused, and she's let out my room."

"Oh, that's ridiculous. Wait, she was talking about her sister coming to stay. I bet you that's the real reason. I'm happy to share a room with you. You don't snore, do you?"

Gloria laughed despite herself. "You're a good egg. Thanks, I'll bear that in mind, but I might see if welfare have another room. I'm sure you want your privacy. I don't understand why she wasn't direct with me. Why don't southerners ever say what they mean? If the room's taken just say so and make it clear. I'll talk to welfare tomorrow."

Bea beamed a mischievous grin. "Or maybe you could ask Cam if her aunt has a spare room."

"I can't do that."

"Why not? I'm sure Florrie would love to have you there too, especially if you sang at home together. And I know Cam would love you being there."

"I couldn't intrude."

"You wouldn't be intruding. I'm sure Cam would welcome it. She's very fond of you."

Gloria twisted her fingers around each other. "And I of her. Well, more than fond. I love her."

Bea grinned. "Good. In that case, you should talk to her about moving in."

"You make it sound so simple."

"It is. But you can't take Lovelace with you, however much she thinks she's your cat."

Gloria laughed. "I can't imagine her around the chickens. I'll miss you."

"I'll miss you too, although they might transfer me to your shift to replace Jamie, and Richard might finally be promoted to the shift supervisor. About time too. He should have been there in the first place, being a very respected Cambridge don, but instead they appointed Jamie."

"Did you know Richard was Jamie's first target to frame when he realised the net was closing in?"

Bea gasped and smoothed down her skirt. "No, I didn't. That does shock me. But I guess it was easier to push the blame on the homosexual."

Gloria only half-listened as Bea continued. Living with Cam and her delightful Aunty Florrie could be fun. They could sing together, play chess, and more. Could she ask? She decided she would see if the opportunity arose. Surprised, she noticed that Bea had stopped talking, and she looked across, sheepishly.

"You're besotted, aren't you? Talk to her after your next shift. Tell her how you feel. Be honest and see where you get to. And if you still need a place to stay after that, I'm sure we can talk Mrs Jones into letting us share a room."

"Thanks." It was kind of Bea, but if there was any room she wanted to share, it was Cam's. The thought made her tingle all over. She checked her watch. It wasn't that late. Maybe she could call now and tell her how she felt. "I might talk to her now: it's our day off tomorrow."

Bea beamed. "'We must take the current when it serves or lose our ventures.' Go, talk to her now."

"Shakespeare again?"

Bea nodded and clapped her hands together, shooing her out.

The air was nippy as she stepped out into the dark street. Her footsteps echoed on the empty pavement, and she squinted to make out shapes of obstructions on her way to the phone box. It was no longer scarlet; it had blacked-out windows and had been painted black except the bottom couple of feet, which were white so that it was visible in the blackout.

She picked up the receiver, put the expected coins in the slot, and piled a few extra on the side in case she needed them. Gloria shifted as she waited, half hoping Cam wouldn't pick up. Why had she needed to talk to her so urgently? It was all Bea's doing; she was such a romantic. Gloria should have waited until tomorrow to talk to her.

"Bletchley 214, Cam speaking."

That voice. Gloria's knees went weak. She pressed button A, and the coins rattled inside as the call was put through. She could hardly speak through the pent-up emotions gathered in her throat. "Cam, it's Gloria."

There was a sharp intake of breath. "Is everything okay?"

"Yes, yes, it's fine. I wanted to speak to you before our next shift." She could almost imagine Cam frowning, trying to discern the emotions behind the words. Why couldn't she just utter the words?

"Can't we talk at work?"

"We were asked not to do anything personal at the Park."

"Oh."

"Cam, I like you. I really like you. I'd like to get to know you better. No, I more than like you. I can't breathe thinking about you. I feel bereft when we're apart, as though I'm missing my harmony.

I'm rambling. Maybe this would be better face-to-face."

"I was going to go for a hike tomorrow morning, then have a late Sunday dinner. Aunty Florrie likes a lie-in on a Sunday. Would you like to come?"

"Ooh, I'd love that. Can we go to Bow Brickhill? I'm told it's the highest peak around here, and I'm missing the Yorkshire moors."

"Of course. Come here first. How does eight thirty sound?"

"Great. I'm looking forward to it."

"I feel you're working up to delivering bad news, that you like me but—"

"There's no but. I more than like you. I want to spend more time with you, sing, play chess, and help with the chickens. I'm trying to say—"

The pips sounded on the telephone, and she pushed more coins in.

"I love you," she said as the coins failed to register and the call disconnected.

She pressed button B but no coins were refunded. She banged the side of the box and sighed. That was the last of her small change. Some kid had probably put a cloth in the machine to catch any returned coins.

Gloria replaced the handset into the receiver and leaned against the taped-up glass. A broad grin settled on her face. Maybe Cam hadn't heard, but she had a date for tomorrow; a date with a delectable gentlewoman she was in love with. Having uttered those three words aloud, the certainty of it clicked into place like a solved cypher, and it filled her soul.

Chapter Thirty-Six

As they cycled to Bow Brickhill ready for their hike, Cam churned through what Gloria had said yesterday. Her initial anxiety had been allayed, but Cam had tossed all night. What had Gloria wanted to say before she was cut off? They couldn't talk properly in front of Aunty Florrie, and Gloria seemed preoccupied as they cycled to the start of the hike, staring out over the fields and enjoying the early summer sunshine.

With the butterflies fluttering from bush to bush, bees buzzing, and the sweet smell of meadow flowers, it seemed incongruous there was a war going on. They came up to a crossroads of two similarly sized country lanes. The hill, because that's all it was despite being the only high ground around here, still seemed to be off to the left. The short cut was left but Cam cycled forward.

"Which way do we go now? I know they don't have signs anymore in case of invasion, but this isn't the way I thought we'd go," Gloria said as she drew level with Cam.

"Ah, I'm taking you a slightly more scenic route, and then we'll take the short cut back home. Aunty Florrie said she's looking forward to seeing you properly again." Cam slowed her pace a little so they could talk easily. "I'm worried about what you want to say. I hope it's not going to be that you don't want to see me anymore, except at work, of course. It's just that I really like having you around. You understand me, my foibles and oddities, and it doesn't seem to bother you. I like your direct speaking and your intelligence. I like not having to explain everything because you know. Even if we didn't work together, I'd still like to see you and be with you. I'm not sure what will happen after the war. Now the

Americans are here, it will surely only be a matter of time before we get victory. I don't know what will happen then. I dread you going back to Yorkshire."

"I won't be going back to Yorkshire. I told my da I could never live with him again, and my mam has gone to live with my sister-in-law to help with my nephew. But I do have to move out of my digs. My landlady says she's rented out my room. I'm sure welfare could find me a dorm or other lodgings somewhere –"

"You must come to us. I'm sure Aunty Florrie would be delighted–"

"I wouldn't want to put you out."

"We'd love you to come. Gloria, I don't know what you're going to say but I have feelings for you. I love you–"

"I love you."

They both spoke simultaneously and laughed, braking to bring their bikes to a halt.

Cam felt weak at the knees and thought maybe it was her wishes rather than what she thought she heard. "Did you really just say you love me? Because I love you."

Gloria stretched over her crossbar to place a gentle kiss on Cam's lips, a kiss that opened her world, that hinted at promise and potential, and she loved it. "Thank you," she murmured against Gloria's lips. As Gloria pulled back, Cam retrieved a handkerchief from her pocket and handed it over. "Sorry, I've smudged your lipstick."

Gloria took it and dabbed around her mouth, but she missed a bit. Cam traced her finger over her soft skin and erased it.

Gloria snatched Cam's fingers and kissed them. "Who cares? I'm proud to have my lipstick smudged by you. This is such a thrill. But I guess we ought to continue if we're going to get back in time for lunch with Florrie." With that, she pushed off and started to sing "Here Comes the Morn."

Cam followed and joined with her part, though it wasn't a flawless performance. When they finished, Gloria repeated it again, and they arrived at the base of the hill, laughing breathlessly. As they pulled up to a fence, another couple clapped.

"Good morning! Very nice rendition."

"Thanks. I'm sure it'd be more musical if I wasn't gasping for air," Gloria said and laughed as she dismounted.

Cam padlocked their wheels to the upright of the fence. Gloria was much better than she was at making small talk.

"You're not from around here, are you? Yorkshire?" the middle-aged man asked.

His wife bobbed her head next to him as if she spent her life agreeing with everything he said. Perhaps she did.

"Aye. Bradford." Gloria smiled, and her accent seemed to get stronger.

"My sister lives in Scarborough. What brings you down this neck of the woods?" He must have caught sight of Cam's scowl. "Oh, sorry, I guess I shouldn't ask. Well, enjoy your walk up the hill."

"Thank you. Have a good walk yourselves."

"And please feel free to serenade us again. It's lovely to hear such beautiful singing."

Gloria laughed and shared farewells. Cam held open the gate until Gloria entered and closed it behind her.

"I'd forgotten how polite you are," Gloria said as she took the uphill path.

"Really?" Cam felt the hackles rising, waiting for the judgment to come flying at her, but Gloria turned and held out her hand.

"I can't tell you how lovely it is to be treated with respect and consideration," Gloria said.

Her fingers were so soft, not calloused and grazed like Cam's. She hoped her palm wasn't too sweaty as Gloria grasped her hand. She looked at Gloria, but there was no disgust there, just unabashed delight at being here. Gloria was so courageous, not seeming to care who saw them.

"Are you okay holding hands?" Cam asked.

"Why not? It's pretty private walking through these shrubs. Is it like this all the way up? I was hoping it would be barren and desolate like the moors around my home. It's hardly got the spectacular grandeur and wildness of Yorkshire. It's more like a pimple, really." Gloria dropped Cam's hand, shrieked, and ran up the path.

Cam gave chase and caught her easily. She pulled her close, intending to tickle her until she submitted, but as Gloria turned, she kissed Cam with a ferocity that radiated throughout her whole body. Cam loved Gloria, and it was reciprocated. She couldn't quite believe it, and yet Gloria was here, holding her hand, kissing her passionately in the slight breeze. Gloria always took her by surprise and opened up a new world in her exuberant zest for life that Cam responded to. That she loved her too was thrilling.

Then Gloria pulled away and ran on. All Cam's emotions unravelled, set free into the wild air, and she opened her lungs to sing at the top of her voice in delight and unfettered joy.

Gloria harmonised, taking each note as if she knew exactly where Cam was going to go with the melody. Together, they created magic. Gloria stopped singing as she reached a steeper part of the slope. Served her right for being so smug and superior about the Yorkshire hills. Cam grinned then powered past Gloria to reach the summit first, delighted she wasn't panting at all.

"Okay. I submit. You win. You're fitter than I am and—oh, wow. There *is* a view from up here. How wonderful. I feel like I'm on top of the world...in more ways than one. Cam, I love spending time with you."

"You do?"

"I really do." She grabbed Cam's hands and pressed them over her heart. "Believe me. You light me up, and I feel so alive when I'm around you. Can't you feel how hard my heart is beating? And that's not just from the run up the slope either. You have my heart, my soul, and body."

Cam shook her head to ensure she wasn't in a dream. "I never thought anyone would want me or like me for me, so I closed off that part of myself..." Worried she was blurting her insecurities, she whispered, "Sorry. Is that too much?"

"No. Thank you for opening up to me and for trusting me. For loving me."

Gloria kissed her again, and Cam absorbed everything she could about her, to savour and remember for ever: the way her curls blew in the wind; the fresh scent of her Pears soap; the warmth of her body; how her dark eyes smouldered with desire. Her breath caught, and her heart raced. Cam was so tempted to take Gloria into the bushes to make love in the open, but her brain finally kicked in. "We've been in enough trouble with the law without being arrested for indecent conduct. We should wait. Let's go back to Aunty Florrie's."

There was a cough and cracking of twigs from behind a bush. Gloria stepped away then swiped at Cam's face where some lipstick had transferred.

"Is my lipstick smeared?" she asked.

Cam wiped away the telltale smudges just as a group of walkers climbed to the top. "Good job there were all these bushes, or they would have seen us for miles," Cam whispered as the group approached them.

Gloria started off down the track. "Good morning. Lovely day, isn't it?"

The walkers returned the greetings. Cam chuckled as she followed. Gloria didn't care what people thought; she was brazen, bold, and beautiful, and she revelled in life. Cam wanted to absorb her energy, take her in her arms and make love to her.

"I'll race you down," Gloria called. "Walking only—no running."

"You cheat. You've got a head start on me—"

"You've got longer legs. Are you scared to lose? Loser washes up at work for a week."

Cam matched her pace and as they approached the gate

where the bikes were parked, she slowed slightly so Gloria could triumph.

Gloria turned, eyeing Cam suspiciously. "You let me win."

"You'll never know. I'd definitely beat you home on the bike, but let's just enjoy the ride. How wonderful to be outside with natural light and no cigarette smoke, where we can breathe and enjoy the view. And I did enjoy the view all the way down the hill."

"I thought as much. You were checking my behind, weren't you?"

Cam laughed. "I couldn't possibly say."

The journey home was much quicker, and it didn't seem half an hour before they were wheeling their bikes into the outbuilding. When they opened the kitchen door, a wall of heat blasted them, and a fog of water vapour rose from the vegetables boiling on the hob. The smell of roast lamb greeted them. Cam wasn't going to tell Gloria that they'd been saving their meat rations all week so she could come to lunch.

"Umm, that smells delicious," Gloria said as they entered the kitchen.

Aunty Florrie stood by the oven, her face as flushed as her flowery pink pinafore. "Oh, good, you've come back in time to take the meat out for me, Cam. Now I can make the gravy. Hello, Gloria, dear. It's lovely to see you again."

Cam strode to the sink to wash her hands while Aunty Florrie gave Gloria a kiss on the cheek. "Aunty Florrie, Gloria is having to move from her lodgings. She was thinking about applying for a transfer to another accommodation—"

"Why don't you come here, dear?"

The immediacy of her offer warmed Cam to her soul. Aunty Florrie welcomed and collected people to her heart, just like she'd done for Cam.

"Cam said you'd say that. But I wouldn't want to put you out."

"It's no trouble. We have a spare room, but it might need a bit of a clear out to make it presentable." Her face crinkled into a cheeky grin, activating her deep wrinkles. "Or you could just share with Cam?"

Cam stared, feeling the heat rushing to her cheeks. "Aunty Florrie, you can't say that!"

"Oh, come on, dear. I can see how close you two are; there's no fooling me."

"How do you know?"

"I've known about you for years, Cam. Whatever cock and bull story your parents gave as an excuse as to why they had to leave you behind on their travels, their judgement couldn't have been more obvious. But their loss is my gain, and I've seen the two of you together. You're like two sides of the same coin. Now don't just stand there with your mouth open. Will you take the meat out of the oven? We need to eat before the vegetables go to mush."

Cam snatched up the thick cloth and carefully removed the tray from the oven. The liquid spat and crackled, and the rich aroma of meat caused her mouth to water. "Why didn't you say anything?"

"I always hoped you'd tell me. But I realise it's difficult."

"And you don't mind?"

Aunty Florrie laughed. "No, of course not. I love you. Who *you* are doesn't change that. Now, will you two go and lay the table while I finish the gravy, please?"

She made a shooing motion, and they retreated to the dining room. Cam opened the canteen with the best silver cutlery. Auntie Florrie had known for ages. Cam had wasted so much anguish trying to hide who she was, and it didn't matter, but she couldn't explore her feelings about that now. "I'll spread out the tablecloth if you can give the cutlery a quick polish with this cloth. Aunty always likes to have a proper set to the table. We're having a main course and pudding."

Gloria picked up a fork and burnished it before setting it down. "Do you think Florrie is like us?"

Cam frowned as she straightened the material, so the overhang was equal either side of the table. "What do you mean?"

"It's just the way she laughed when you mentioned it, as though nothing you could do would surprise her."

"How can you get that just from one sentence?"

Gloria straightened the knife she'd polished. "Intuition."

"I don't have that."

"Not about people maybe, but definitely about patterns and codes."

"But I've never cracked the code of relationships."

Gloria took her in her arms, and Cam didn't care if Aunty Florrie came in or not as she responded with a kiss, deep and intense and full of hope and expectation for the future.

Gloria pulled back and smiled at her. "You've certainly cracked the code of love."

Cam groaned.

"What? Too corny? Okay then. You've decrypted my heart."

And somehow, it was like when a code revealed its secrets. It was impossible not to see the truth as the jumbled words gained meaning. They had unlocked the most beautiful message. They loved each other.

Epilogue

8 May 1945, Victory in Europe Day, London

GLORIA PULLED CAM CLOSE as they weaved through the crowds. She could see Cam getting more agitated by all the people, so she tilted her head at Richard, wordlessly asking him to hurry. Cam had gone very pale, and beads of sweat formed on her forehead. Her mouth was set in a thin line of determination.

"Not long now, I promise. We're going down that side street over there," Richard said.

Across the road, revellers propped each other up and engulfed the cars trying to inch their way through. The noise of out of tune popular songs assaulted her ears. Richard led the way, threading through a disappearing gap in the churning mass of people.

A drunken sailor grabbed Gloria on her way through. "Hello, darlin'. Up for a good time?"

Gloria shrugged him off. "Having one already, ta."

Cam gave a thin smile as Gloria tugged her through the crush of happy faces and finally into the dark alley. "This is like my worst nightmares."

Gloria squeezed her hand. "I know you'd prefer to be back home with Aunty Florrie and the chickens, but there is only one Victory in Europe night. This is history."

Richard smoothed down his thinning hair. "True. Now we just need to finish off the war in Japan."

He seemed slightly out of step with all the beautiful people in uniform. Sometimes Gloria wished they had a uniform. People would treat them with more respect because their service and sacrifice was more obvious. She hurried after Richard who'd raced down the cobbled street towards an unmarked black door.

"Do you know what you're doing after the war?" Gloria asked as they fell into step, her thoughts and anxieties bubbling to the fore.

Richard puffed on his pipe. "Yes, I'm going back to Cambridge in October. I'm hoping I can entice you back to my department, Cam. We need your skills."

Cam inhaled and raised her hand. "But—"

"And Gloria. If you'd like to study for a degree, I'm sure Girton or Newnham college would welcome you with your talents, especially if I put in a good word."

Gloria had forgotten that Richard was a world-renowned mathematician. For the past few years they'd all been equal, working towards the same goal. Now the new realities were setting in. She couldn't go back to what she'd been doing before the war. She'd tasted freedom and didn't want to give it up. It was in these offhand unscripted conversations that opportunities often arose, and she didn't intend to squander them. "I might take you up on that, depending on what Cam decides to do."

Cam exhaled, and they shared a look full of gratitude and longing.

Richard laughed. "You two are inseparable. It's not a very well-hidden secret that you live together."

Cam sniffed. "We live with my aunty."

Richard winked. "Is she your chaperone?"

Gloria shared a shy glance with Cam. Her clothes were stored in the attic room, but they slept—and did other things—in Cam's big bedroom. Afterwards, when they were sweaty and shaking with the afterglow, she would snuggle into Cam's arms and be surrounded by Cam's scent and love. Fortunately, Auntie Florrie was quite deaf or chose not to hear.

Cam lifted an eyebrow that expressed so much. She was

clearly remembering their lovemaking this morning before their new cockerel, Winston, crowed.

Richard chuckled. "Come on, before you get us all arrested." He knocked on the door.

Gloria nudged him. "Are you going to tell us about this friend of yours we're meeting here?"

Richard's whole face lit up from within, shedding years from his face. "His name's Hal, and he's here with another friend from his squadron."

"So you've got yourself a fly boy then?"

"I have."

A metal shutter slid across at eye level, and Richard gave a code. Within seconds, bolts unfastened, and the door opened a crack.

"Don't dawdle," someone barked from behind the door.

Inside was cramped and chaotic. Gloria wasn't sure how long Cam would cope. Cam was already receiving admiring glances, although she seemed oblivious. You can't have her, she's mine, Gloria wanted to shout.

Men slow-danced with men. Women kissed women. Some were dressed in three-piece suits but none were as handsome as Cam, whose shoulders relaxed a few inches as she probably realised they were amongst their kind.

Richard pushed through the dancers to the far corner. A younger RAF pilot caught sight of Richard, flung his arms around him and kissed him on the lips. This was another side to Richard, not the slightly stuffy mathematician who chain-smoked a pipe. Richard turned around, his joy radiating from every pore as he turned to Gloria and Cam. The RAF officer's friend had moved forward to meet them too.

Richard reluctantly released his officer. "This is Hal and his friend Terry. They're in the same squadron."

"Pleased to meet you Hal and Terry. Which squadron?" Gloria asked.

"Number one squadron flying spitfires in Tangmere," Terry said, straightening to attention.

Gloria had to breathe more slowly and inhale deeply. "I know it's a bit of a long shot, but did you know Ben Edwards?"

"Edwards? Yeah, he was a great guy. How do you know him?"

"He was my brother."

Terry's smile faltered. "I'm really sorry for your loss. We still miss him."

"Do you know what happened? We never got a full answer."

Terry blinked as if he was debating with himself how much to reveal, or maybe he was reliving the moment, which couldn't be easy.

"There was nothing he could do. It was our third sortie that day. It was the height of the blitz, and the air was full of planes. He said on the radio he had one in his sights. The next thing, his plane was on fire and he was going down. I guess he didn't see the one behind him. I'm sorry, but it was really quick."

Relief and sorrow rushed over her, and Gloria held her hand to her chest before she could speak again. "Thank you. Maybe I can take your details down. I think it might help my mam; she's never got over his death."

"Of course. Here's my better half with our drinks."

He seemed relieved to change the subject. It must've been so hard for him for them to see so much death and to lose friends in the blink of an eye. She wasn't aware she'd started crying until Cam offered her a handkerchief. "Thanks."

"Do you need to go for a walk in the fresh air?" Cam asked.

"No, but thank you. Enough of that. Ben would have loved this celebration. I'm not sure what he would've said about us. Probably, 'I've seen everything now.'"

Cam squeezed her hand, and the pressure of her long fingers and warm skin grounded Gloria.

Terry accepted his drink from the man whom he introduced as Mike. "Pleased to meet you."

His accent was pure East London, not what she expected in a flying officer. It was yet another example of how the war had shifted the perceptions about class. Da was probably disappointed the war had ended as his gravy train would come to a halt. He'd have to go back to making belts and chains for agriculture and industry.

Two women in the smart uniform of the air transport auxiliary joined them.

"These are my dear friends, Beryl and Odette," Mike said. "They're the real pilots among us, flying anything to anywhere for the ATA."

Gloria had a little uniform envy. These were the glamour girls, so smart and self-assured. By contrast, she and Cam couldn't talk about what they did; they just had the secret knowledge that what they did mattered.

She spared a glance at Cam, who was asking one of the women, Beryl, about flying different aeroplanes.

The other woman, Odette, turned to Gloria. "What have you been doing during the war?"

Faced with that difficult question to answer, Gloria said, "Just working in the Foreign Office." Hoping Odette didn't ask for further details, she smiled. "How about you?"

"We've just flown a plane back from Belgium."

The woman's accent was too thick for Gloria to discern its origin. "Is that where you're from?"

"No. Originally, I'm from France. We didn't land there, but I couldn't believe the destruction we saw from the air. But now it can be rebuilt." A sorrowful expression slipped across her face, and she sipped her drink.

"Will you return there?" Gloria asked.

"No, I'm hoping to stay in England and fly with Beryl."

Odette looked across at Beryl with such an adoring expression, Gloria had to grin. She probably had the same doe-eyed look when she gazed at Cam.

Cam must have seen Gloria staring as she raised an eyebrow at her and nodded at Richard, sharing the joy at seeing him come alive as he chatted to his young man. She conveyed so much without words. Cam had come to this noisy place with people she didn't know, and it was probably purgatory for her, but she hadn't complained. It must be love.

More people squashed into the bar area, and Cam put her arm around Gloria's waist. The sensation of the physical touch in public caused Gloria's heart to race. When there was a pause in the conversation, Gloria whispered, "Thank you for coming, Cam, even though you probably hate this. I love you."

Cam directed her intense focus on Gloria and everything else drifted into background noise, constant but irrelevant.

"I love you too, Gloria. There's no way I would've come here normally, but I'll do anything for you. I love the fact that people can be themselves here. It's confirmation that we're not alone. My fourteen-year-old self would never have believed somewhere like this existed."

"My twenty-three-year-old self hardly believes this exists either."

Cam kissed her in full view of everyone, and it was liberating and intoxicating. If this is what peace brought, there was such hope for the future, for the country, and for them.

Maybe they would continue at Bletchley Park, or maybe they would settle in Cambridge where she could study for a degree. Aunty Florrie and the chickens were as much a part of her family now, and they would come too. Everything was feasible.

She inched back and gazed into Cam's eyes, wanting to fix this moment in her memory. "When I solved that crossword puzzle, I would never have believed I would make friends with some of the most intelligent people in the country and do a job that stretched my brain. But all that is nothing compared to a future with you. You've shown me real love. It's more than what we read in books or see all around us. It's in that respect and devotion of a hundred little things. It's in the power and pleasure of the physical and spiritual, blending and expansion to the glories of the universe when we sing or make love. I love you."

Cam brought Gloria's knuckles to her lips and kissed them. "I love you too. You've changed my whole world, given me meaning, and opened me up where I was closed off. You made me believe I could be loved for who I am. You've unlocked the code to my heart."

It wasn't so much unlocked as deciphering what was already there and had been from the moment they met. Gloria would face whatever the future held for them as long as they could do it together.

~ The End ~

To read more about Bea's story with Maud, why not check out Warm Pearls and Paper Cranes? And you'll find Beryl and Odette's story in Virgin Flight.

I really hope you enjoyed reading *Encrypted Hearts*. If you did, I'd be very grateful for an honest review. Reviews and recommendations are crucial for any author, particularly one early in her career. Just a line or two can make a huge difference.

Thank you,

E. V. Bancroft

Other Great Butterworth Books

Caribbean Dreams by Karen Klyne
When love sails into your life, can you climb aboard?
Available from Amazon (ASIN B09M41PYM9)

Encrypted Hearts by E.V. Bancroft
Even amid the chaos of war, love is the hardest code to crack.
Available from Amazon (ASIN B0DKG7BHMJ)

Unwritten by Helena Harte
No strings is fun 'til it unravels.
Available from Amazon (ASIN B0DGQFFHYB)

Chucking Putty at the Queen by Simon Smalley
A heartbreaking, humorous, and courageous exploration of what it takes to be ones authentic self.
Available from Amazon (ASIN B0DGGBV22W)

The Promise by Addison M Conley
When the world keeps pulling you under, who do you reach for?
Available on Amazon (ASIN B0DDY9FH6Z)

Back to Back by Jo Fletcher
."When Fred and Ruby's worlds collide, can love rise from the rubble?"
Available on Amazon (ASIN B0D6M499K2)

Sanctuary by Helena Harte
Passions ignite and possibilities unfold. Welcome to the Windy City Romances.
Available from Amazon (ASIN B0D4B42RRW)

Heart of the Storm by Ally McGuire
Sometimes a storm is just what you need to clear the skies ahead.
Available on Amazon (ASIN B0CYTSQXWW)

Brave Enough to Love by Valden Bush
In a dance between truth and sacrifice, can they rewrite the rules of love?
Available on Amazon (ASIN B0CQP8PMVB)

Stolen Ambition by Robyn Nyx
Daughters of two worlds collide in a dangerous game of ambition and love.
Available on Amazon (ASIN B0BS1PRSCN)

Cabin Fever by Addison M Conley
She goes for the money, but will she stay for something deeper?
Available on Amazon (ASIN B0BQWY45GH)

Breakout for Love by Valden Bush
They're both running from their pasts. Together, they might make a new future.
Available from Amazon (ASIN B0CWHZ4SXL)

The Helion Band by AJ Mason
Rose's only crime was to show kindness to her royal mistress...
Available from Amazon (ASIN B09YM6TYFQ)

That Boy of Yours Wants Looking At by Simon Smalley
A riotously colourful and heart-rending journey of what it takes to live authentically.
Available from Amazon (ASIN B09V3CSQQW)

Sapphic Eclectic Volume Five edited by Nyx & Willows
A little something for everyone...
Available free from the Butterworth Books website

Of Light and Love by E.V. Bancroft
The deepest shadows paint the brightest love.
Available from Amazon (ASIN B0B64KJ3NP)

An Art to Love by Helena Harte
Second chances are an art form.
Available on Amazon (ASIN B0B1CD8Y42)

Music City Dreamers by Robyn Nyx
Music brings lovers together. In Music City, it can tear them apart. Available on
Amazon (ASIN B0994XVDGR)

What's Your Story?

Global Wordsmiths, CIC, provides an all-encompassing service for all writers, ranging from basic proofreading and cover design to development editing, typesetting, and eBook services. A major part of our work is charity and community focused, delivering writing projects to under-served and under-represented groups across Nottinghamshire, giving voice to the voiceless and visibility to the unseen.

To learn more about what we offer, visit: www.globalwords.co.uk

A selection of books by Global Words Press:
Desire, Love, Identity: with the National Justice Museum
Aventuras en México: Farmilo Primary School
Times Past: with The Workhouse, National Trust
Young at Heart with AGE UK
In Different Shoes: Stories of Trans Lives

Self-published authors working with Global Wordsmiths:
Steve Bailey
Ravenna Castle
Jackie D
CJ DeBarra
Dee Griffiths
Iona Kane
Maggie McIntyre
Emma Nichols
Dani Lovelady Ryan
Erin Zak